Rihanna's Dream

The Story of a Miracle

Mozaffar Sālārī

Translated by Blake Archer Williams

Lantern Publications
info@lanternpublications.com
www.lanternpublications.com

Ordering Information:
Quantity sales. Special discounts are available on quantity purchases by corporations, associations, and others. For details, contact the distributor at the address below.

Shia Books Australia
www.shiabooks.com.au
info@shiabooks.com.au

ISBN- 978-0-6489869-5-9

First Edition

In the Name of God,
the Most Compassionate, the Most Merciful

Prayers of God's Peace and Blessings

In keeping with the Islamic practice of showing respect for the name of God, and sending prayers of God's peace and blessings whenever the name of His blessed Prophet, Lady Fātema, and the Twelve Imams ﷺ is mentioned, as well as for asking God to hasten the reappearance of the Lord of the Age on the Earthly plane, one or more of the following Arabic symbols have been employed throughout the text. They are repeated for their great rewards.

 Used exclusively after the name of God, meaning "the Sublimely Exalted", or, as a prayer, "[May His name be] Sublimely Exalted".

 Used exclusively after the name of the Prophet, meaning "May the peace and blessings of God be unto him and unto [the purified and inerrant members of] his family"

 Used for any of the Twelve Imams or past prophets of God ﷺ, meaning "May God's peace be unto him".

 Used for two or more of the Twelve Imams or past prophets of God, meaning "May God's peace be unto them".

 Used for Lady Fātema, meaning "May God's peace be unto her".

 Used for a plurality of the Fourteen Immaculates, meaning "May God's peace be unto them all collectively".

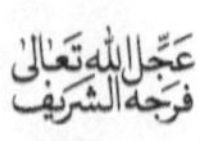 Used for the Lord of the Age (the Twelfth Imam), meaning "May God hasten the advent of his noble person".

Author Note:
[The character in the novel named] Abū-Rājeh's being visited by
the Lord of the Age ﷻ, and the miraculous nature of his cure as
it is described in the book, are true events.

Al-'Abqarī ol-Hesān, Volume 2, Page 192.

(*Al-'Abqarī ol-Hesān* is a nine-volume work about the Lord of the Age
ﷻ written in Persian by Hājj Sheikh Alī-Akbar Nahāvandī in 1364 of
the lunar Islamic calendar (1944). The volume and page number refer
to the Persian edition – Translator.)

Chapter 1

I went down a few stone steps. That's all it took. And in less than a month, I went through an adventure that completely changed my life. I sometimes think that the adventure was a dream, or that I am still asleep, and that I will realize that it was nothing but a dream once I awaken. I can't describe it as anything but a miracle. Sometimes reality is so incredibly strange that one becomes discombobulated by it. When I think back on my past, I think of my going down those few stone steps as the beginning of my amazing adventure.

Grandfather says, "True, it was indeed strange, but we must believe that it actually happened! Life itself, and the heavens and the earth, are so wondrously strange that at times it is as if we are living in a sweet dream. When one comes to have faith in the Creator, one will believe that He is capable of absolutely anything."

It all started from a seemingly insignificant decision. I don't know what prompted Grandfather to make this decision, but he suddenly came to me and said, "Hāshem,[1] you have to come downstairs with me." Thus, I had no choice but to follow him downstairs. It was after this act that I realized how a seemingly insignificant event can change the course of one's life.

God ﷻ, in His infinite grace, has endowed me with an unusual quantum of good looks. Grandfather, who is still a handsome man, would say on occasion, "You need to sit at my side in the store" – his jewelry shop, that is – "and help me handle the customers, rather than wasting your time in the workshop."

He would say, "I have become frail and my wits are not as sharp as they used to be. You need to take charge of the affairs of the store so that I can rest assured you'll be able to run the store as well as the workshop after I am gone." And I would respond by saying, "Allow me to achieve a mastery of goldsmithing so that I would be peerless, at least in Hilla,[2] for if I am not sufficiently skilled in my trade, I will not be able to command the confidence either of my apprentices *or* of the customers."

Grandfather would look with approval at my designs and creations and say, "You might not be aware of this yourself, but you are already a master."

I would say, "I do not want to be respected on account of your wealth and success. My desire is for all of the people of Hilla and Iraq to envy your having trained a skilled grandson."

He would smile at my words and give me a big hug. And sometimes he would let out a deep sigh and tears would well up in his eyes and he would say, "When your father, God ﷻ rest his soul, died at a young age, there was a time when I didn't think I would recover my optimistic outlook and sense of hope in life. May God ﷻ forgive me for all of my negativity and ingratitude, and for all of my complaining to God ﷻ. I had entrusted the business to my apprentices, and couldn't focus on the work at hand in the workshop or in the store. I would spend most of my time in Abū-Rājeh's *hammām*. If it weren't for Abū-Rājeh's words of encouragement, I would have lost the business and slipped into a deep depression. But Abū-Rājeh would take me to communal prayers and the Friday congregational prayers, and would swing by and take me with him to the festivities of the Eid al-Qurbān, the Eid al-Fetr[3], and the anniversary of the birth of the Prophet ﷺ, to bring me out of my depression. It was in those same days that your mother remarried at the insistence of her father and went to Kūfa, where her hardhearted husband refused to take you in. That was when your guardianship was entrusted to me. You were just four years old at the time, and the care of such a young, motherless and fatherless child was difficult for me. Omm-Hobāb took on the motherly responsibilities for your upbringing and raised you, and your coming into our household became the occasion for my coming out of my depression, and I became occupied with your education. May God ﷻ be praised! It was as if they had given me your father again."

I paid him my full attention, even though I had heard this story many times over. Abū-Rājeh would say, "Hāshem is the only memento you have of your son. Strive to raise him with care, and he will be like a tree that bears a good harvest of fruit." He would say, "I can see from your grandson's forehead that your will realize in him all that which you had hoped for in your son."

I liked Abū-Rājeh. He was the owner of the large and beautiful public bath or hammām of the city of Hilla. Grandfather would take me to Abū-Rājeh's hammām from when I was very little whenever he took me to the jewelry store so that we could spend time with Abū-Rājeh and look at and play with the beautiful goldfish which were in the pool in the middle of the changing room. Later, Abū-Rājeh would bring his little girl Rihanna to the baths on occasion. I would take Rihanna's hand and we would frolic in the bazaar and caravanserais and while away the time. But when Rihanna reached the age of six, Abū-Rājeh no longer brought her with him to the bathhouse, after which time I only saw her occasionally. She would come to the jewelry store with a pot of food, cover her face closely [with her *chādor*⁴] and say, "Hāshem, go and give this to my father."

She would then quickly take her leave. She didn't like visiting the men's section of the bathhouse. It had been years since I had seen her. Once, when Grandfather was feeling contented and full of vitality, he said, "Hāshem, you are all grown up now. You need to start thinking about getting married. I want to see you dressed as a groom before I die. If God ❀ were to grant me a long enough life to see your children, all the better! I would have no other wish after that."

I don't know why the thought of Rihanna crossed my mind at that very moment.

One day, when Grandfather had just come back from Abū-Rājeh's hammām, he climbed the stairs to the workshop and without any preamble, blurted out, "Too bad this Abū-Rājeh is Shī'a, else I would ask for the hand of his daughter Rihanna in marriage for you."

My heart started beating faster upon hearing Rihanna's name, which surprised me. I didn't think my childhood playmate would have any significance for me now. I feigned nonchalance and asked, "What made you think of Rihanna?"

He sat on a stool and proceeded to wipe the sweat off his face with a white silk kerchief. "I hear his daughter is a *hāfez al-Quran* – one who knows the whole of the Quran by heart, and that she teaches the Quran and the ordinances of God's sacred law to women. How good it would be for one's wife to have attained to such perfections of character!"

He arose, and as he started to descend the stairs, he leaned against one of the pillars of the workshop and said, "This Abū-Rājeh has only two faults – and a great man once said that it suffices the nobility of a person's character that his faults can be counted on the fingers of one's hand."

He had repeated this adage about Abū-Rājeh on numerous occasions. I took the initiative and said, "I know. Firstly, that he is Shīʿa, and secondly, that he is not very handsome."

"Exactly! Well done. These are indeed his only two faults. If I were to place the entirety of my wealth with him in trust, I am certain that he would not violate his trust by as much as a farthing. He is a devotee of God ﷻ, and a man of knowledge. He is a man of righteous character and conduct, makes for pleasurable company, and is always at the ready to help others. But it's too bad that it is as you say, that he is not very pleasing to look at, and follows another religio-legal rite (*madhhab*) than ours." After all, a Shīʿa is a Shīʿa, and a Sunni is a Sunni."

At this point he suddenly turned his face towards me, turned around, made two pillars of his arms on my workbench and, said in a voice that was lowered so that the apprentices would not hear, "The proprietor of a public bath does not need to be handsome, but a goldsmith must be handsome, so that when he places a piece of jewelry before a customer, they will want to purchase it."

I was setting a ruby in an expensive necklace. He placed his hand on the necklace, and looking at me with wide-open eyes, said, "Get up and let us go downstairs! From this day forward, you must work downstairs in the store."

I picked up a roll of papers on which I had drawn the patterns for some fine and expensive jewelry from a shelf and unfurled them on the bench and said, "Grandfather! *You* be the judge! Look closely, now. Which is more important, my continuing to work on these designs, or my being a salesman and hackling with the ladies?!"

He rolled up the patterns calmly and tossed them to his most senior apprentice who was a master goldsmith in his own right, who caught them in mid-air.

"No'mān! From here on out, you will be tasked with making all of Hāshem's designs. And I expect you to work in such a way as not to afford him any opportunity to find fault with your work."

No'mān kissed the scrolls and said, "Your instructions will be obeyed, Master."

I shook my head in dismay. Grandfather was glaring at me. I said, "Then let me finish this one first…"

He placed his hand on the necklace again.

"Right this minute!"

His tone was calm, but determined. I could not look him in the eye. So I got up, untied my work apron, threw it on a stool, and followed Grandfather down the stairs to the surprise and interest of the apprentices.

Chapter 2

It had been a few days since I had been away from the kiln and smelting pan and crucible and hammer and metal file and workbench of the workshop. I was growing used to my position as a salesman. Abū-Naʿīm's jewelry store had the most beautiful storefront in the whole of Hilla's great bazaar. The walls and ceiling of the store were covered with fine mirrorwork. Grandfather and I, together with two other salesmen, sat among the glass display cases and mirrored chests, and presented various pieces of jewelry and fine ornaments to our customers. These were either of our own design and manufacture, or were items we had imported from various other cities and countries. The glass display cases behind us nearly reached the ceiling. The incline of the upper shelves was set at a shallow pitch so as to allow the customers to inspect the most expensive pendants and necklaces on the ruby and emerald colored satin cushioning that covered the shelving.

I had just opened the door that morning. The cobblestones in front of the store had been washed down, and the scent of their dampness was intermingled with the expensive fragrance that Grandfather wore. The sound of pigeons fluttering their wings could be heard coming from under the high domes of the bazaar. The air was cool and refreshing. Two Indian traders who had made an appointment earlier had come to show us a few large pearls. Grandfather was examining the pearls with a magnifying glass and haggling over their prices. It was a many-year custom of the two traders to bring us their pearls. The pungent scent of the fragrant oil that they wore was familiar. One of the salesmen brought them some mango nectar and a plate of dates. Grandfather insisted on receiving a discount. The Indian traders smiled and shook their heads in their own inimitable way and said, "Nay, nay."

There were not many customers in the bazaar in the mornings, and so, whenever there weren't any customers in the store, I would work on my template designs. Someone had brought news from the Sultan's palace that the Sultan's family intended to pay our store a visit in the next few days, and I wanted to show them my most exquisite designs.

I was sure they would be pleased with what they saw. One of my designs was a diamond ring with two dragons, one on either side of the gemstone, whose gaping mouths held the gemstone in place. It was one of the few rings that was worthy of adorning the fingers of the Sultan's daughters and wives.

The Indian traders kissed the dinars which Grandfather had given them and placed them in a leather pouch, held their hands together before their faces in a gesture of gratitude, bowed low, and took their leave. Grandfather wrung his hands together with pleasure and examined the pearls again with his eyeglass, this time murmuring some tune under his breath. One of the salesmen who also kept the accounts opened his large ledger and entered the record of the transaction in it.

Two women who were completely veiled save for a narrow slot for their eyes entered the store. They looked at the display cases and the mirrored chests for a minute or two. The quality of the fabric of their *chādors* told me that they were not wealthy. They looked mostly at the earrings. It looked to me like one was the mother and the other her daughter. There were no other customers in the store, and I saw no reason why they should not take as long as they wanted to look at the jewelry. I felt like the one who looked to be the daughter cast an occasional glance at my designs. The woman drew near to Grandfather, greeted him with a *salaam*, and said, "We are not strangers. We have come first thing in the morning before the store gets busy with your customers to buy something good and be on our way."

Feigning concern and coming to mock attention, Grandfather placed the pearls in a large thimble and said, "I do apologize, Madam. My store and I are at your service."

Many customers introduced themselves as friends and acquaintances in order to get a discount. I grinned and continued with my work. They did not seem to be people we knew. The accountant took the thimble of pearls and placed it in the large metal safe, locking it. There was a small cushion on top of the safe, on which the accountant now sat.

Grandfather asked the woman, "Are you from Hilla?"

The woman nodded and let out a gentle chuckle. "I am Abū-Rājeh's wife, the hammām-keeper."

Both of us froze in place. Grandfather started to cough and said in a happy tone, "Oh, how wonderful! You have brightened our day! You are most welcome! Why did you not let us know beforehand that you would be giving us the pleasure of your company? Why did you not introduce yourselves immediately so that we could welcome you with the honor that befits you? We are ashamed [for not having given you a proper welcome]. We trust that we will be forgiven for this breach of decorum. I beseech you not to relay anything of our misconduct to my friend and brother Abū-Rājeh!"

"Not at all! You are too kind."

"Believe me, I don't have my wits about me. I must be dreaming that Abū-Rājeh's wife is gracing our store with a visit. I am grateful for your considering us to be worthy of your custom. And the lovely young lady with you is Rihanna, I take it? Have I guessed right?"

The mother turned slightly towards her daughter and said, "Yes."

Rihanna uttered a *salaam* in a low voice and lowered her head. I could not believe she had grown so tall.

"*Alaykom as-salaam*, my daughter. How tall you have grown! May God ☙ protect you. It is as if it was only yesterday that you and Hāshem rushed headlong into the store hand in hand, saying, "There is a dwarf who is a magician who says that if we give him a coin, he will make a camel go into a bottle!"

Grandfather smiled. Rihanna and I looked at each other abashedly for a brief moment.

"And this is Hāshem. As you can see, he too has grown into a veritable young man. May God ☙ have mercy on his father's soul. Sometimes I imagine that his father is sitting here working on his designs. He's the spitting image of his father. I start to miss him if I do not see him for more than an hour! See how bashful he is, and how he blushes like a girl! His preference was to sit upstairs in the workshop and make jewelry, but I would not allow it. I wanted him to be by my side. This way, I can rest assured that all is well with him."

I gave Rihanna's mother my *salaams*, which she returned and, turning to Grandfather, said, "Truly, children grow up faster than a squash plant! May God ☙ protect him for you, and keep your patronage over both of us!"

Grandfather dabbed his eyes with his silk kerchief. "What you say is indeed true. These kids grow as fast as shadows at sunset. And then they marry and pursue their own lives. It is as if it was just an hour ago that the halva street vendor had taken hold of Hāshem's hand and was pulling him after himself, with Rihanna running behind them in tears, trying to keep up. The vendor came in and said, 'This boy has taken a dirham's worth of halva from me and has eaten it together with his sister. And now that I demand payment he tells me to go and get it from Abū-Naʿīm!' He thought Hāshem and Rihanna were a couple of street urchins who had never tasted halva in their whole lives!"

Rihanna's mother chuckled and said, "God save us from these children! So it was not for nothing that Rihanna would insist every morning that she wanted to go and play with Hāshem!"

I also smiled at this. But this time I made sure not to look at Rihanna so as to avoid the possibility of our looking into each other's eyes again.

"Do you know what I told that halva vendor? I asked him how much he wanted for his whole tray of halva. When he said that if you were to buy it all, it would cost five dirhams, I gave him the sum and told him to go and divvy up his halva among the street-vendor children, and to thank God for these little customers of his!"

Grandfather let out a hearty laugh. "You should have been there to see the look on his face. He just stood there, not knowing what to say; but then bowed and left."

It was interesting for me to see how clearly Grandfather remembered everything.

"This boy was a playful one. And he can be stubborn at times even now. He does not pay due consideration to the condition of this old man. He is bashful like a girl. He wants nothing more than either to mess around with the kiln and smelter in the basement, or to sit upstairs in the workshop making earrings and bracelets. I had to pry him away from all that to bring him to work next to me. You see? He is still making all these patterns on paper. Every day he presents me with a new design of his. Abū-Rājeh admonishes him plenty, but will he listen?"

Grandfather felt that he had talked too much. "Forgive me. When one grows old, one doesn't give one's tongue a rest. Seeing you has made me so happy that I've gotten to rambling on about nothing. May God be praised!"

Rihanna's mother pointed to a pair of earrings. "We've come to buy a pair of earrings for Rihanna. She is accustomed to being satisfied with her lot in life, and does not pine for ornaments and jewelry, but for our part, we too have a duty to fulfill."

I took the pair of inexpensive earrings out of their case and placed them on a pink satin cloth which had an embroidered border. I didn't know what I was feeling. I was confused. I couldn't believe that I was seeing Rihanna after so many years. It was as if the person who was the dearest to me had just returned from a long journey. I wanted to carry myself with dignity and poise, but couldn't. I kept looking back and forth, and I was afraid that Rihanna and Grandfather would become aware of my erratic behavior. Rihanna's mother picked up the earrings and showed them to her. Childhood memories rushed into my mind. At one time, Rihanna and I were playmates, but now it was not acceptable for me even to cast a glance in her direction. We were no longer the children of yesteryear. Father Time had erected an invisible wall between us with the contents of his satchel. Grandfather extended his hand with a pleasant frown toward Rihanna's mother, who placed the earrings in the palm of his hand.

"No, madam. These earrings are not at all worthy of our Rihanna. One who knows the whole of the Quran by heart and teaches the Quran and knows the ordinances of God's sacred law and the science of interpreting His sacred writ ought to wear earrings that have been handed down from Heaven. Alas, we do not have any such specimens at hand, but allow me to see which of our earrings are worthy of my daughter."

Grandfather stepped out from behind the display cases and pointed to a beautiful and expensive pair of earrings of my own design and manufacture. I was happy to see him choosing these for Rihanna, although I doubted that her mother would take on the burden of their expense. I took the earrings out and gave them to Grandfather.

"The design and workmanship of these is Hāshem's. They are truly exquisite!"

Rihanna's mother took the earrings and examined them. "They are indeed beautiful, but we are after something less expensive."

Grandfather returned to his spot. "A moment, if you will. I would like to know what Lady Rihanna thinks. What do you say, my child? You are very reticent."

I looked at Rihanna with curiosity to see what she would say. I could see an outline of her face in the light. She was the same Rihanna that I knew from way back when. From the time she had entered the store, she kept her gaze on the mirrored casement next to her. It was as if the jewelry on display in the store had no attraction for her. She opened her closed fist and displayed the two dinars that lay in the palm of her hand.

"You are as kind as ever, but I believe that these two coins speak for themselves."

The melody of her voice was familiar but melancholy.

Grandfather chuckled and said, "How precise and to the point!"

Rihanna's mother placed the earrings on the velvet and looked around in search of the previous earrings. Grandfather placed the expensive earrings in a small ruby-colored velvet-covered box and slid the box over to Rihanna's mother.

"It so happens that the price of these earrings is two dinars."

I extolled Grandfather in my heart. I had prayed to God that Rihanna would become the owner of those earrings, whose true value was ten dinars. I had worked on them for a whole week. Four women entered the store. Grandfather assigned them to two salesmen, after which Rihanna's mother returned the box to Grandfather.

"I know that their price is much higher than that. I cannot take these."

Grandfather frowned and returned the box to where it had been. "Upon my word of honor before God, you must take them! These earrings have Rihanna's name written all over them. Pay the two dinars and take them with you. It will be between me and Abū-Rājeh. After all, he and I do have some accounts to settle after thirty years of friendship."

Grandfather had a salesman's gift of the gab, and, one way or another, prevailed on them to take the earrings with them. When Rihanna placed the two dinars on the embroidered satin, her mother said, "These are the earnings from the rugs which my daughter has woven. They are pure and *halāl* – free of any taint of ill-begotten gains."

Grandfather took up the coins and kissed them, then placed them in my hands.

"I must give these coins that are charged with *baraka* (or divine blessings) to Hāshem, so that he too can be compensated for his efforts."

I again saw the outline of Rihanna's face in the light of the store. It was the face of the Rihanna I knew, but something had changed in her that sent my heart aflutter. This mysterious thing prevented me from looking at her and talking with her and laughing together, the way we used to in the past. But most important of all was the passionate melancholy that I saw in her eyes, which was as if she had just been roused from a convalescent sleep. At the same time, I was taken aback by her beauty, which was mingled with a modesty of character and praiseworthy shame (*ḥayā*).

They bid us farewell and left. Rihanna's last look aroused such a passion in my heart that I felt that she has reached in and snatched my heart out of my chest and taken it with her. I decided to keep those two coins forever as a memento of our meeting again on that day. Grandfather let out a sigh and said, "See the mysterious way in which God works? Who would have believed that this beautiful and worthy child would be Abū-Rājeh's daughter?"

Chapter 3

I left the store on some pretext. After Rihanna and her mother left, I couldn't focus on my work. Grandfather nodded and said, "Come back soon!"

When I put a foot out the door he said, "Give my regards to Abū-Rājeh!" When I looked back at him, he handed me a grin.

The bazaar had become crowded. The noises and scents surrounded me. No one felt alone in the hustle and bustle of that busy bazaar. Traders would yell out the descriptions of their newly arrived wares. A blind beggar recited poetry and prayed for the souls of the passersby. Columns of light made their way past sunshades and canopies, and were cast on the wares of street-vendors and shopkeepers who had spread their trinkets in front of their shops and on the front walls of their shops. Specs of dust twirled around and climbed the columns of light. I spotted a row of tired and dusty camels when I passed by the caravanserai. Porters were busy unburdening them of their loads. In the section of the bazaar where the apothecaries and spice merchants had their shops, the smell of coffee, pepper, frankincense, and musk titillated the nose.

Merchants, servants, bondsmen and bondmaids, and men and women with horses and donkeys and shopping baskets were busy going back and forth. I wanted to occupy my mind with the sights of the bazaar, but couldn't. An old man was making a delivery of a camel-load of water to a coffeeshop where they sold mango juice and my favorite coconut pastries. I stopped by there every day, but on that day, I had no appetite for any mango juice or sweet pastry. A water vendor who carried a large skin on his back extended his copper goblet toward a passerby. I was thirsty but passed him by distractedly. A small boy was wailing, trailing behind his mother, while his mother moved along quickly with a heavy basket on her head, not paying any attention to the child's cries. My heart went out to everyone, and I wanted to help them. I wanted to purchase whatever it was that the boy was crying out for, and to carry his mother's basket to the door of their house. I never used to pay attention to these things, and realized I wasn't being my usual self.

Every forty steps or so, there would be a short flight of steps in the main thoroughfare of the bazaar, which would descend in keeping with the lay of the land. Abū-Rājeh's hammām was located at the crux of a fork in the road. It was only a hundred steps to my Grandfather's store. My strides were unhurried. Occasionally, someone would brush up against me as they passed by. The cloth merchants would hold up their bolts of cloth one by one, singing their praises. Most of their customers were women. A snake-charmer had gathered a throng about himself in another corner. He was busy getting a Cobra to come out of its basket, and had another snake coiled around his neck and shoulders. Two constables were resting their hands on their sword handles and were standing in the semi-circle formed by the crowd. They had one eye on the crowd and another on the bazaar.

I stood up. It had been ages since I had seen Rihanna. Her sudden visit had taken me by storm. It had shaken me to my very foundations. I didn't know how I was feeling. I didn't know what had happened to me during those few minutes. I was feeling downhearted. I squeezed the two coins I was holding in my hand. Perhaps the two coins had spent some days in her company. Perhaps she had felt them on more than one occasion. It was as if they still held the warmth of her touch. The coins pulsated, as if they had a heart. Never had seeing Rihanna had such an effect on me. I wanted to laugh. I wanted to cry and shed tears. I wanted to run so that everyone would be startled and pull aside and make way for me. I wanted to hide in the close quarters of a dark cellar in the bazaar, or to climb to one of its rooftops and shout out at the top of my lungs.

Two women passed me by. I shivered at the thought that they might be Rihanna and her mother, but it wasn't them. I started to walk again. Were they still in the bazaar? No; they had come early to avoid the crowds. A bondmaid saw me and snickered. Maybe she had cottoned on to what was taking place inside me by the look on my face. Maybe Rihanna was back to weaving mats now. Or maybe she was holding her Quran classes for women. My only hope was that she was also experiencing whatever it was that I was going through. Did the earrings that I had crafted hold the same significance for her that her coins did for me? Was she wearing the earrings? What was the meaning of the bondmaid's giggle?

These questions were preoccupying my mind. I was concerned that Abū-Rājeh would also get wise to my inner state, and that I would have no choice but to reveal all to him. I remembered Grandfather's words, who said, "Too bad Abū-Rājeh is Shī'a, else I would ask for the hand of his daughter in marriage for you." I do not know what it was that put a distance between us and the Shī'a. They performed their ritual devotions just as we did, fasted as we did, recited the Quran as we do, and performed the Hajj pilgrimage like we do. If there was a way, I could perhaps prevail on Grandfather to ask for Rihanna's hand in marriage for me. A hulking black man bumped up against me. An old street-vendor had placed a tray of eggs in front of him. Strings of garlic were hanging down from the wall behind him. When I was bumped up against him, I nearly stepped onto the eggs. A rug merchant was leaning up against a pile of his rugs and kilims, smoking a hookah, and was amused to see me almost fall over. When he recognized me, he raised his hand and touched his mantle and gave a slight bow. I tried to pay more attention to what I was doing.

I had reached Abū-Rājeh's hammām. Even if Grandfather could be prevailed upon, Abū-Rājeh would never give his permission. He and his daughter were Shī'a, and my grandfather and I were Sunni, and I did not know what had placed such a distance between us, both of us being Muslim. This distance irked me more than ever. Would that they would adopt our ways. Then there would be no obstacle in the path. But how was such a thing possible? Abū-Rājeh was someone who was knowledgeable and well-read. He would read books and take notes in his spare time. Rihanna had been raised and educated in his house. In all likelihood, she was devoted to her religious ways, like her father.

I reached the fork in the road. On one side, the bazaar continued, with its expansiveness and hustle and bustle. The other tine was a narrow, serpentine alley populated with two- and three-story buildings. Abū-Rājeh's hammām was nestled between the two tines of this fork. It was not clear whether it was a part of the bazaar or part of the winding alley. A towel was hanging on both sides of the door to the hammām. A pleasant scent greeted one when one entered the hammām. A short corridor led to a short flight of stairs that led down to a large and pleasing changing room. On each side of the changing room there were benches and rows of wooden lockers in which customers placed their garments. In the middle of the changing room was a large stone pool. When one came through the main hall of the hammām and before one reached the changing room, Abū-Rājeh would place a towel on one's shoulder. One would then bathe one's feet in a small stone foot-wash pool, and would then climb onto the platform by the lockers to dry oneself and get back into one's street clothes. The ceiling of the changing room was elevated and domed, in the sides of which thin plates of marble had been worked that let sunlight through, which made its way down to the pool below. These windows lit up all of the changing room. Abū-Rājeh's hammām was built by an Iranian master builder. A flower-patterned cloth hung over the entryway, after which there was a small room made of wood paneling in which Abū-Rājeh or his helper sat and collected the fee from the customers. The thing that attracted one's attention right away were two beautiful swans that were floating on the pool, which had been brought for Abū-Rājeh by an Andalusian merchant. There were no other swans in Hilla. Many people came to the baths just to look at the swans, and would bathe and see to their personal hygiene as an afterthought. Abū-Rājeh loved his swans and took good care of them.

Abū-Rājeh was sitting on the wooden platform talking to several customers who had already changed back into their street clothes.

Chapter 4

When he saw me, he got up and came towards me. He took me by the hand and took me to the platform where the others were standing, who also stood up as a gesture of respect. When we were all seated, Abū-Rājeh lauded Grandfather and myself to the others, in response to which I said something to the effect that he was being too kind.

With the social niceties out of the way, Abū-Rājeh finished telling an interesting story whose conclusion had been interrupted by my arrival, after which his customers stood up, placed a coin on the counter of the wooden alcove, and left. Abū-Rājeh made a sign to his young attendant Masrour, who went and brought a bowl of grapes. Masrour had been working there since he was a child. When he placed the bowl of grapes in front of me, I saw from the look on his face that, as always, he was not happy to see me. He had a grudge against me ever since our childhood, when he saw that Rihanna liked me. He had to remain indoors in the hammām while Rihanna and I played and cavorted outdoors. Abū-Rājeh took me by the hand and said, "You look preoccupied. Has something happened?"

Surprised, I said, "To you, I am like a crystal vase: with one glance you can see everything that is on my mind and in my heart."

He squeezed my bicep and smile.

"Whenever Abū-Naʿīm was upset or depressed, he too would come and see me."

I looked at his kind face. How could I tell him that my problems were connected to him in some way? He looked off-color, as usual, and his hair was thin and wispy. His large, yellowed teeth were displayed whenever he smiled. It was strange to see that his kindness and nobility of character shone brightly in his eyes despite his ailing and gaunt appearance. His eyes were those of Rihanna's. Years ago Grandfather had said, "No one can believe that a girl as beautiful as Rihanna could be the daughter of a father such as Abū-Rājeh, unless they were to pay close attention to his eyes."

The sound of falling water and the indeterminate conversations of customers could be heard from the main hall of the hammām. Masrour approached a man who was coming out of the main hall and handed him a towel. The man wrapped the towel around himself and dipped his feet in the pool. The swans drifted to the opposite end of the pool. Three people were drying themselves off and putting on their clothes on the platform on the other side of the pool, and two others were preparing to enter the bathing hall. For his part, Masrour would place the towels that he took from each customer in a specific spot so that he could place them back on the shoulders of their respective owners upon their return from the baths. The first and last gaze of the customers was to the swans.

I wanted to be as courageous as to be able to tell Abū-Rājeh all that was in my heart. I knew that he would listen to what I had to say with equanimity, but I did not understand why such a thing as one's religious beliefs should put a distance between us. How much easier it would have been to talk about Rihanna, and how much happier I would have been if no such distance existed! In order not to prolong the silence, I said, "I nearly stepped on the eggs of a street vendor on the way over."

Abū-Rājeh said, "Your mind and heart are elsewhere. Wherever it is that they have gone to, you must do something to bring them back."

"A salesman who saw me almost trip over myself laughed at me. A bondmaiden snickered at me too. I've never felt so disoriented."

Abū-Rājeh covered his mouth with his hand and gave out a hearty laugh. "May God help you, my son! The things that you say are signs of someone who has fallen in love! I imagine that some beauty has stricken you with the arrow of her looks, and you are not even aware of what happened."

Masrour was sitting in the wooden alcove with his chin resting on his hand, waiting to collect the fees of the customers on their way out. I knew he was curious to know what we were talking about.

"You've got it right, Abū-Rājeh. I don't know whether what has come over me is love or some other affliction. Until recently, I was contentedly minding my own business in the workshop. But Grandfather was so insistent that I join him in the store that I eventually relented and started to work in sales. He would say, 'A goldsmith must be handsome so as to prompt the customers into spending their money.' So this is the result!"

"Salesmen mustn't be ugly and uncouth and ill-mannered. But being too handsome has its disadvantages too. It shouldn't be the case that a customer becomes so taken by the handsomeness of the salesman as to be taken in rather than being able to evaluate their decision to purchase with peace of mind. And this is especially so in the jewelry business, in which most of the customers are women. Masrour and I don't have to worry about this; neither of us are particularly handsome, nor do we have to deal with womenfolk in our business."

I smiled again. I said, "Under the circumstances, it would have been only natural for someone to fall in love as I have, but now it is me who has been stricken like this. I have always striven to lower my gaze and to be conscious of what I allowed my eyes to linger on. My Grandfather says, 'You are like a modest maiden and do not raise your eyes to look at women.' Believe me when I tell you that sometimes, love steps into the abode of one's heart uninvited! The path of two people's sights cross, and that which ought not to occur, occurs!"

We were not sitting at a great distance from Masrour, and he could hear our voices. Abū-Rājeh nodded his head and gently squeezed my arm. He had great empathy and did not pass judgment hastily. He said, "Love is a good thing when it occurs within the bounds of the sacrament of matrimony, but if no such bond of a life lived together in marriage is involved, then love becomes the cause of anxiety and strife. In this latter case, the problem that falling in love presents can be cured by maintaining one's virtue and chastity. You must choose between these two actions. See if that maiden is suitable to be your wife, and if so, marry her. But if she is not, keep your distance from her so that in time you will be able to forget her."

"Is that possible?"

"If you do not see her for a while and ask God for help, you will forget her. There is a cure for every ailment, and the cure for futile and troublesome love is just as I have said."

"But Abū-Rājeh! She is perfectly suited to be my wife. If you knew who she was, you would affirm that I could not hope for a better wife."

"That is not how love works. What one sees with one's eyes makes us blind to the faults of one's beloved, and magnifies their merits a thousand-fold."

"Grandfather also thinks that she is the most suitable of candidates and would make the best wife for me."

"Abū-Naʿīm is a man of great experience and understanding. So then I do not understand what the problem is. You like her, and your grandfather is not averse to the bond. The only thing that remains is for you to ask for her hand in marriage."

I was staring at the swans. They did not have to deal with problems that human beings faced. I needed to tell the truth.

"She and her family are Shīʿa."

Abū-Rājeh was taken aback and remained quiet for a while, then stood up and got off the platform.

I don't know how he would react if he knew who it was that I was talking about. He went and sat on the edge of the pool and wet his hands in the water. The swans approached him, and he proceeded to pet them. Without looking at me, he said, "In such cases, suitors are frequently turned down. So nothing can be done but to be patient and wait."

I placed the bowl of grapes to the side and got up. Our conversation had reached a sensitive pass. On my way to the baths, I had foreseen Abū-Rājeh giving me this advice. Masrour had chosen to remain in the alcove in order to see what was afoot. His ears were perked up and he was pretending to be busy with counting the coins. I wouldn't be surprised if he had figured out that I was talking about Rihanna.

I scooted over to the edge of the platform. Sounds carried and echoed in the space under the dome over the pool. I said quietly, "It has been many years since the time I became aware of the distances that exist between our families. We are like brothers. We work together and have business dealings with each other. We perform our ritual devotions together and pray together. We come to each other's aid. We love one another as brothers, and see each other socially. So then why is it that there should still be this distance between us, when we are both Muslims and we both believe in the same sacred writ and in the same prophet?"

Abū-Rājeh turned to me with a smile and said, "It is a very important question." He stood up and came over and sat on the edge of the platform. "And what is more important is for you to find a suitable answer to this question of yours."

I went over and sat next to him. "You provide aid and succor to anyone who is in trouble. So then help me too so that I can understand."

"There are, of course, certain distances… but they are not as great as some would have us believe. There are differences and distances between two intimate friends also. It is only natural. But these differences and distances do not hinder their friendship. Each person has his own peculiarities and is occupied doing his own thing and living out his own life in his own house. It is entirely possible for the awareness and intelligence of two brothers to be different from each other. Nor are different people's faith and piety the same. The problem stems from a different source. The Caliph has appointed a wicked person such as Marjān-e Saghīr as the Sultan or ruler of the city, and this man happens to be an enemy of the progeny of the Prophet ﷺ and of their followers or partisans (*shī'a*). The Sultan's dungeon is full of Shī'a who are innocent of any crime. This is the situation in a city whose residents are mostly Shī'a. Before this, Shī'a and Sunni Muslims lived in peace and tranquility with each other. Now what the authorities want to do is to create an atmosphere where someone such as yourself thinks of me as your enemy.

The way they treat us is worse than the way they treat infidels and outsiders. They have tried to dilute the strength of the Shī'a majority by settling thousands of people of the Jewish faith here. We are no longer protected under the law of Islam, and our property and our very lives can be taken at will by anyone, without their having to fear for the consequences of their actions. They spread false rumors about us and demonize us. The great scholars among us, such as Sayyed Eben Tāwūs and Allāma Hillī respond to these aspersions and false accusations with respect and with solid reasons, but they are not concerned with the truth and continue to carry out their program against us. It has been almost a hundred years since the fall of the Abbasid dynasty[5], but the anti-Shī'a mindset that they propagated rages on unchecked. The *nāsebīs*[6] are still around, and if they were to gain a handhold on any real power, they would undoubtedly massacre the Shī'a. Rather than preaching equality and brotherliness, they sow the seeds of discord and rancor, and oppress the Shī'a in order to curtail the possibility of our rising up against them. Rather than putting an end to their injustices and self-indulgent lifestyle, they do nothing but add to their iniquities and oppression. They are rotting from within and are concerned about imaginary threats to their reign. You can see that it is us Shī'a who suffer more as a consequence of the distance that exists between us."

"I accept all this, but a question has been on my mind for a long time which you Shī'a must answer. The problem might be solved in this way."

"By all means. I will listen to your question attentively and answer it if I can."

"There were no denominations or sects during the time of the Prophet ﷺ. So why do sects exist now? Maybe the Caliph and Marjān-e Saghīr's policies are aimed at bringing about unity between us again."

"I would like very much to talk about these subjects, but I have been told that the Sultan's court has me under surveillance and is unhappy with the most innocuous things that I say. All sorts of people come and go here, and the Sultan's snoops are everywhere. So we must continue our conversation somewhere where we have privacy."

I glanced over to Masrour. He was now spooning cedar chips and henna out of a couple of bags and placing them into small bowls.

"Who do you mean by 'snoops'?"

"I'm not exactly sure. It could be that some come to the baths under the guise of being customers and report things that they allege I have said. One who has no fear [of the consequences of his actions before the judgment] of God is capable of doing anything!"

A venerable customer who had a shaved head and hennaed beard came out of the courtyard. Abū-Rājeh gave him three premium towels with flowers embroidered on them; one to wrap around his waist, and the other two for his head and shoulders. He gave his neck and shoulders and arms a rubdown and took some musk from a jar and rubbed it into his customer's henna-colored beard. Masrour tidied the bowl of grapes and placed it before him, and then helped him into his clothes.

A disturbing thought had occupied my mind. Maybe Abū-Rājeh wanted to give Rihanna's hand to Masrour. In all probability, if Masrour was to ask for Rihanna's hand in marriage, he would not be turned down. He had worked for Abū-Rājeh since childhood and Abū-Rājeh needed his services. I had seen Masrour on numerous occasions praying in the Shī'a fashion, with the arms held straight down. Abū-Rājeh would undoubtedly prefer to give his daughter to Masrour, so that his groom could run the hammām for him when old age prevented him from being able to run it himself, and so that his grandchildren would inherit it. Everything was arrayed against me. It was as if the heavens and earth had joined forces to take Rihanna away from me.

That venerable customer spent some time looking at the swans, and then gave Masrour a good tip on his way out. Masrour gladly placed the gentleman's shoes before him, and then accompanied him for a few steps past the exit before returning. I had heard that his grandfather was bed-ridden. Abū-Rājeh took care of that debilitated old man too, helping him out every once in a while. Occasionally, when Masrour was not at home, he would send Rihanna and his own wife to their home to give the place a good going over. Once I saw that he had placed what remained of a meal which Rihanna had brought for him aside so that Masrour could take it home with him. I had no doubt that Masrour awaited the day when he would see Rihanna as the lady of his house.

Masrour brought the bowl of grapes over again and placed it in front of me. He tried to smile. I was bewildered at the twists and turns of fate. At one time, Rihanna and I were playmates and I was the subject of Masrour's envy, and now Masrour saw Rihanna within his reach and was the subject of my envy.

Abū-Rājeh came over and sat next to me. Masrour placed the bowls of cedar and henna on a shelf that was within the reach of the customers. Abū-Rājeh smelled of musk. For the first time, its smell bothered me. I could not like Abū-Rājeh like I used to. I wanted to leave. I felt I was a stranger there. The scents of the hammām that were always pleasurable for me were now weighing on me and were overpowering. Maybe Masrour had already asked for Rihanna's hand in marriage and I wasn't even aware of it. Maybe the earrings had been purchased for the wedding. Masrour would be pleased when he saw the earrings, and Rihanna would be even more beautiful. Nor would she ever mention the fact that I had designed and crafted them. And even if she did: what possible importance could that have for Masrour? He might even scoff at me and my grandfather.

The swans had separated. One was grooming itself with its beak, and the other was still and was slowly going around itself in gentle circles as a result of the ripples that were caused by the water-fountain.

Abū-Rājeh gently scratched my nose. I snapped out of my thoughts and managed a smile.

"Don't let all these thoughts carry you away, my dear Hāshem! Place your trust in God! Who know, maybe the person you are thinking of is indeed the one that you're destined to marry. Or maybe it is someone else. If she is the one, then you will marry her. And if it is someone else, I will pray that she will be many times better than this one, and for the two of you to live happily together. Someone in your position can even marry the Sultan's daughter."

The swan who had turned its back on its mate was pecking at the grapes that had fallen into the foot-wash pool. I tried to think my situation through logically in order to keep the thoughts that tormented me at bay. I was rich and handsome. Why did I have to be so feeble and lame as to allow myself to be the plaything of the whims of the daughter of a hammām-keeper? Masrour was more suited to Abū-Rājeh than me. If Rihanna wanted to live with Masrour, I needed to expect that she was worthy of nothing more than this. With bitterness, I tried to get myself to accept the notion that the only reason Rihanna and her mother had come to our store was so that they could get a good discount. They had reckoned correctly that by giving two dinars, they could get a discount of eight dinars! But they probably could not believe it themselves.

I reached into my pocket and felt the two dinar coins. It no longer felt that they had a pulse, and they felt cold and dry. I wanted to bring them out and to toss them into the pool. But then Abū-Rājeh would be surprised and curious to know why I did something like that, and I would look distractedly behind myself and say, "You'd better go and ask your daughter what it means!"

I squeezed the coins in my hand and stood up. I wanted to escape from that dank and suffocating environment. I thought that I might feel a little better if I went for a swim in the Euphrates. Abū-Rājeh held my hand in his and said, "You must come tomorrow so that we can sit in the private room and talk."

I looked into his kindly eyes. I felt ashamed of all of the bizarre thoughts that I had let into my heart. How had I allowed myself to have such thoughts about Rihanna? I recalled her noble modesty, which was unadorned and angelic. Suddenly the sound of heavy footsteps could be heard from the corridor of the hammām. Someone dressed in the uniform of the Sultan's court quickly drew aside the curtain that covered the entrance of the hammām and said, "His Eminence the Vizier will be entering momentarily. Prepare to show your respects!"

Chapter 5

The Vizier was a gaunt man with a long beard. He donned a thin mantle with gold-embroidered edging on his shoulders. He sat on one of the steps of the platform and, after casting his gaze around the hammām, stared at the swans. Masrour held the bowl of grapes before the Vizier, who waved him away with his hand. He tried not to look at Abū-Rājeh.

"You have a nice hammām, Abū-Rājeh!"

In a gesture of respect, Abū-Rājeh lowered his gaze and said, "If it pleases your honor, allow me to help you to disrobe and escort you into the inner chamber of the hammām so that you can see its beautiful vaulted ceiling as well. It is a wonder to behold!"

The Vizier turned away from Abū-Rājeh.

"There is no time. I was just passing by your place and thought I'd stop by to see these two beautiful birds."

He looked at the swans again. He had beady eyes that moved sharply back and forth.

"They are just as beautiful as I was told they would be. It is as if they are heavenly creatures who have wound up in your place due to a bizarre twist of fate, the poor things!"

He chuckled mirthlessly, then became aware of my presence.

"Who is this handsome young man? He has the looks of a Persian Prince about him."

Abū-Rājeh wanted to introduce me, but the Vizier motioned him to remain quiet.

"He has a tongue of his own. I want to hear his voice."

I said, "My name is Hāshem. Abū-Na'īm the goldsmith is my grandfather."

"Abū-Na'īm is still alive, then?"

He laughed without humor again and showed his two incisors. It was evident that he was a person who enjoyed his position of authority and was ready to act in any way he pleased.

"Yes, God be praised."

"I hear you are a competent goldsmith. What brings you to these parts? This hammām is not a suitable place for a handsome young man such as yourself. It would have been better if you had been accompanied by your grandfather."

I decided to take a risk and said, "Neither have you been accompanied by the Sultan."

He let out a loud belly-laugh. The sound of his laughter echoed under the domed ceiling.

"You have boldness. I like that. But I do not dare come here unaccompanied! That is why I bring my guards with me. Wherever Abū-Rājeh happens to be is a dangerous place."

He looked at Abū-Rājeh, expecting him to say something. For his part, Abū-Rājeh remained silent, knowing that the Vizier was looking for some pretext. The Vizier guffawed and said to me, "In any event, I shall take seeing you and these beautiful swans as a good omen."

He turned to Abū-Rājeh.

"Although Almighty God has not deigned to give you much in terms of beauty, He nevertheless has endowed you with exquisite taste. What a beautiful hammām! What beautiful swans! And handsome customers with such grace, and smart-alec answers at the ready, too!"

Abū-Rājeh said, "Allow me to have a lime cordial brought for you."

"Never mind that. I fear you might poison me!"

He pointed to the swans.

"I do not think there are any other specimens such as these in the whole of the Land between the Two Rivers.[7] In the Sultan's inner chambers, there is a pool made of jade out of which Chinese sculptors have carved flowers. These swans deserve to be in *that* pool. I was at the service of the Sultan yesterday. Your name was mentioned. It has reached the Sultan's ear that you have been disparaging him and denigrating his authority and administration. Make sure that this is not true! Someone told me that there were such birds in Abū-Rājeh's pool. He had described their beauty in such a way that the Sultan instructed me to arrange for them to migrate to the jade pool if they are as beautiful as it is said they are."

His smile exposed his teeth.

"What an eloquent phrase, 'to migrate to the jade pool'! Now I have done you a kind turn and come to visit you on my own cognizance to suggest for the sake of eliminating any misunderstanding – if for nothing else – that you should present the swans as a gift to the Sultan."

Abū-Rājeh sat next to the pool. The swans swam toward him. He said, "These are my boon companions. I have grown used to their company. And my customers are fond of them too. They have spurred my business."

The Vizier said impatiently, "You are an inconsiderate person. It would be better for you to cease your stubbornness and think of the consequences of what you are saying! You might not be presented with an opportunity as good as the one

I am offering you again. I would say that your choice is either to present them to the Sultan as a gift, or to accept payment for their value."

"Why do you not instruct a merchant to procure a few pair of these birds for the palace?"

Signs of anger were now visible on the Vizier's face.

"Don't be a fool, Abū-Rājeh! Think a little, man. That would take several months. The Sultan would like to see these birds in the pool of his private chambers this very day, so that he forgives you your sins. The Sultan's patience wears thin, whereas you can ask whoever it was that brought these birds for you to bring you another pair."

One of the guards who was standing at the entryway of the hammām turned a customer away. Abū-Rājeh shooed the swans into the middle of the pool and stood up.

"If I have committed any crime, I ask the good Lord to forgive me."

He turned to the Vizier.

"Very well. I accept. Neither do I want the Sultan to be upset with you, nor for him to treat me unfairly. So I will give my swans as a gift to Marjān-e Saghīr."

The Vizier nodded his head in satisfaction. "You are a clever man!"

"If I am to forego my swans, it would only be fair for the Sultan to give me a gift that would be worthy of his station and munificence."

The Vizier pointed to Abū-Rājeh and said, "But this would then be a business transaction. The Sultan would not approve."

"I am sure that you can bring him around, having such a wily tongue as you do."

"Watch your tongue! What is it you want?"

"Two of my friends have been thrown into the dungeon without their having committed any crime. I would like them to be freed."

The Vizier narrowed his eyes in concentration. He tried not to show his anger. He stood up. "It would have been better if I had not called on you personally and had sent a ruffian to expropriate the swans and deliver them to me at the palace. Your life and property have no legal standing."

"But I have not asked for anything untoward, surely. Try to remain calm, I beseech you. It was only a suggestion; a request."

"What else did you want to say?! In a flagrant violation of the norms of decorum you claim that we have imprisoned two innocent men who are friends of yours. Did you know that if you are unable to prove this claim, you would have to join your friends in the dungeon? This is over and above the fact that you are presently accused of serious crimes yourself, the penalty of which would indeed be the dungeon. But in any case, your request is denied: the Sultan will not forgive them their crimes."

"There is no evidence of their criminality. Everyone knows that they were sent to the dungeon without trial!"

The Vizier approached Abū-Rājeh and slapped him violently across his face. The sound of the slap reverberated under the dome. Abū-Rājeh, who had a frail disposition, teetered for a step or two, then fell to the ground.

"Shut your mouth, you ugly baboon! The penalty for anyone we feel poses a threat to the public order is imprisonment in the palace's dungeon! If you were to see a scorpion here, would you wait for it to sting you??"

I helped Abū-Rājeh get back on his feet.

"Would that I had not stepped foot in this place! It is true what they said, that you have a bitter and biting tongue, like the sting of a scorpion."

Undaunted, Abū-Rājeh said, "If you had sent a ruffian to take my swans away from me by force, he could not have acted worse that this! So now that things have taken such a turn, I will neither give my swans as a gift, nor will I take money for them. I have said so in the past and I will repeat it now: the way you treat the Shīʻa is worse than how your treat non-Muslims and infidels. And it is plain for anyone to see the truth of what I say."

The Vizier went to the exit and clawed the curtain to one side, saying on his way out, "Keep your blasted swans for yourself! Given the situation you have created, if I see them in the palace pool, they will do nothing but remind me of you, and I never want to be reminded of you again. Truly, your existence is a pestilence!"

Abū-Rājeh wiped the blood that was bleeding from his nose with a handkerchief and said, "You come to my hammām like an abhorred extortionist. You speak with nothing but arrogance. You became angry for no reason. You assaulted me like a madman. You wanted to deprive me of the swans that I like so well and who have helped to grow my business, with threats of violence. And worse than all of this, you humiliated me in front of everyone present and struck me. And you act like *I* am in *your* debt?! If there was a modicum of fairness in you, you could judge for yourself whose existence is a pestilence!"

The Vizier's eyes moved rapidly in anger. A thought came to his mind and he gathered his wits about him. He said with a voice that quivered with anger, "I see that you no longer care whether you live or die! But you are right. *I* am the evil one. So know that I will not rest until I have brought the roof of this hammām down on your head!"

"I take refuge in God from you and the Sultan's court! It seems that you do not believe that there is such a thing as a day where you will be held to account for all of your actions. Your position and power, which are ephemeral, have deceived you. So do whatever it is that you are wont to do!"

The Vizier nodded his head and said, "I am surprised that you did not take advantage of my coming here in person. You could have parted with these birds pleasantly and seen me off in a happy state of mind. It would have been to your advantage."

Abū-Rājeh showed the Vizier the bloody kerchief. "That was indeed my intention. My only mistake was that I asked that justice be done. Nor has anything of great consequence taken place now. I have been slapped, that's all. This should not cast a shadow on your mind! Take the swans and leave. I will miss them dearly for a few days, but I will comfort myself with the thought that they will have a better life in the palace, where they will be cared for lovingly by the Sultan's attendants."

Before the Vizier disappeared behind the curtain, he said, "I am distraught now. Let the swans stay here while I come to my decision."

I was shocked by the scene I had witnessed. Abū-Rājeh washed his hands and face. I took him to the room that was off the corridor so that he could get some rest. When he reclined on the backrest, he said, "I am done for. In the best possible scenario, I will be sent to the dungeon. I don't think this incompetent Vizier will leave me be. He is a spiteful man."

The window of the room opened onto a small inner courtyard. Abū-Rājeh's prayer rug lay open by the window. His books sat in a row in a shelf. Masrour brought in the bowl of grapes, placed them in front of Abū-Rājeh, and left. Abū-Rājeh tried to make light of the situation, saying, "That was not a pretty scene. I didn't want you to witness such a scene after your coming to see me after all this time. But at least it took your mind off your unrequited love sorrows for a few minutes."

Abū-Rājeh chuckled, and I began to laugh too, despite myself.

"If your poor grandfather finds out what happened here, he will not let you come to see me anymore."

We laughed again. It was as if nothing untoward had happened. Abū-Rājeh picked up a cluster of grapes and offered it to me and said, "Here, take it and enjoy it, as it is our lot and daily sustenance."

I took it and started to pick at the grapes with gusto. Masrour stopped by to see what was happening. He could not believe that we were smiling. Seeing his bewildered stare made us break out in laughter again. "It is good that you stayed and saw with your own eyes how the government treats us."

Chapter 6

Grandfather had been summoned to the Sultan's court on several occasions to show and sell the best specimens of his jewelry and personal ornaments to the Sultan's family. But it was the first time that the family of the Sultan were due to come to the store, examine everything up close, and to select anything they liked right there and then. Grandfather instructed his staff that in addition to cleaning the store, the workshop and basement should be given a thorough cleaning as well. It was not out of the realm of possibility for the ladies to decide to visit these areas as well.

Two negro guards entered the store. Without offering any word by way of explanation, they proceeded to the basement and up to the workshop where they inspected everything, including inside the chests and wardrobes and cabinets, until they were satisfied that nothing suspect was inside the store. The curve of their scimitars was clearly visible under their robes. When the ladies entered, the guards took their positions outside the store and monitored the situation.

The company of the ladies numbered around twenty people. The wife of the Vizier and the wives of the functionaries of the court were also present. The Sultan had several daughters, all of whom were married except the youngest, who had also come along. The ladies stood further back than the Sultan's wife and deferred to her. But the Sultan's daughters, not concerned with standing on such ceremony, would point to the jewelry that was on display and express their opinions on a piece's beauty or worth. Other than three women servants, the other ladies had covered their faces with a thick piece of silk cloth in such a way that only their eyes were visible. Two goldsmiths had come down from the workshop and helped out by serving lime cordials and confections.

I had a feeling that I had seen the Sultan's youngest daughter before. She had paid the store a visit on a few occasions in the last few weeks and had purchased some expensive jewelry. Grandfather had said that she was probably the daughter of a rich merchant. When I saw one of the women servants, I became certain that our rich customer was none other than the daughter of the Sultan. Each time she had come to our store, she had been accompanied by this servant and by no one else. I thought to myself, "I feel sorry for the future husband of this woman, given her appetite for so much expensive jewelry!"

I knew that her name was Qanwā. All of the young men and women of Hilla knew this. She was famous for being adventurous. Sometimes she would roam the bazaar and streets of the city incognito. I had even heard that she had at times dressed as a young man and acted out the role of a street vendor and even played a magician in the bazaar.

I unfurled the scrolls of my designs and showed them to the wife of the Sultan. Qanwā stood beside her listening to my explanations with a smirk on her face. Her sisters stretched their necks from behind her to get a glance. As I had thought, my designs of the diamond ring with two dragons, the one with one on either side of the gemstone whose gaping mouths held the gemstone in place, had caught their attention. Qanwā looked at me and said, "I want a complete set in this design. Highly refined and delicate, and on the double."

I saw the outline of her smile. She was relishing her moment. It was clear that she was the beloved of her mother and older sisters. They had spoiled her rotten, to the point that she thought she could have anything she desired. The store accountant wrote down the orders as fast as he could. I told him to take the following down: "A complete set, inclusive of a ring, a bracelet, a necklace, an armband, a belt, a foot bracelet, and a hair clasp, in the two-dragons design."

Outside the store, the guards told the customers to leave or to stand back at a distance if they wanted to wait until the shopping spree of the ladies of the palace was over. The ladies finally had their fill of the store after about an hour and began preparing to leave. They had made purchases and placed orders that totaled the equivalent of a whole week of the store's business. The Sultan's wife told Grandfather: "So send Hāshem to the palace tomorrow to collect the payment for what we have purchased."

Grandfather gave her an invoice for the purchases with a bow and said, "As you wish, madam. But if you will allow me, I should like to call on the palace personally."

The ladies wanted to leave the store when Qanwā signaled her mother, reminding her of something. Her mother said, "Send someone to clean and polish the palace jewels and ornaments, and to make any necessary repairs."

Grandfather said, "If it pleases my lady, the jewels can be dispatched to the store where all manner of detergents and special cleansing agents are available at the ready, as are the special tools required for buffing and polishing jewelry."

"Transporting all that jewelry outside the palace grounds is both difficult and imprudent. The person you send will have to begin work at the palace from the day after tomorrow."

Grandfather gave this some thought and said, "No'mān is suitable for this task. He has a good understanding of the polishes and cleansing agents, and is a master when it comes to repair work."

Qanwā said, "It is better that you send Hāshem. He has an aristocratic look about him."

Her mother looked me over and asked Grandfather, "What is his work like?"

Grandfather scratched an itch behind his ear under his turban and said, "His skill as a goldsmith is good. The most beautiful works that you purchased were of his design or craftsmanship, but I would not like him to stray far from me as he is still very young and does not have a sufficient familiarity with palace protocol. If it pleases my lady, permit No'mān to be at your service."

Qanwā narrowed her eyes and said, "Don't keep repeating yourself! I like the designs of this young man. If my time permits, I should like to see how he goes about his designs. We shall see him in the palace."

Her mother turned towards the exit. "We shall set him up with a room that will act as his workshop. And he will be paid upon the completion of his work."

Before leaving, Qanwā said to me in a low tone of voice, "You will make the jewelry that I ordered at the palace. I want to see how you work."

I said, "Making those requires a fully equipped workshop."

Qanwā shrugged. "Whatever is necessary shall be provided."

When the ladies had left, Grandfather said to me, "You were right. I should not have had you come down from the workshop to the store."

But my curiosity had been aroused and I wanted to see the inside of the palace.

Chapter 7

My room was on the second floor of our house. I had arranged it to my own tastes. I had hung some of my designs on its walls, together with mementos of my father and some fine art that I had bought in my travels. My bed was positioned next to the window, and at night I would gaze into the night sky until I fell asleep. Before I had seen Rihanna in the store, I felt good about life. I would lay down on my bed, well worn out after a hard day's work, and, content with a life that was free of any anxiety, would entrust myself to the journeys that my dreams had prepared for me. Occasionally, Grandfather would come to my room an hour or so after dinner, bringing with him two cups of some calming herbal infusion that Omm-Hobāb had brewed. We would spend a few minutes talking and laughing and making plans for the future.

I was restless that night, as I had been the previous several nights since Rihanna's visit. I wasn't able to sleep until the early hours of the morning. I kept my eyes on the gentle swaying motion of the palm trees under the dark clouds, and thought about my uncertain future until dawn. I could not see any way out; every avenue led to a dead-end. There was a wall between Rihanna and I in which not a single opening was to be found.

I kept going over and over the scene of Rihanna and her mother's visit to the store in the tranquil and portentous heart of the night. I wanted to understand the mystery of love. What was it that made a single glance and smile into a snare that hooked an erstwhile freeman into its claws? Between the waking and dream state, I wanted to know what it was about Rihanna's being that had so discombobulated me. Was it nothing more than the outline of her face? Was it the mere crossing of our lines of sight? Her poise and dignity? The tone and melody of her voice? Was it all of these? Or none of them? It was all of these and none of them at the same time.

I was hoping to be able to forget her after the passage of a few days, but couldn't. I was like an ensnared animal who became more ensnared the more it struggled to free itself. I sat in my bed, confused and without hope of relief, clutching at my hair. I needed to find a way out of the darkness that engulfed me, back into the light. That was the only solution to my situation. But how?

I determined to pay a visit to Rihanna and her mother on the morrow and reveal all that was in my heart. An hour later, I had decided the better course of action would be to go to Abū-Rājeh and shout out, "That customer who stole my heart while purchasing those earrings is your daughter!"

When my thoughts and mind came across yet another escarpment-like dead-end after having run an unpromising alley to ground, I would throw myself on my pillow and beg Sleep to come take me away to the Land of Dreams. In those nights, sleep was like a light-footed hare who increased the distance between us the more I chased after it.

I wanted to see Rihanna in a dream and tell her, "All of our childhood memories were set in motion by a single glance of yours." I aspired to go for a stroll with her in my dream, next to the bridge over the Euphrates, and to tell her all about the woes of my heart. I could not find peace even in sleep. I saw her, but she was with Masrour and they were walking away from me.

One night I dreamed that Masrour snatched Rihanna's earrings and threw them into the river from a bridge. As I had been watching them, I dived into the river after the earrings. I found them on the riverbed, but they had grown to such an enormous size that I was barely able to dislodge them and bring them back up with me to the surface. I looked at the bridge. No one was there. The weight of the earrings pulled me down into the water. When I looked behind me, I saw Rihanna and Masrour in a boatful of grapes that receded from me no matter how much I struggled to reach it.

In the morning I made my way down the stairs slowly. Grandfather was sitting on a wooden bed in the front yard, waiting for me. He stood up when I approached him. He held my shoulders and stared into my eyes.

"What's the matter? Are you not feeling well? Why did you not come down for breakfast?"

I was confused and disoriented. I could barely stand up. I sat on the bed.

"I don't know. I couldn't sleep last night. And when I finally fell asleep, I had all these weird dreams. It has been like this for so many days now that I dread the approach of the evening."

"You better stay home today and get some rest. You must go to the Sultan's palace tomorrow, and you can't go there in such a state and looking like this."

Grandfather called our maidservant, who was a kindly old woman.

"Omm-Hobāb!"

Omm-Hobāb stuck her head out of a room on the other side of the yard.

"Yes, master."

This child is not feeling well. He will be staying at home today. You must see to his every need and ensure that he makes a full recovery and deliver him back to me as good as new by noon."

"Yes, master. Don't you worry about a thing."

Grandfather turned to me and said, "I am familiar with these states. You have fallen in love with Rihanna, am I right? I had guessed as much. Now what is to be done? I cannot think of any way to bring about your marriage to Rihanna. It is not as if we did not have enough troubles without this one being added to the lot! And from how Qanwā acted yesterday, it would seem that she has found her future husband."

I could not hide my surprise.

"What are you saying, Grandfather?"

He came over and sat next to me and put his arm on my shoulder.

"You are so simple, and Rihanna has so taken over your heart and mind that you are no longer even aware of your surroundings!"

I went to stand up, but swooned.

"If that is the case, then I will not go to the palace."

He helped me sit back down and stood up himself.

"Don't rush to a decision about that. When I think about it, I see that it isn't so bad after all. It is to your advantage to prefer Qanwā to Rihanna. Marjān-e Saghīr is a *nāsebī*, it is true. He is malevolent toward the Shī'a. But a bond of marriage with him is a great honor. If you gain access to the Sultan's court, it won't be long before you forget all about Rihanna. What I mean to say is that you really have no other choice."

I held my head in both my hands.

"No, Grandfather. No!"

"Calm yourself, my son."

"You are among the well to do of this city. You are thinking of my future, I know. But it is not within your power to give me that which I most desire."

My helplessness and hopelessness set off tears that silently made their way down my face. A few drops landed on my shirt. Grandfather took me in his arms.

"My dear, crazy son! I had no idea that you had fallen so head over heels in love with her. It is my own fault for dragging you out of the workshop. You would not be going through all this torment if you had stayed where you were."

Omm-Hobāb who was stout and tall rushed in panting for breath.

"I will strangle that godless butcher with my own hands! The meat he sold me yesterday was rancid, and now he has poisoned this poor, motherless child."

Her quivering jowls made me smile. When she saw my smile, she took in a deep breath and said, "O, thank God! So you are not feeling that bad after all, and my wanting to strangle the poor butcher was for naught. May God forgive me my trespasses."

Grandfather who didn't know what to say, said to Omm-Hobāb, "Go and fetch the lad some herbal tea or something. He didn't have a proper meal last night either."

Turning to me he said, "I need to think to see what can be done. But take today off and get some rest."

"I have been raking my mind day and night; there is no solution!"

Before leaving, Grandfather said, "We must entrust our affairs to God. The key to every closed padlock is in His hands."

I stretched out on my bed. Omm-Hobāb prepared an elixir in no time and brought it for me. I felt a little better after I had taken it. I related to her everything that had happened. She felt really sorry for me. She had raised me from the time I was nothing but a toddler, and loved me a lot. She wiped her tears away and blew her nose. I told her that Rihanna teaches the Quran to ladies, as well as holding classes on the ordinances of the sacred law. I gave her the address to Rihanna's house and asked her to go there and see if she could bring me some news of her. I took the two dinars that were in my pocket and held them out to her, but she was very offended.

"I used to change your diapers, and now you hold out a couple of coins for me?"

I knew that this was how she would react. I replaced the coins in my pocket and reclined again onto my bed.

"Forgive me, Omm-Hobāb! You have enough troubles of your own. It's not your fault that I have come to such a pass!"

She sat on the corner of the bed and started to rub her knee. She was weighing her options.

"Alright. I might go there tomorrow. *May*be. I'm not up to it today. My knee is killing me."

I turned away from her in disapproval.

"You know, you should be ashamed of yourself for falling in love with the daughter of a hammām-keeper."

"You have to go this very day! You have not even seen her. When you do, you will change your mind."

"All I know is that none of the girls in Hilla are worthy even of being your maidservants."

"I can't stand it! You have to bring me some news of her. If you truly loved me, you would get up and go there right now."

"Don't even *think* about that! You should know better than to force a poor old maid to do something. I don't know what on earth this love business is that afflicts you foolish young people and turns your minds to mush. Thank God that there were no signs of such madness in my own life! I loved my late husband, may God have mercy on his soul. And he loved me. But if he ever went on a journey, neither of us would fall apart and act like the world had ended."

I stood up and acted like I had blacked out.

"You are right. I should not put you to the trouble. After all, it is me and not you that has fallen in love. I will go myself, come what may. If it gets dark and I have not come back by then, don't worry on my account."

"Sit back down, you silly boy. I can't be responsible for answering the complaints of that grouchy old man. Alright, I'll go. But don't be put out if I put an end to this self-indulgent girl!"

I was so happy that I thought I could fly.

"Don't talk about her like that. One day she will come to this house and help you with the chores. Then you will love her so much that you will not be able to live a single day without her."

"Yeah, right! How is Abū-Rājeh going to give the hand of his daughter to someone such as yourself who is not even Shī'a?!"

With these parting words, she went to get ready to go out. When she was leaving, with a shopping basket in her hand, she said, "Don't you move from your bed. And eat up all of your breakfast. Then get plenty of rest so that some fresh blood can reach that crazy brain of yours."

When she stepped over the door's threshold, she said, "Think good and hard, and see how you will answer God's questions. You're sending this poor old woman with bad knees to the other side of the bazaar for what? For nothing!"

"Remember, she mustn't know who you are!"

"Don't think I will waste my time talking to her! I have to get back right away and prepare lunch. It is not as if I have nothing to do!"

She had not even turned the corner of the alley before I left the house too. I couldn't stand to be confined indoors. I needed to see Abū-Rājeh.

Chapter 8

Abū-Rājeh was not in. The swans were motionless in the pool. Masrour was counting more coins in the wooden alcove. When I asked where Abū-Rājeh was, he shrugged and pretended that if he stopped counting the coins, he would lose count of them. So I waited for him to finish what he was doing. When Abū-Rājeh was not at the hammām, it was as if it was dark and lifeless. Masrour counted the last of the coins. He looked at me without enthusiasm and remained quiet.

"Now tell me where Abū-Rājeh is."

He unhurriedly placed the coins into a leather pouch which he placed in a small chest next to him.

"He didn't tell me where he was going."

I sat on the edge of the platform.

"So I'll just wait for him to come back then."

"He might have gone to the Station of His Eminence the Mahdi[8] in order to offer his ritual devotions."

I was getting ready to leave when he said, "It would be better if you didn't come around here."

I went up to him and asked, "Why? Has something happened?"

"Did you know that Abū-Rājeh is being monitored by the authorities?"

"How do you know?"

He couldn't look me in the eyes. He had turned away and was looking at a man who was dressing his child on the platform.

"You saw how the Vizier treated him. The government doesn't like Abū-Rājeh. It is to your advantage to keep your distance from him. Nor is he happy for you to get yourself entangled on his account for no good reason."

"So then why have you stayed here?"

"My situation is different. Everyone knows that I have been his apprentice for many years, and that I must keep the doors of the hammām open under any and all conditions. This is Abū-Rājeh's own instructions."

I had made my way to the curtain. I said, "I thank you for thinking of me and for your counsel, but I thought it would have been your duty to defend Abū-Rājeh in the face of the Vizier's accusations. After all, he is your patron."

"It is Abū-Rājeh's own wish that I not interfere in these matters. Suppose he is arrested and sent to the dungeon. Would it be better for me to be imprisoned with him, or for me to stay here and run the hammām?"

I left the hammām and started to run towards the Station of His Eminence the Mahdi ﷺ through the back alleys of the city. The Shī'a believed that their last leader (or Imam) had gone into a state of occultation (or absence from the earthly plane) at God's behest, and that he will reappear whenever God wills it. The Shī'a cemetery was next to the Station of the Mahdi ﷺ. The Station was known as a place where the Mahdi ﷺ had appeared. Grandfather would say, "How is it possible for a person to live for hundreds of years?" About five hundred years had passed since the disappearance of their Imam. I was surprised at Abū-Rājeh for believing that his Imam was still alive.

The Station consisted of a simple mosque. It was said that Marjān-e Saghīr had decided to raze it. I entered the Station. A few people were busy offering their ritual devotions. One of them was praying for the freedom of those who were imprisoned in Marjān-e Saghīr's dungeon. His face was wet with his tears.

Abū-Rājeh was not there, but I saw him in the cemetery. He was sitting next to a gravestone reading the Quran. I went up to him and sat down next to him. He smiled when he saw me. His eyes had become red. It was clear that he had been busy praying to the Lord earlier at the Station of the Mahdi ﷺ. I recited the *Fāteha*.[9] It was a nice and tranquil place.

"Hāshem. What are you doing here? Why are you so pale?"

"I was not feeling well. Grandfather told me to stay at home and rest. But I could not stay put once he left. I was feeling really depressed, so I thought I'd come and talk to you for a while."

"How are you feeling now?"

"Much better. I could not get to sleep last night. All I can do is think of that Shī'a girl. Ever since I have fallen in love with her, all of my nights are spent thinking of what to do about her. I am terrified of nightfall now. If only it were possible to pick off the nights like the dried and shriveled up berries of a cluster of grapes and throw them out!"

He laughed.

"You're turning into a bit of a poet."

I said, "How can you laugh? If things continue like this, it will not be long before I wither away. I am dying. I can't eat. I can't motivate myself to work. Who can help me?"

He laughed again.

"May God help you!"

"Maybe you do not want to help me. Maybe it's because I'm not Shī'a that you want nothing to do with me."

"Come now, don't say such things, Hāshem."

"What I am saying is that what I am going through is not that important to you."

He shook his head sadly.

"I love you like my own daughter, Rihanna. What difference is there between the two of you for me? I prayed for you today too, in this sacred place."

Hearing Rihanna's name made me swoon. I asked, "How is Lady Rihanna, anyway?"

She was afflicted with an unknown disease a while back. She was very ill and was bedridden for a while. We didn't allow her to do any more carpet-weaving. She's been feeling a little better for the last week or so."

"Thank God! What great times we had when we were kids. Has she not married yet?"

"No, not yet."

I had untethered myself and had ventured out to see.

"I hear she knows the whole Quran by heart and holds women-only courses on Quranic exegesis and on the ordinances of the sacred law. You have expended much effort in her upbringing and training. Such a young lady probably has a large number of suitors as well. May God keep her safe. From when I remember her, she was a very kind-hearted person."

I blinked a couple of times to clear the tears that were gathering in my eyes.

"You are absolutely right. She has many suitors. Masrour has approached me on this subject as well."

I almost fainted. I leaned on the low wall of the grave to stop myself from falling over.

"Masrour? How did you respond?"

"Rihanna says that she has been shown her future husband in a dream. She says that she will only say yes to this suitor."

I breathed a sigh of relief.

"How very interesting to think that one's husband-to-be would be indicated to one in a dream. Godspeed to her!"

"Of course, I have not mentioned Masrour's asking for her hand to her as of yet. It would not surprise me if she has seen Masrour in her dream but is too bashful to make mention of it."

I began to lose heart again. It was as if the cemetery, with all its graves and surrounding palm trees, was whirling around my head.

"No matter how much her mother insisted that she say who the person is, she refused to divulge his identity. Perhaps she does not know him. All she has said is that the young man held her hand in his, and that a young and handsome version of me held them both in my arms. I do not know whether such a dream is or is not a true dream, you know, those that come to pass. In any event, I gave her a year to see if her dream will come true. If nothing happens within that time, then she will have to marry a suitable suitor.

"What does she say about that?"

"She said that if her dream is a true dream and it is God's will, that the young man will ask for her hand in marriage within the year."

"What a story! How much time is left of that year?"

"Two or three weeks."

My mouth went dry. Everything was aligned against me. I wished that there were eleven months and thirty days remaining! In that case, I could rest assured somewhat, for a little while anyway. I had no doubt that I was not the person

Rihanna had seen in her dream. For how could she hold out hope for marrying someone who was not Shī'a??

I didn't ask any more questions as I was afraid that Abū-Rājeh might get a whiff of the secret I held in my heart of hearts. My only hope was that Omm-Hobāb was with Rihanna at that very moment, and that she would be able to bring me some good or at least interesting news. Just to change the subject, I asked, "Whose grave is this?"

He let out a sigh and said, "Ismael Harqalī's."

"The name is not familiar to me."

"He died fifty years ago. His story is a very strange though interesting one. Do you want to hear it?"

I preferred that he would talk about Rihanna, but my curiosity had been aroused and I wanted to hear the story. The man's story must have been important if it had brought Abū-Rājeh to read the Quran by his gravesite. We were seated in the shade provided by the palm trees. The sun was climbing up and about to show herself to us from above the fronds of the palm trees. I reproached myself for not having had a bite to eat for breakfast. I was starving!

Chapter 9

"I heard this story from Ismael Harqalī's son. May God have mercy on his soul. He was a hardworking and righteous man. The story is so well-known that many of the people of Hilla and Baghdad still remember it. Your grandfather must have heard it too."

"I don't remember him saying anything about it."

"When Ismael was a young man, he was afflicted with a large abscess the size of the palm of one's hand on his thigh. This abscess or boil would burst every year in the spring, oozing out infected puss and blood. Can you imagine? The poor man couldn't live a normal life. You know how the village of Harqal is near Hilla. Well, that is where Ismael lived."

"Yes, I know where it is. Our caravan made a stop there a couple of years back."

"Ismael made his way to Hilla. When he asked around for the greatest scholar of Hilla, the people directed him to Sayyed Eben Tāwūs's house, telling him that Eben Tāwūs was the most knowledgeable and most pious scholar, and that the Sunnis as well as the Shī'a seek his help in solving their problems. So, Ismael goes to Eben Tāwūs and shows him the abscess on his thigh. Eben Tāwūs tells him with good cheer that he will help him recover from his affliction."

"I have heard things about Eben Tāwūs' knowledge and nobility of character."

"The Sayyed called upon the surgeons of Hilla to come and examine and cure Ismael's abscess. The surgeons said that the abscess was positioned on a critical artery, and that the only cure was in its excision. Sayyed Eben Tāwūs tells them that there is no choice, and to proceed with the excision. But they respond by saying that there is a high probability that the critical artery will be severed or damaged during the surgery, leading to the patient's death. So Sayyed Eben Tāwūs takes Ismael to Baghdad, where he shows the abscess to the most skilled surgeons there. These surgeons tell him the same thing that the surgeons of Hilla had said. Sayyed Eben Tāwūs wanted to return to Hilla, but Ismael said to him, 'Now that we have come this far, it would be good to make a pilgrimage to the shrine of the Imams ﷺ of Sāmarrā. And so, they make pilgrimage to the shrines of Imam Ali an-Naqī and Imam Hasan al-Askarī ﷺ, who are the tenth and eleventh of the Shī'a Imams. They then go to the 'Sacred Cellar', where they ask for the Lord of the Age[10] ﷺ to intercede with God for the sake of curing Ismael's abscess."

"Where is the 'Sacred Cellar'?"

"It is a cellar from which the Lord of the Age ﷺ disappeared and started his period of occultation.[11] Many people have had the honor of being at the service of His Eminence the Twelfth Imam in that cellar. Ismael stayed in Sāmarrā for a few days, spending most of his time in supplication and prayer to Almighty God, and in seeking intercessory recourse (*tawassol* [12]) with the Imams. Ismael performed a major ablution (*ghosl* [13]) on a Thusday in the Tigress River outside of the city, and then puts on a clean set of clothes, in further preparation of a final visit to the pilgrimage sites of the shrines of the two Imams and the 'Sacred Cellar'. When he reaches the city wall, he sees four riders on horseback before him. Three of them were young men, and the fourth was an old man. One of the young men was endowed with a greater dignity and grandeur than the other two. The riders greet Ismael with *salaams*. Ismael believed them to be notables and dignitaries among the ranchers of the region. The man who had a great dignity and awesomeness about him asked him, 'Will you be returning tomorrow?' To which Ismael replied, 'Yes, I will be returning to Hilla on the morrow.' The man then said, 'Come forward so that I can examine that thing that has been tormenting you and causing you so much anguish'."

Abū-Rājeh continued with his story, "Ismael was unwilling to let the man touch his abscess. He was afraid it would start to ooze puss again and soil his clothes, which would then no longer be ritually pure, and would need to be changed before he could make his pilgrimage with peace of mind. Nevertheless, he did as he was asked to do and went forward, being under the influence of the stranger's awe and grandeur. The man then bends forward while still mounted on his horse and, placing his right hand on Ismael's shoulder for support, places his other hand on the abscess and applies pressure to it, causing Ismael to feel a slight discomfort. The man then raises himself up and sits erect again on his horse. The older man among the four says, 'You have prospered, Ismael!' When Ismael shows surprise that the man knew his name, the old man continues, 'His Eminence is the Lord of your Age ﷻ.' Ismael approached his Imam happily and with excitement, and kissed the Imam's foot, who in turn set his horse in motion. When Ismael ran to keep up with the company, the Imam told him to return. Ismael who was so excited that he didn't know what to do said, 'Now that I have seen you, I shall not abandon you.' The Imam replied, 'It would be better that you return.' But Ismael insisted, 'I shall not part company from you!' At this juncture, the old man says, 'Have you no shame, Ismael? The Lord of your ﷿ has twice instructed you to return to your affairs!' Ismael finally comes to his senses and stands still, and His Eminence disappears with his companions."

"Ismael, who had become bewildered and saddened by the departure of his Imam, sat right there and wept for about an hour. When he felt better, he returned to Sāmarrā and went to the shrine. When the keepers of the shrine see Ismael's distraught state, they ask him what had come over him. When he relates the story to them, they ask him to show them his thigh. Ismael shows them his left thigh, but they see that there is no sign of any abscess or scarring on it. He thinks that perhaps he is mistaken and that the abscess must be on his other thigh. But when he exposes that thigh also, there is no sign of any abscess or scarring on it either. At this point, the crowd that had gathered around him start to pick at pieces of his clothing, shredding it and taking pieces of it as *tabarrok*.[14]"

How could I believe such a thing?! I said, "It is a strange story!"

Abū-Rājeh continued, "Ismael went back to Baghdad, where Sayyed Eben Tāwūs fainted after hearing Ismael's story and examining his thigh. When he gained consciousness again, he gathered the surgeons of Baghdad around and pointing to Ismael, said, 'Proceed with the cure for the abscess of this man's thigh.' The surgeons reiterate, 'As we have said before, the only option before us is to cut the abscess out, and if we do that, he will surely die.' Sayyed Eben Tāwūs asked them, 'If the abscess is excised and the patient does not die, how long would it take for the wound to heal?' The surgeons replied, 'At least two months. But a concavity will remain at the site of the excision, and hair will not grow on the scar tissue.' Sayyed Eben Tāwūs asked, 'How long has it been since you last examined the patient's abscess?' They said, 'Two days.' Sayyed Eben Tāwūs then showed Ismael's thigh to the surgeons, whose mouths gaped in astonishment. One of the surgeons who was a Christian cried, 'This is the work of the Lord Jesus!' Sayyed Eben Tāwūs replied, 'We know full well whose handiwork this is.' When Ismael returned to Hilla, the people went to visit him in droves and examined his thigh."

I said, "It's hard to believe! How is it possible for someone to live for hundreds of years and still appear to be young?"

Abū-Rājeh stood up and washed the tombstone with a jugful of water he had brought with him.

"Do you not know that the prophet Noah lived to be around a thousand years old, and that Khezr and Jesus are still alive? Perhaps the old man who was with the Imam was none other than Khezr. Is it not in the power of the Almighty to grant a person such a prolonged lifespan and to keep him young? Is it not the case, after all, that in Heaven, everyone stays young and healthy? Nothing is beyond the power of the Almighty."

I remained quiet. I didn't have anything with which to respond. We strolled together close to the bazaar, and when we reached a crossroads, he went towards the hammām and I headed home. I needed to get back as soon as possible. Abū-Rājeh's words had distressed me. I hoped that at least Omm-Hobāb would bring me some good news.

Chapter 10

I threw myself on the platform bed. I was tired. My limbs were shaking. Omm-Hobāb had not yet returned. I felt very strange. I felt confined in the large expanse of the yard. The walls were taller and closer than usual. I could not wait for Omm-Hobāb to get back. My talk with Abū-Rājeh had not given me any encouragement. I was completely despondent. How was it possible to believe that the Shī'a had such a loving leader who was unaffected by the passage of time and who could perform prophet-like miracles? It was hard to believe! But on the other hand, Abū-Rājeh was not a liar. Could it be that Ismael had faked an abscess on his thigh, and then wiped it off and claimed that the Lord of the Age ﷿ had cured him of it? But the surgeons of Hilla and Baghdad together with Sayyed Eben Tāwūs had examined his thigh. He would have been found out if it was a lie. Whatever the case was, what was certain was that Abū-Rājeh believed in their Imam with such strength of faith that it was as if he was living among them. How was I supposed to believe that their Imam had lived for close to five hundred years and was still alive, and a young man at that? On the other hand, I reasoned with myself that if such longevity is impossible, then how did the prophet Noah live for twice as long as the Imam of the Shī'a? I knew, of course, that God had the power to do anything.

I heard a sound. I thought that Omm-Hobāb was behind the door. I got up and opened the door, but it was a raggedy beggar who hadn't had a decent meal in days, from the look of him. On an impulse, I took the two dinars that were still in my pocket and gave them to him. I had imagined that he would jump for joy and be all over me with gratitude, but he looked at the coins unsurprised and smiled. I said, "Pray for me, brother! I am in love with someone whom I cannot marry."

He said, "It seems you are truly stuck. Few people are willing to part with two dinars[15] and give them to a beggar who is a stranger to them. Would you like to have them back and give me a dirham instead?"

What he said was true. He was a stranger; I had never seen him before. I replied, "These coins are very dear to me. It is best that I give them as a gift to God."

He smiled again and said, "I hope that God accepts them from you! I have heard that at times, God afflicts his devotees with a trial in order to draw them closer to Him."

After the fakir left, I closed the door and stood right there behind it. How could I have parted with those coins? Had I not determined to keep them forever? Maybe I felt that their presence tormented me and would be a constant reminder of Rihanna. I asked myself, "Was that man a real fakir, or were his tattered clothing fake and taken me in? I cursed Satan. But there was a certain sincerity in his face that caused me to want to help him. The dinars were nothing more than a memento for me, but they could be the start of a new life for him.

I was still feeling depressed. I mumbled to myself, "Your tardiness will be the end of me, you lazy woman!" I collapsed on the bed again. I was starving, but could not muster enough motivation to get up and pay the kitchen a visit. I couldn't wait for Omm-Hobāb to come back so that I could put all sorts of questions to her right there at the front door.

There was a canopy above the bed that blocked the sun's rays. But that same canopy seemed oppressive to me. It was as if a heavy quilt had been thrown on me. I was frightened by my own condition; it was very distressing. I was receding away from the window of hope and the shoreline of life. I cried out, "Help me, Lord!"

Then in a lower tone of voice I added, "God, if that young man really exists and cured Ismael Harqalī, I beseech you on [the right of] his soul to save me from this anguish and torment! It is not as if I was thinking of Rihanna; it was You who showed her to me out of nowhere in all her beauty and grace, and cooked my goose. So then *You* make it so that she will be within my reach! She is goodness personified. Is it wrong to love that which is good? Lord, could it be that I am the young man whom she has seen in her dream? Is she waiting for me to ask for her hand in marriage? Was there such a request hidden in that enchanting look of hers that lit me like a candle and melted my heart and soul?"

I struck my forehead to the bed's headboard. I said to myself, "Don't fool yourself with these childish thoughts, you dolt! Whyever would she dream of you and be waiting for a non-Shī'a suitor?! *You* think of her night and day, meanwhile, *she* is thinking of Masrour or some other Shī'a fellow, and how he will make her happy after their marriage. It has been several years since Rihanna has laid her eyes on you, you miserable wretch, so how is she supposed to have dreamed of you as a befitting suitor? If she had seen you in her dream, she would have waited for you to ask for her hand in marriage and to lay a chest of the most exquisite jewelry at her feet, rather than to come and purchase a cheap pair of earrings for two dinars. And besides, even if she *has* seen you in her dream, what use is that when Abū-Rājeh would never consent to give the hand of his lovely daughter to a Sunni suitor?!"

The key in the locked door shifted and I heard the familiar sound of someone's panting. The door swiveled on its heel. It was Omm-Hobāb. I jumped out of bed enthusiastically and went over and picked up the basket that she had placed on the ground, and brought in into the house. I expected her to start complaining between her panting, but she came in and sat down calmly on the bed. She was deep in thought. I sat in front of her on the floor, next to her shopping basket.

"What took you so long, Omm-Hobāb? Did you not consider that I have been waiting for you here all this time? I thought that maybe you decided to stop by Baghdad on the way!"

She smiled gently and said, "All I can say is that you have excellent taste! I didn't think that there could be such a gem in all of Hilla. I was completely overwhelmed by her kindness."

That made me very happy. I said, "So tell me, Omm-Hobāb! Tell me every little detail!"

She looked at me and asked, "Why are you so pale? Have you had your breakfast? No?"

She bent down and picked out a couple of mangos from the basket.

"God! What am I going to say to Abū-Naʿīm? First, I will fix you up with a bowl of mango juice, sweetened with date syrup. Once you drink that and start to feel better, we can sit and talk properly."

I grabbed the mangoes from her clutches and chucked them back into the basket.

"Don't do something that will drive me crazy and make me go out into the desert like a madman!"

Her eyes opened wide in astonishment. "God forbid!"

"You can be sure that I won't eat a thing until you tell me everything!"

She frowned and shook her head in disapproval.

"It so happened that I arrived at their house at a time when she was holding one of her classes. They have a small house. Everyone was gathered in the house's largest room, and Rihanna was addressing them in a serene tone of voice. I entered the room and sat down in a corner. She smiled at me and said, 'Welcome!' Her face was so luminous that one would think that it lit up the whole room. She explained a verse of the Quran, then proceeded to answer people's questions. Then, at the end, she recited a portion of Hosayn ibn Ali's Testament (*shahādat-nāmah*) in a very melancholy tone of voice, causing everyone in the room to shed tears. Her recitation was so beautiful and full of emotion that even a stone-hearted person would have been moved to tears. I wept for the Imam too."

She went quiet and began to rub her knees. I said, "Is that it? What happened next?"

She said, "I wish I could attend every day. I learned many things. I couldn't believe that a girl as young as Rihanna could be so knowledgeable! And so humble! She paid attention to everyone equally. What a kind and lovely person she is."

She again went quiet and started to rub her knees once more.

"Did you not speak with her?"

"Did you expect me to ask for her hand in marriage for you right there too?"

"Noooo, but…"

"When the class was over and the ladies started to leave, I stayed put. She and someone else who I found out later was her mother came and sat next to me. They lovingly asked how I was doing. I said, "I have come from two districts over so that I can learn something in my old age. Too bad it is such a long walk, otherwise I would come every day." Rihanna went and fetched me some dates and fruit juice.

Omm-Hobāb didn't say anything more and stared at my face. I asked, "What else happened? Why do you stare at me like you're seeing a ghost?"

"Believe me, if it is your lot to marry Rihanna, you will have the best possible mother in law in the world! Rihanna was brought up by her, after all. The way she talked with me was so kind and loving, it was as if we had known each other for years. Rihanna's mother then asked me a question, which got me thinking to use my noggin'."

She went quiet again. She smiled at what she had done as she rubbed her knees. Impatiently I said, "What did she say?? Why do you stop between every other sentence and rub your knees?"

"Be patient, child! It is not as if I spent a year over there to have stories to tell about it all night. What was I saying?"

"Her mother had asked you something that made you use your brain."

"Right. She asked, 'Where do you live? We might be in the neighborhood one day and might be able to stop by'. I said, 'You must have heard the name of Abū-Na'īm, the goldsmith…'."

I yelled, "Omm-Hobāb, you weren't supposed to say who you were! Just one time you had to use your head, and you ruined everything!"

Knowing better, she gave me a dirty look. "Patience! Listen, *then* say what you have to say. I said, 'You must have heard the name of Abū-Na'īm, the goldsmith?' Rihanna's eyes brightened. Her mother said, 'Yes, we know him.' I said, 'We are neighbors.' At that point, Rihanna exposed the earrings that she was wearing from behind a thicket of hair, and said, 'We bought these earrings from their store'."

She went quiet again and cracked a knowing smile. I lost it.

"What do you mean by all these coy smiles? Why have you gone all quiet again??"

She rubbed her knees.

"You are a real dolt, aren't you? Did you not pay attention to what Rihanna said?"

"Which part?"

"Rihanna is an intelligent girl. She chooses her words carefully and with deliberation. She didn't say 'We bought these earrings from Abū-Naʿīm's store.' She said, 'We bought them from *their* store.' Do you know what that means??"

I had no idea what she was talking about.

"No. I have no idea."

"It means Abū-Naʿīm and *Hāshem*'s store!"

"And?"

"She was giving you a hint!!"

"So, what does it mean?"

"It means that she likes you too!"

I set the basket of meat and groceries aside. "For the love of God, don't jump to ridiculous conclusions! Something as simple as that can never have the kind of meaning that you read into it!"

"Then what kind of meaning *does* it imply, Mr. Know-It-All?"

"Because she knows I am Abū-Naʿīm's grandson and that I work in his store, she said 'their' store, that's all. So now tell me what happened next."

She rubbed her knees with a big frown on her face.

"Alright," I said, "you might be right. Please continue!"

She didn't wipe the frown from her face, but continued, "I said, 'What beautiful earrings! Bravo to Abū-Naʿīm and his creativity!' But then Rihanna's mother said,

"These were made by Hāshem, his grandson." I looked at Rihanna. When she heard you name, she blushed and held her head down."

"Tell the truth, Omm-Hobāb! You're just saying these things to placate me."

She ignored me.

"I asked, 'Is Hāshem that tall and handsome young man?' You should have been there to see how Rihanna looked at me when I said that! Her mother said, 'Yes, that's the one'."

"Omm-Hobāb!"

"Believe me when I tell you that Rihanna's looks told me she is even more lovestruck than you are! I asked her, 'Are you not feeling well, my child?' Her mother then said, 'She's been very ill and bed-ridden for a couple of weeks'."

"I knew that already. Abū-Rājeh had told me. I figured she was not well when she came to the store."

"We women understand these things better. You don't 'already' know anything."

I couldn't believe what she was saying. She was willing to exaggerate and stretch credulity just to placate me.

"If only it were as you say it is."

"Then I said something that I shouldn't have. May God forgive me! I said something over which that poor innocent child will lose her appetite and sleep."

She was a master storyteller. Those were the days when her stories would put me to sleep. I remained quiet so that she could continue her story.

She continued, "I said, 'Have you heard that the Sultan's daughter is sweet on him and stops by to see him in their store? The Sultan's wife has invited Hāshem to the palace to polish their jewelry.' Would that I had not uttered these words. I saw that suddenly a light went out in that beautiful face. She said with a quiver in her voice, 'I wish him well! He and I were playmates when we were kids. Now he is a prosperous and notable young man. Qanwā could not hope for a better husband than Hāshem'."

I cried, "From this statement of hers, it is obvious that she doesn't give me a second thought."

"You are very mistaken, Hāshem. You should have been there to see her when we said our goodbyes. She could barely walk straight. She was in the same state as you are in. She walked with me for a few steps past their house. Maybe she wanted to ask me something about you but was too bashful to come out with it. She has a great sense of modesty."

"That's enough, Omm-Hobāb! And I thank you for the trouble you have gone through. You just had an ordinary conversation together. But your interpretation is nothing but the elaborations of your own mind. I for one cannot believe what you say. Do not expect me to entrust my rational faculties to your whims! Too bad I wasn't there to see what transpired for myself."

"Don't make me laugh with your talk of *reason!* So far, all you have done is to entrust what little reason you don't have to your heart."

"If only you hadn't said anything about Qanwā!"

Omm-Hobāb stood up and took her shopping basket to the kitchen.

"Serves her right! If you are to suffer on her account, then it is only fair that she should suffer on yours. I'm going to go and fix you some food and fruit juice. You'll need all your strength for tomorrow."

She let out a mischievous laugh.

"Qanwā awaits!"

I knew right then what a terrible night I had in store. I would no doubt lay in bed going over Omm-Hobāb's and

Rihanna's words a thousand times, trying to make sense of them, struggling between hope and fear until dawn.

Chapter 11

There was a row of beautiful aristocratic mansions along the river, the most beautiful of which was the Sultan's palace. The greater the distance from the river, the smaller the houses got, and the large, stone houses gave way to small, adobe ones. The palace grounds were green and lush. Two tall, dark-skinned guards were stationed outside the large wooden door to the palace grounds. Between the two guards sat a middle-aged man who was short and stout. He answered to the name Sendi. He had a large, unattractive belly, which made him look as if he was permanently holding onto a barrel. He had been sitting on that stool of his for years. I went over and offered my salaams, which he ignored. He asked me what my business was by a silent twirl of the stubby fingers of his hand. I gave him a very summary statement of the situation. He stood up with reluctance. He had sweated so profusely that his clothes were stuck to his back. He pulled his shirt off his back and slouched toward the door. There was a peephole built into the door, which was of solid wood that was covered by metal strapping and large iron studs. He knocked the door's knocker three times. When the peephole opened, I was able to see part of the face of a sleepy guard.

"Open the door. This young man is a goldsmith. He says that he is supposed to make some jewelry for the Sultan's wife and daughter."

The door's dry bolt was thrown back and the door swiveled open on its heel, revealing the palace grounds to my gaze. A magical moment had arrived where I could see the palace's courts and pavilions and entry hall. I had wanted to see the palace and all of the people who worked at the Sultan's court since I was a child. Grandfather used to say, "Although the Sultan's palace in Hilla is not like the mythical palaces of the *Thousand and One Nights*, but it is beautiful enough to remind one of the palaces of Baghdad."

Sendi dried the sweat of his jowls and the back of his neck with the end of his turban. He gently growled in my ear, "Do your work well so you get a good reward. Then you will give me a coin or two." His breath smelled of the pumice stones used on feet in hammāms. It seemed he knew as much, as he was busy chewing away at a stalk of mint. His rotten teeth and dark lips were covered by a greenish slime. When he shooed me in with his hand, he gave me a smile that was neither pleasing to look at nor at all friendly. The door closed behind me, making the same sound.

The first impression of the palace grounds was that it was a place of great beauty. Great trees that reached to the heavens shaded the grounds with their lush canopies. Hilla and its environs were full of palm plantations, but the palace grounds only had a few palm trees among a great variety of other trees. The path that winded through the trees was paved with cobble stones. It seemed the attendant who accompanied me to the palace entrance was mute, as he directed me with hand signals.

The cobblestone path came to a beautiful series of water cascades. Crystal clear water entered small and large pools of water, and then cascaded into a streamlet that meandered its way and disappeared into the trees. The size and elevation of the pools varied. Some smaller ones were positioned above larger ones. The largest pool was a pond that contained several islets. The quavering image of the entry portico was reflected in the cascade pools. A few people were seated on the steps next to the water cascades, carrying on conversations. And there were a few others who were reclining on wooden platform beds that had been placed in various nooks and crannies within the gardens. The sound of laughter would occasionally break the tranquil silence. The attendant indicated that I should wait until he came back for me. There was a guard positioned on each side of the palace entryway. And there were a few additional guards patrolling the grounds to make sure no one snuck a peek into the palace windows. From where I was standing, the faint sound of music and a woman's singing could be heard.

Contrary to my expectations, I got a good night's sleep thanks to the elixirs and infusions that Omm-Hobāb had prepared for me. I was hoping that I would be so awed by the grandeur of the palace that the thought of Rihanna would leave me alone and stop tormenting me. But alas, that was not to be. Without Rihanna, the palace had no attraction for me. I was willing to turn back from the palace and go to the shack of the poorest person in Hilla, as long as I could hear Rihanna's voice from behind a wall or through a window there.

What kept appearing in my mind and continued to torment me was the thought that Rihanna had to be ready to marry in less than a month. And the fact that Masrour had already proposed was yet another source of torment. I wished that Rihanna was the daughter of the Sultan, and would sit next to me when I worked on that special ring for her, and observe my workmanship.

In the moments that I was awaiting the attendant's return, I was daydreaming about whether or not it was possible for me to see the day when I would be busy with my work, and have Rihanna bring me a meal that she had prepared with her own hands, and sit next to me so that we could eat together and talk about whatever came to our minds. I was deep in these thoughts when I heard the sound of footsteps coming from the courtyard. It was a man who was scared out of his wits, holding his turban in his hand and being ushered rudely forward by a burly guard. The people who were reclining on the steps sat up in alarm.

"Get the hell out of here! You upstarts won't learn until you are thrown into the dungeon. The guard shoved the man down the stairs with a slap on the back of his neck. The man tried to keep his balance, but failed to do so and fell to the bottom of the stairs. It took a minute or so for things to return to normal. The person who was closest to me looked me up and down and said, "You might as well get comfortable. It'll be a while before they let you in. I've already been here an hour myself, and there's still no indication of when I'll be allowed entry."

There were a couple of stubborn flies that wouldn't leave us alone. It was not clear why they preferred our company to all the lush greenness of the grounds and to the clear water of the pond. I asked, "What brings you to the court of the Sultan?"

He pulled out a pouch full of coins which he had slipped under his cummerbund, and jingled the coins.

"What else? I've come for the privilege of paying my taxes. You see, one has to wait in line to pay taxes too. His Highness the Emir is still getting his beauty sleep. Do you have a good connection with the court?"

"No."

"But I know the steward. Maybe he will be able to get me a good discount with the Emir. If you are here to pay your taxes, I can have him put in a good word for you too."

"No. Thank you."

The man pursed his lips and turned his gaze to the water cascades. The sound of footsteps on the cobblestone walk could be heard again. Everyone turned around to see who was coming over. It was the attendant who was hurriedly coming back towards me. After making a bow, he said, "I am sorry for having kept you waiting, sir. Please come this way."

The man who had come to pay his taxes looked at me with a surprised look in his eyes and tucked his money pouch back underneath his cummerbund. I started to walk toward the main hall. I could feel my pulse quickening. I had no idea what the inside of the palace looked like, or what adventures awaited me within its walls. Grandfather had counseled me about how I was to talk and behave. But I was so excited that I had forgotten everything he had said. We crossed the courtyard and entered a vestibule leading to a beautiful hall from which an extremely large garden could be seen that was spotted with two- and three-story buildings. The attendant tried not to walk in front of me. As a result, he constantly had to direct me with hand movements. We descended a short flight of steps and crossed the yard, which included a large pond. Several ducks and geese and pelicans were wading in the pond under the shade of some trees.

The waterworks consisted of a series of small interconnected plots with rose bushes and short but bushy trees. We entered another hall. There were a few people there who were sitting on slatted platforms beds doing office work and haggling. We came to a flight of stairs beside which a sentry stood and by which a young woman awaited my arrival. The attendant bowed to me and left. The woman smiled at me.

She was obviously one of the special attendants of the Sultan's household.

"My name is Amīna. I am Lady Qanwā's special attendant."

She indicated that we should go up the stairs. I remembered her. She was the one who had come to the store with Qanwā and the other ladies of the Sultan's court. We went up the stairs side by side until we reached the second floor. We passed a row of stone pillars, in front of which there was a carved wooden railing. From there, the entirety of the palace gardens could be seen. The garden looked even more beautiful from this vantage.

We reached a wooden door that led into a large and bright hall with a tall and ornately patterned ceiling. Amīna opened the door and said, "This is your workroom. Arrangements will be made for you to come and work here every day without having to go through the normal security measures."

I followed her into the room. The room was large and pleasant. It had two arched windows that looked onto the palace grounds. The floor and the platform in the back of the room were covered with carpets. The windows were dressed with expensive curtains. Amīna drew the curtains back, revealing a view of a portion of the palace grounds, a vista of half of the city, the Euphrates river, and the Euphrates bridge. She opened the windows to air the room out.

When Amīna saw that everything was in order, she bowed and left. I went over to the platform. Next to the cushions and fur throws, there were bowls full of grapes, pomegranates, and mangoes. The room hadn't the slightest resemblance to a workshop. Grandfather was right: Qanwā and her family had other plans for me, otherwise they would have given me a small room in some dark corner on the ground floor.

But the room I was standing in was suited for hosting important guests and people who were near and dear to the Sultan.

An hour or so passed, and nothing happened. Sometimes I would get up and stand by the window, and would then make my way back and sit on the edge of the carpeted platform. The thought occurred to me a couple of times to go and ask Amīna or someone else when and how I was to begin my work. There were a few bejeweled scimitars and daggers and shields affixed to the walls. I took one of the daggers in my hand and passed its scabbard through my silk cummerbund. I stood in front of a stone-framed mirror which had been built-in to a wall. I turned around and looked at myself in the mirror. I drew the dagger out of its scabbard. It had a fine blade that glistened in the sunlight, and the gemstones in its handle and quillon had been placed and secured expertly. I thought that I was perhaps to start my work by cleaning and polishing these armaments. I maneuvered the dagger in the air and thrust it at an imaginary enemy, repeating this action several times. Imagining I was a prisoner intent on making my escape, I went and hid behind the door, then opened it suddenly.

I froze when I saw what was before me.

Chapter 12

a black boy stood opposite me, holding a small wooden chest. He cried out in a soprano voice and pulled back in fright. Amīna was standing behind him. She too was taken aback for a moment. Ashamed, I stood aside to let them in. I clumsily drew the scabbard out of my cummerbund, sheathed the dagger in it, and returned it to its place on the wall.

"Forgive me. I was bored, so…"

Amīna said, "You should never apologize to a servant or to a black slave." The black slave whose head was wrapped in a royal-purple turban bowed and lowered his head.

"Jowhar[16] is deaf and mute. He will assist you with your work."

I said, "What good is a deaf-mute slave to me!? This room is too large and luxurious for a workroom. And where are my tools and instruments? There is nothing here. Am I to work somewhere else?"

Amīna signaled Jowhar to place the chest on a shelf. Without turning to me, she said, "These questions have nothing to do with me. You may ask my Lady Qanwā such questions when she arrives."

Jowhar placed the chest on a shelf incompetently and waited there for his next instruction. Amīna signaled him to open it. The chest was filled with expensive jewelry and ornaments.

"This is one of the several chests that will be entrusted to you for you to work on. Its contents have been fully inventoried. They all belong to Lady Qanwā. For today's work, you are to examine the contents of this chest and determine which items need to be cleaned or repaired. When you return tomorrow, you will see that everything you need will be ready for you."

Amīna made another bow and left. The fact that these poor souls had to bow a hundred times a day made me laugh. I went through the jewels. Some of them had been purchased from us. And none of them were in any real need of repair or even of cleaning. I turned to Jowhar and said, "Someone such as Rihanna spends all her time weaving kilims, yet cannot afford to buy a decent pair of earrings. And someone like Qanwā has so much gold and jewelry, she doesn't know what to do with them. And that's not to mention the difference between Rihanna and your Lady Qanwā!"

Jowhar pursed his lips and shrugged his shoulders. He had no idea what I was saying. I pointed to the fruit bowls and said, "Have some if you'd like. There is enough for over twenty people there."

He smiled and nodded, and took the chest over to the fruit bowls and emptied the jewelry onto the fruit before I had an opportunity to react. I couldn't believe how asinine he was. I made the sign to him that he was to return the jewels back to the chest. He nodded and this time placed all the grapes in the chest! For good measure, he topped off his creation with a couple of pomegranates and a few mangoes and squeezed the lid of the chest closed with some difficulty, then turned around and looked for my approval. When he saw that I was dumbfounded, he smiled and grabbed the jewels by the handful and placed them in the empty grape bowl. I wanted to intervene, but he didn't stop until he had placed the bowl of jewelry onto the shelf.

I realized he was insane. I pointed at him angrily that he was to stay there and not to make another move. Instead, he emptied the contents of the bowl onto the shelf, and sat down and placed the empty bowl on his lap. I was flabbergasted. If Qanwā or her mother had entered the room when it was in such a state, my days would have been numbered. They might have sent us both straight to the dungeon. I was wondering what to do with this calamitous madman. I pointed to the exit and yelled, "Get out! Right now!!"

He held his hands over his face in fright. When he raised his arms, his forearm was exposed, which was white. I could hardly believe my eyes. I staggered backwards in shock. I sat on the platform and stared at him.

"Who *are* you??"

He became aware of his exposed forearm, shook his head in dismay, and struck his legs with his clenched fists. With a scratchy voice that stuttered he said, "I was careless. I wanted to have a little fun, but it cost me my life." I was about to have another bout of vertigo and started to feel ill, like I had earlier.

"What is going on here? Who are you?"

I got up and went to the door to call Amīna. Jowhar crawled over toward me on his knees. He pleaded with me, "Have mercy! Amīna said you are a kind-hearted man."

I stopped short of the door. He was standing erect now, but still on his knees. He said, "My name is Hilāl. As you can see, I am not a deaf-mute. I am Amīna's betrothed. The Sultan wanted to wed Amīna to the Vizier's son. So I killed the

Vizier's son and made myself out to be a deaf-mute black slave. Amīna put the word out that Hilāl escaped by night through the palace's secret passageway."

I asked, "If the Vizier's son was murdered, why do the people of Hilla not know about it?"

"The Sultan preferred to keep the news of the Vizier's son's murder from the Vizier. They buried him at night and spread the word that, fearing his being made to marry Amīna, he escaped with me through the tunnel."

"But Amīna is both beautiful and kind. Why would anyone fear marrying her?"

"Don't look at her surface appearance! To date, she has killed two of her suitors by releasing venomous vipers in their beds when they were asleep. Who knows, maybe that is the fate that awaits me too. Amīna swore that I am different from the others and that she loves me. But women's words are not to be trusted. As you can see, I am not handsome. Oh! If I were handsome like you, my troubles would be at an end!"

He was right; he was not handsome. Suddenly, the door opened and a group of women entered, making a ruckus. I almost fainted. My eyes swooned in fright. Qanwā's mother and her sisters were among the women, and they were followed by a stout and grouchy man. The maidservants bowed. He was probably Marjān-e Saghīr. Amīna stood in a corner holding a washtub in her hands that contained a silver urn of water. She was staring at Hilāl with concern. The Sultan looked at the jewels on the shelf and smiled. He came over to me, and I greeted him with a salaam, but he didn't return my salaam. He turned and looked at Hilāl.

"Amīna is very loyal, but her loyalty is to us. She informed us of how you had turned yourself into a black slave and called yourself 'Jowhar'!"

Hilāl said in a plaintiff tone, "How could you do that to me?!"

Amīna shrugged nonchalantly. With the Sultan's signal, Amīna placed the washtub in front of Hilāl.

"Wash your hands and face so that everyone can once again see your ugly and ominous face."

Amīna held the urn up and poured water for Hilāl to wash up. It was exceedingly strange to see that Amīna could not keep from smiling. I saw that Hilāl was right to be concerned. There was not an ounce of loyalty in Amīna. Maybe she was actually enjoying what was going on. The ladies were hiding their smiles behind their silk handkerchiefs. The Sultan cried, "Silence!"

Everyone went quiet and stood to attention. Amīna placed the urn in the washtub, which was now full of dark water. She knelt in front of Hilāl and began drying his hands and face. Some of his face and hands still had some black soot on them. She was drying off Hilāl's hands and face with a verve and enthusiasm that I had rarely witnessed. So she obviously loved him. Amīna turned to the Sultan and said, "I have served your daughter Lady Qanwā faithfully for years. I entreat you to forgive Hilāl on account of my years of faithful service!"

The Sultan roared, "Impossible!"

Amīna embraced Hilāl and said, "I will perish without him! If Lady Qanwā was here, she would soften your heart and prevail upon you to forgive him."

The Sultan roared again, "The better that she is not here. She is the one who is responsible for all of this business!"

He looked around. "Hmmm, well, where *is* this mischievous child of ours?"

I too was wondering where Qanwā was, as I could not see her in the crowd. The Sultan went towards the platform and opened the chest. When he saw the fruit stuffed in it, he cried, "What's going on here? What kind of nonsense is this? Why is the jewelry on the shelf? And what is this fruit doing in the chest?? Who is this young man? What business does he have with Hilāl in this room? Somebody speak up!!"

He was staring at me. I was panting for breath. Amīna said, "The truth is that this stranger is responsible for everything! Nobody knows what he is doing here. He might be a thief for all we know. Or a spy, even!"

Goosepimples broke out all over my skin. I was thinking of throwing myself out the window and making a run for it if I survived the fall. Hilāl said, "A moment, if you please! Do not rush to judgment. This young man's name is Hāshem. He has murdered the Vizier's son and kidnapped Lady Qanwā and secreted her away in a hiding place whose whereabouts is known only to him."

Amīna said, "That is the God's honest truth of the matter. And now he has come back to steal Lady Qanwā's jewels and precious ornaments."

I was utterly flabbergasted. I wanted to put some distance between them and myself when the Sultan's puffy eyes bulged out as he said, "Don't you make a move!"

The Sultan sat next to Hilāl and said to him, "I knew you were innocent. You have suffered much, and in order to compensate you for all that you have gone through, I am willing to inflict whatever punishment you deem appropriate on this young man."

The ladies gathered around Hilāl. They sat around the tub and fixed their eyes on him. I thought of Grandfather, and how he was sitting at ease in the store at this very time, oblivious of what I was going through. Hilāl looked at me angrily and said, "Leave him to me. I know exactly what to do with him."

His voice had suddenly gone up an octave and become feminine. He fished out two tiny rolled up pieces of cloth out of his nostrils, allowing his nose to return from its enlarged state to normal. He then took out a couple of leather-like objects from behind his lower and upper lips and chucked them in the tub. I could not believe it, but it was Qanwā! She removed her turban, allowing her hair to fall on her shoulders. I lowered my gaze. Amīna placed a head-covering on her head. The Sultan and the ladies had burst out in fits of laughter. Qanwā was not laughing. She was holding her head up so that Amīna could wipe the soot away from around her face.

I could not smile. My knees were still shaking in fright. I was still shocked at all of the deliberate mischief that Qanwā had gotten up to. The Sultan got up and came over to me. He ambled a few steps around me, looking me over closely, and then nodded his head in a gesture of satisfaction. The ladies got up and formed a circle around me. The Sultan broke through the circle and moved towards the door.

"Governance is an arduous task. It does not countenance any emotion. This little play caused me no small measure of entertainment. And now, I trust that nothing will sully the luster of my mind today!

The Sultan exited the room and closed the door behind himself. After a few minutes, the entourage of women followed his wife and daughters, who were still laughing and imitating him, out the door. Qanwā sat on the platform, placing an arm on a cushion. She had tired herself out. Amīna busied herself tidying the room. I just stood there, not knowing what to do.

"I better leave. I have had more than enough of being the brunt of your practical tricks."

"Did you not like the show?"

On Qanwā's signal, Amīna went and stood in front of the door and crossed her arms. I looked out the window.

"I had always wanted to see the palace. But I have had more than my fill for the day. And frankly, for a whole lifetime!"

"But this was a celebration in your honor! It's not like we put ourselves out like this for any old person that happens to come along," she pouted.

"I am not your plaything!"

She yawned and stretched her limbs.

"Sometimes, a little fun is necessary. Are you averse to a little fun and games?"

"You have brought me here for fun and games?"

"Thanks to you, I did not go back to sleep after performing my morning devotions, preparing this play. Where is your gratitude?"

"I am a goldsmith, not a clown."

"You will be paid for your time, in any event."

"I have no need of payment for anything such as this."

She stood up and came closer to me. It seemed the game was still ongoing.

"Even if the payment is equal to the value of the jewels I purchased from Abū-Na'īm's store?"

"I don't follow you."

"Why do you think we came to your store and spent so much money there?"

She came and stood next to me and looked around.

"I started a game that I must finish, otherwise poor Abū-Na'īm will not be able to collect the funds for the goods that he has sold so effortlessly."

"I have a right to know what game you are playing at."

"It does not concern you."

"I do not want to be sacrificed in this game of yours."

"You have been chosen for this role. No harm will come to you from it."

"What is my role?"

"The person whom I am attracted to. Nor will I answer any other question about it."

She went and sat back down, brushing Amīna aside.

"Who is this Rihanna, anyway?"

I remembered that I had mentioned her name.

"She is someone I am attracted to, that's all. Nor will I answer any other question about her."

Some moments passed in silence. Amīna continued placing the jewelry silently into the chest. Qanwā asked, "You have a lot of earrings. Why don't you give her a pair? Although, when you marry, she will have all of the best jewelry she could ever desire. But why should a wealthy and handsome young man such as yourself be attracted to a poor kilim weaver? And why have you not married her?"

I was looking at the bridge. There was a large river between me and Rihanna without there being a bridge for us to cross to reach each other.

"She will never consent to a life with me."

"Are you serious? Maybe Abū-Naʿīm will not allow it, is that it? After all, you are a distinguished young man, and she is from a poor family."

I turned to her. She tossed an apple to me, which I caught with one hand.

"She is Shīʿa"

Qanwā laughed.

"Then you better forget her. I have no doubt that all of the gorgeous girls of Hilla dream of having a husband like you."

"My Grandfather says the same thing. But how can I forget her?"

She let out a sigh.

"People who do not have wealth and power think that if they had these things, they could have anything they wanted.

But they are mistaken, of course. Love is a case in point. Sometimes, a poor girl and a poor boy fall in love with each other and marry and live a life of contentment that eludes kings and princes."

I moved towards the door.

"And I wish to be nothing more than an ordinary apprentice to a goldsmith, as long as I could live with the person I love."

"I'll see you tomorrow."

A minute later, I was making my way through the palace grounds. I was sure that Qanwā was watching me through the window. She could keep an eye on me from her vantage point until I reached all the way to the Euphrates Bridge. I felt like watching the flow of the Euphrates from the crown of the bridge.

Chapter 13

I told the story of the day's adventure to Grandfather.

"I wish that you had sent No'mān to the palace instead of me. It's not like I didn't have enough troubles of my own, to have this one added to them."

"Be patient. You'll start your work there before too long. This is what the women of the palace are like. They're all bored and looking for an excuse to be entertained and have some fun. What do you expect from a bunch of rich and powerful people who have nothing to do and time on their hands? *I* don't want you to go there either, but I fear that if you do not go back, they will make trouble for us. I am more concerned for you than I am for myself."

I went to Abū-Rājeh's hammām in the afternoon, where I found Abū-Rājeh in the changing room. Masrour was seated on the edge of the platform. He seemed agitated and angry. He did not return my salaam. I couldn't figure out what was upsetting him. It was clear that he had no patience for me.

Abū-Rājeh was doing some reading in his own room. It was a small room off the half-landing of the stairs that led to the rooftop. When I sat next to him, he closed the book and placed it on the shelf. After asking him how he was feeling, I said, "I envy you for having a quiet place of your own where you can do your reading without a worry in the world."

"I am content to have nothing but this little room, as long as the Sultan's court leaves me in peace."

"Why was Masrour so agitated? He didn't even answer my salaam."

Abū-Rājeh let out a sigh and said, "Do you remember how he had asked for Rihanna's hand in marriage?"

Blood rushed to my brain.

"Sure, you told me so yourself."

"I told Rihanna that he had proposed."

"What did she say?"

"Her answer was a single word: 'No'."

I breathed a sigh of relief and thanked God. That was good news. I could understand why Masrour would be upset.

"I told Rihanna that if her dream did not come to pass within the time limit that I had set, that she would have to think more seriously about Masrour's proposal."

The danger had not yet passed completely. A twinge of anxiety came back to haunt me. But I was happy to know that Masrour was not the person in Rihanna's dream, because if he was the one she had dreamed of, I would have lost all hope. Masrour was not worthy of Rihanna. I questioned whether or not I was worthy of her. What other merits did I have beside my Grandfather's wealth and the fact that I was born naturally handsome?

"My wife tells me that you are to work at the palace for a while."

So Omm-Hobāb had indeed said certain things about this to Rihanna and her mother.

"How did your wife learn about this?"

"An old lady who is apparently one of your neighbors told her."

I related the story of what happened in the palace that morning, adding Grandfather's opinion on the matter.

"Your connection with the palace would be very useful, as long as it does not temp you into committing any sins. Do not permit them to use you as a toy or as their plaything. If you give in to their whims, they will ride you for all you are worth and humiliate you. But if you maintain your dignity, they will have no choice but to treat you with respect."

"How can my connection with the palace be to my advantage when I do not want to marry Qanwā?"

Abū-Rājeh stared at a spot ahead of him. "You are not Shī'a, but you know full well that a group of the best and most righteous sons of Hilla are imprisoned in Marjān-e Saghīr's dungeon for no other reason than that they are Shī'a. News has reached me that the condition of some of them is dire. One of my friends who is called Safwān, and his son, Hamād, are prisoners there. Using the pretext of wanting to see various parts of the palace, you could ask Qanwā to have the guards let you into the dungeon. I will be obliged to you if you succeed in bringing news of their condition to me."

I was willing to do anything to make him happy. I wanted to say that I will do this for you on the condition that you agree to give Rihanna's hand to me in marriage, or at least to promise that she will never marry anyone else. But how could I utter such a thing? In order to point out the importance of the task, I asked, "Is it not a dangerous thing to do? If the Sultan finds out, he will probably punish me."

"I don't want to force you to do something like this. The choice is yours. Seek God's help and use your intelligence. I pray that the Lord of the Age ﷿ will be by your side."

I remembered the story of Ismael Harqalī's miraculous cure.

"If I was disturbing your reading, I should leave."

He laughed and said, "You know that I love you and love talking with you. I feel there is something on your mind that you want to mention, but are in two minds about doing so."

I wanted to confess that I loved Rihanna, but right at that point, I wanted to ask about something that had occupied my mind for a long time and for which I had no answer.

"You figured right. Why should I not be able to marry a Shī'a girl? Are we all not Muslims, after all? Why should a Muslim not be able to marry another Muslim? You haven't even asked who she is, even once. Maybe we can do something about it."

He replied with kindness in his voice, "Husbands and wives must have certain minimum compatibilities. They must think the same way in terms of their creed and basic beliefs, so that differences do not arise between them in their conformance to the ordinances of the sacred law and in their performance of their devotional rituals and obligations. Such differences place a distance between a husband and wife, and cause occlusions in their relationship, as well as having a negative effect on the upbringing of their children. A husband might treat his wife harshly in order to get her to change her *madhhab* or religio-legal rite. On the other hand, let us suppose for the sake of the argument that you succeed in marrying a Shī'a girl. In such an event, your and your wife's relatives will, in all likelihood, ostracize you both. This is why I do not see your marrying a Shī'a girl to be in either of your interests."

I hadn't given these matters any thought. Like her father, Rihanna was a knowledgeable Shī'a and would never consent to marrying a man who was not Shī'a like herself.

"You know that the number of non-Shī'a Muslims is much greater than Shī'a ones. Why do you not follow the *madhhab* of the majority of Muslims so that we become united as one?"

"We would have to see which one was in the right, the Shī'a or those who are not Shī'a. Being a majority is not a reason for their being in the right, for if that were the case, we would all have to convert to Christianity because the number of Christians is greater than that of Muslims. The number of the Muslims in its nascent period was very little, and so, according to the logic of majoritarianism, they should have followed the idolaters who greatly outnumbered them. And this is over and above the fact, of course, that non-Shī'a Muslims are not fully united with each other and are divided into different sects and *madhhab*s themselves. Sunnis are divided into these four *madhhab*s: the Hanbalī, the Shāfe'ī, the Mālekī, and the Hanafī. Why do *they* not unite? Thus, the best thing is for them to formally recognize the Shī'a *madhhab* as another *madhhab* alongside the four Sunni *madhhab*s. Unfortunately, the policies of those who hold the reins of power runs counter to this. Marjān-e Saghīr's actions are a good case in point."

Abū-Rājeh stood up and said, "It would be better for us to go to the river. I am used to this room, but you are young and I know that you like open, pleasant spaces."

His suggestion gladdened me. Masrour became even more upset and became grouchy when he learned that Abū-Rājeh and I intended to go somewhere together. Maybe he was thinking that I had proposed to marry Rihanna, and that we were now off to go and speak to her and her mother about it. I felt sorry for him.

Chapter 14

a young husband and wife were leaning against the wall of the bridge, looking at the river and its surroundings. They clearly loved each other very much. Their smiles never left their faces. I had no other wish but that one day, Rihanna and I would stand next to each other like this couple, smile at each other with loving kindness, and talk about whatever came to our minds.

A portion of the palace and some of the houses of Hilla could be seen from the bridge. I did not know what kind of play Qanwā had prepared for tomorrow. A cool breeze sent ripples through the surface of the river, which wound through the houses and dense date-palm plantations of Hilla in a serpentine fashion. Abū-Rājeh said with a smile, "Did you know that our *madhhab* is older than yours?"

I asked with surprise, "Do you really mean to say that such a thing is possible?"

He laughed and said, "The founders of the four Sunni *madhhab*s, who were Mālik ibn Anas, Abū-Hanīfa, Mohammad ibn Idrīs ash-Shāfiʿī, and Ahmad ibn Hanbal, were all born about a century after the migration of the Prophet ﷺ from Mecca to Medina, which means that the four-fold

Sunni *madhhab*s did not exist in the first Islamic century. The Muslims who lived in the nascent period of Islam and in its first century predate the followers of the four Sunni *madhhab*s, and if these *madhhab*s had not been created at the time, the people of the community of Islam would still be Muslims."

I asked, "What about the Shī'a *madhhab*, when did it come into being?"

"From the time of the Prophet ﷺ, and it came into being at the Prophet's own behest."

I was hearing strange words which I found difficult to believe.

"You are well-known as a truthful and righteous person, but is what you just said really true?"

Abū-Rājeh leaned against the bridge railing, taking pleasure in the breeze.

"Yes, it is as true as this river and bridge are real. The Prophet ﷺ called on the community of Muslims to follow his Ahl al-Bayt[17] ﷺ, and said, "I leave among you two precious and weighty trusts, one being the Book of God and the other being my Progeny. These two legacies will never be separated from each other, and if you lay firm hold of them, you will never go astray." We Shī'a follow the Prophet ﷺ and his Ahl al-Bayt ﷺ. His Eminence the Prophet ﷺ stated that his Ahl al-Bayt ﷺ consisted of Ali, Fātema, Hasan, and Hosayn, unto all of whom be God's peace and blessings. By the way, do you know anything about the Sermon of Ghadīr Khomm, Hāshem?"

"All I know is that you Shī'a have a holiday of the same name."

"Numerous Sunni scholars have related the sermon and the events relating to it in the most authoritative collections of hadith[18] reports. In the last year of his life, when the Prophet ﷺ was returning from his last major (Hajj) pilgrimage, he gathered the people around at God's command in a place called Ghadīr Khomm. He told them that his time on the earthly plane was nearing its end, and after enjoining them to follow the Quran and his Ahl al-Bayt ﷺ, he said, 'O People! Almighty God is my lord and master (*mowlā*), and I am your lord and master. Of whomsoever I have [hitherto] been lord and master (*mowlā*), [so too] this [here] Ali ﷺ shall [henceforth similarly] be his lord and master.'[19] The Prophet ﷺ is authoritatively reported to have said elsewhere: 'Know that the example of [the purified and immaculate members of] my House (*ahl baytī*) ﷺ is like the example of Noah's Ark: he who boards it is saved and he who does not shall drown'. The Shī'a are those who have acted on His Eminence the Prophet's ﷺ instructions and guidance. And so, I would turn the question around and ask you: when there are so many solid reasons for us to follow [the purified and immaculate members of] the House (*ahl al-bayt*) ﷺ of our Prophet ﷺ, why would you expect us to abandon them and follow others?"

What Abū-Rājeh said was so disconcerting for me that beads of sweat broke out on my forehead despite the cool breeze.

A few minutes later, we boarded a boat. The boat's owner paddled it gently, causing it to cleave the water's surface as it moved forward.

"I know it must be difficult for you to believe that what I have said is true. I pray to God to guide us to that which is right."

There were a few other boats on the river. Children were swimming in the river's shallows. Abū-Rājeh said, "Furthermore, the Prophet ﷺ pointed to his Twelve Successors, who are our Twelve Imams ﷺ, the first of whom is Imam Ali ﷺ, and the last of whom is the Lord of the Age ﷺ. Remember that everything that I have said can also be found in your most authoritative books of hadith. I hope and trust that this will be an introduction that will spur you to give more thought to study the sacred history we hold in common."

I had enjoyed going for a stroll and riding in a boat with Rihanna's father, but the things he said with such conviction had more than ever completely destroyed me. The story of Ismael Harqalī, and what he had said that day about the Prophet ﷺ enjoining us to his Ahl al-Bayt ﷺ, and his designation of his successor, did not accord with our *madhhab* or with the beliefs of our denomination. I wanted to know who was truly in the right.

I accompanied Abū-Rājeh to close to where his hammām was located. When we were saying our farewells, he took my hand in his own and said, "Commit Safwān's and Hamād's names to memory. Hamād, Safwān's son, is about your age. They arrested Safwān on the charge of vilifying Marjān-e Saghīr. When Hamād went to the Sultan's court a few days later to see what was happening with his father's case, they sent him to the dungeon as well. I think that this will be the fate of any other Shī'a who tries to follow up on their cases and who tries to proclaim their innocence. You remember how the Vizier dealt with me, right?

I was still holding onto his hand. I said, "You have always been a good friend and guide to me and to my grandfather. The time has now come for me to return a small portion of the favors you have shown us; if it is within my power to do so, of course."

He drew me into his arms and kissed my forehead.

"Allow me to make a confession. It saddens me that the difference in our religious denominations has erected a wall between us, despite all of the love that we have for each other. If it were not for this wall, I would have liked to give Rihanna's hand in marriage to a worthy young man such as yourself."

His eyes were kinder than ever. Hearing these words set my soul ablaze. I wanted to control myself, but I saw no good reason to do so. I said with a voice that trembled with happiness, "I too thank God for giving me a friend such as you!"

If only we had parted ways right then! As if a fleeting thought had occurred to him, he said, "Hamād is a good boy. He works in his father's dye works. Perhaps he is the one that Rihanna has seen in her dream."

With these words, every ounce of happiness took flight from my being.

"Rihanna has seen and perhaps grown fond of Hamād in one of the days when they had come over to our place, or when we had gone over to theirs."

This time I tried to control the quiver in my voice.

"You can ask her. Maybe it is not the case."

Abū-Rājeh shook his head in dismay and said, "That's not a good thing to do and it upsets Rihanna for me to go and ask her whether she has seen such and such a young man in her dream every time someone comes to mind."

It had only been a couple of hours or so that I had started to rest assured that Masrour was not in the running, as it were. It seemed it was my lot for the concerns that had been lifted from my mind with such alacrity to be transformed into a large raven that circles around and comes to sit on the roof of my mind once again. I had not yet seen Hamād, but from that moment on I considered him to be my rival, or to put it more accurately, my enemy. What other name could I put on anyone who could take Rihanna away from me?

Chapter 15

We were having breakfast when Grandfather said, "Don't go if you don't want to. It's not important, even if they don't pay for what they have taken."

Omm-Hobāb poured us some milk. She was pursing her lips, which is what she did when she was thinking.

"See, Abū-Naʻīm, how he eats with such gusto? Qanwā provides a good distraction for him. What were you willing to pay for a group of jesters and magicians to entertain this boy? Well, the palace has put on a show to entertain the child for free! What's not to like in that?? Let him go to the palace so he learns that there is more to the world than the jewelry store and gold and jewelry."

Grandfather gave her a dirty look. "Don't mislead Hāshem with your words, woman! We have no idea what their intentions are."

But Omm-Hobāb was undeterred. "What intentions, sir?! A spoiled young girl wants to show her father or someone else what a handsome young man she has managed to ensnare, that's all. All of this show is for nothing more than this. Mark my words."

Grandfather was about to place a morsel of food into his mouth, but placed it back on his plate and said, "Good heavens! What wayward path have we taken?! The world has turned upside down! First, a beautiful and seductive young makebate comes to our shop unannounced and turns our life upside-down. And then a mischievous and sly young maiden forces us to go to the Sultan's palace and gives us ultimatums! The world is being run by a bunch of girls and old women. Whatever will be next?!"

Omm-Hobāb didn't say anything else and started clearing the breakfast tablespread. Before I left, Grandfather put a hand on my shoulder and said, "Decide for yourself. But if you decide to go to the palace, have your wits about you more than ever. I entrust you to God's good graces."

I could only think of Hamād, which is why I wanted to return to the palace. When I came before Sendi, there were no more traces of yesterday's anxiety or curiosity. Sendi got up and gave me a welcome with a nod of the head and a show of his rotten teeth. At the same time, he knocked on the door three times.

I drew up to the water cascade without paying any attention to the surroundings. I felt I was being watched from the windows of the palace. The stubborn flies of the palace grounds had also come over to greet me. The few people who were sitting on the steps waiting to be received automatically stood up in deference to my arrival. They must have thought I was a high dignitary, from the nonchalant way in which I strolled towards the palace courtyard.

Amīna was the only person in the room. She was dusting the mirror. A carved chest had been placed in a corner of the room, but other than that, the room was no different than it was yesterday.

"Has a different room been arranged for me to do my work in?"

Amīna pointed to the chest.

"According to my lady's instructions, you are to work in this room. Everything you will need in terms of tools and instruments is in this chest.

I approached the chest to open it but it was locked.

"Where is its key?"

Amīna came over and tried the lock.

"I don't know. I wasn't told anything. Two servants brought it and left without offering any explanation. Maybe they forgot to unlock it."

I sat on the edge of the platform and bit into a ripe mango.

"Instruct them to come and open the lock. The sooner I start my work, the sooner I will finish."

Amīna bowed and wiped a silver candelabra that was sitting on a shelf holding a few camphor-scented candles.

"I will go in a minute."

I went to the window and looked at the river and the bridge. It was a beautiful view. I would have loved for my own room to have such a view.

"What game have you arranged for today with your Lady Qanwā?"

"She is no longer in the mood for any games."

"Well, I can't exactly blame her. It is not easy to blacken one's face every day for some silly performance."

Amīna came over and said with a surprising anger in her tone, "Please mind your manners, sir! It is *you* who does not like her and wants to make a plaything of her, but I will not allow it!"

I recalled Abū-Rājeh's and Grandfather's words of counsel to me. I was to maintain my cool at all times.

"Is there a new game afoot? I didn't know I was supposed to like her."

"You should be so lucky! My Lady's attraction to you will not last. It won't be long before you are shown the way to the palace exit."

"Is that right? Hmm. So Qanwā is attracted to me, and you, who are a lowly servant, envy me! You can't face the fact that Qanwā will marry one day and go and pursue her own life outside the palace. She has many suitors, and will marry one sooner or later."

"I grant you that my Lady will marry, but I will always be in her service."

"Then you will probably envy her husband, and Qanwā will have no choice but to let you go."

"She would never do such a thing!"

"When you yourself marry, you will no longer be able to abide taking orders from a mischievous child."

"Pity Lady Qanwā who thinks you would make a suitable husband for her!"

"When I saw you standing by the stairs yesterday, I thought you were an intelligent girl with a good upbringing. How wrong I was! You'd best mind your business and not talk to me. Do not forget that you and I are here to work. As for me, I would not have stepped foot in the palace if I had a choice in the matter. My grandfather insisted, and so I came. Now that I am here, please allow me to think only of my work."

Amīna sat on the chest. She wiped away a tear with the back of her hand.

"It is a strange story. Rihanna loves someone else while you are in love with her. Qanwā loves you, while the Vizier's son loves her. And I am in love with the Vizier's son, and this… it's a long story."

"I do not want people talking about Rihanna here."

She blurted out a hearty laugh.

"Rihanna?! A poor girl who weaves kilims, and the grandson of Abū-Naʿīm the goldsmith, the owner of several jewelry stores and date plantations, in love with her! That's very funny!"

I reckoned she wanted to arouse my ire by whatever means she could. I sneered at her to let her know her arrow had missed its mark.

"The fact that Rihanna weaves kilims and her father is not wealthy are not important to me. If the Vizier's son is a good actor like Qanwā, they are well-suited for each other. And you had better think of yourself, for, how else are you going to bear the fact that your Lady Qanwā has taken your beloved out of your clutches?"

Amīna lost it. She sprang up and grabbed a sword from the wall and drew it out of its sheath. I tried not to be afraid.

"Ah, a scene from another play for Qanwā's amusement! Is she watching from some spyhole, then?"

I picked out an apple from a fruit bowl and tossed it toward her. She swung the sword to cleave it in half, but the sword missed and the apple struck her forehead. Suddenly a peal of laughter rang through the room. The sound originated from the chest. Amīna lowered the sword and started to laugh.

"Ah, another game!" I cried.

Amīna removed a key from her pocket and opened the chest's lock. When she opened the chest, Qanwā stood erect within it like a statue. Amīna helped her out, and she took hold of the sword as she continued to giggle. The chest contained nothing else within it. Without giving Qanwā a second glance, I went over to the window and fixed my gaze outside the room. Qanwā said to me, "Now you must go inside the chest! We'll have a couple of the servants take you before my father and we'll tell him that we have brought him another leopard!"

Without turning to her, I said, "Amīna or the Vizier's son are more suited for this role."

"You had better do as you are told, or you'll be sent to the dungeon. You have already said more than your share of impertinence today. Do not forget where you are and who you are talking to!"

I gave her words a quick thought and said, "As a matter of fact, I think that's a good idea!"

"So you'll get in the chest?"

"No, but I would very much like to see the dungeon. If I am not to do any work today and am only here to entertain you, then I might as well have some fun too."

Amīna, who had turned back into being a well-trained servant, said, "Why the dungeon? There are many other interesting places to see in the palace. The dungeon is a horrid place. You'll regret having gone there."

Qanwā said, "My father has a leopard, a hunting hawk, and a beautiful horse. And my mother has several Persian cats and a peacock. And I have two monkeys and a few talking parrots. Would you like to see them?"

I turned to face them.

"On the condition that we stop playing these games and I start my work from tomorrow."

Qanwā shrugged her shoulders.

After seeing several animals that had been trained and were kept in cages of assorted sizes, we went to the stable and saw all the horses, including the Sultan's personal horse, as well as Qanwā's, which was piebald. She stroked its long mane and said, "Let's go horse-riding tomorrow after you have done some work, what do you say?"

I could not accept. If we did that, the news would spread throughout all of Hilla, and worst of all, it would reach Rihanna's ears as well.

"I thought we agreed that there would be no more games."

Qanwā said quietly, "As a matter of fact, a game *is* afoot. I shall turn myself into a young boy in such a way that even you won't be able to recognize me! I've done so successfully many times."

"The word will eventually get out. Just as the word got out that you had dressed up as a vagrant and a beggar and a street merchant in the bazaar."

Qanwā pouted, "But if I don't do these things, I'll go out of my mind with boredom!"

She played coy so expertly that I was unable to tell whether she was sincere or still putting on an act. We stopped by different places within the palace grounds and saw its various sights. Qanwā continued to insist that we go horseback riding along the riverbank tomorrow.

"I've been planning it for a couple of days now."

"Then why don't you and Amīna dress up as boys and go riding without me?"

"Don't be a spoilsport. We'll go to the river, go over the bridge, gallop to the plantations outside of town, and then come back to the palace."

"I still don't know what these things have anything to do with polishing jewelry."

"Don't be so boring! Do what is expected of you and you will be paid."

"I smell trouble. I think I have become the victim of a dangerous game. I might even end up in the dungeon. So it would be best for us to go and take a look at it. Let's go to the dungeon today, and then we can talk about tomorrow's horseback riding."

Qanwā relented but said, "My father has grown used to my strange antics, but I am sure that he would be surprised if he found out that I had taken you to see the dungeon. We had better forget it."

"You can wait outside. I'll take a look inside and come right back out. You're not afraid of the dungeon, are you?"

"The dungeon is a foul, dangerous place. Some of the prisoners have infectious diseases. There are rats there to whom cats offer their salaams with deference. It is a dank and depressing place that reminds one of Hell. The prisoners there are neither dead nor alive."

"You have riled up my curiosity. I'll go horseback riding with you, but only if we go to the dungeon first. If I change my mind, you'll think I'm scared. A group of people live there; why should we not be able to spend an hour among them?"

Qanwā said to Amīna, "We'll go there. You don't have to come. Or you can come later if you change your mind."

"Going there is not right. Your father will be angry."

With this, Amīna bowed and left.

Qanwā said, "I thought she'd never leave me alone."

We went through a passageway that was in semi-darkness and got to a heavy wooden door that was reinforced with metal strapping and large iron studs. At the time, all I wanted to do was see Hamād.

Chapter 16

Qanwā raised the knocker and struck it to the door. The door squeaked open. A sentry stuck his head out and said, "What is your business?"

"I am Qanwā, the Sultan's daughter, and this gentleman is one of our dear and honorable high-ranking guests who must remain anonymous. He has come to inspect the dungeon."

The sentry stood back and said, "Enter."

We stepped into another walkway that was shorter and which veered to the right. When we made the turn, we arrived at a large courtyard which was surrounded by rooms, each of which had a short door with a window. The sound of moaning could be heard from one of the rooms. Some people were tied to stakes in one of the corners of the courtyard. All of their shirts were discolored with bloodstains.

A tall and brawny man came out of a room that looked different from all of the others and made his way toward us. He bowed to Qanwā and said, "Welcome! I am the warden. What brings you here?"

"We have come to inspect the dungeon. Provide us with a tour."

"It would be better if you obtain written approval from your father, ma'am, so that my actions would not be questioned."

"If it were necessary, he would provide written approval. Rest assured you will not be questioned about this."

"Your wish is my command. And who might this gentleman be?" He pointed to me.

Qanwā said coolly, "Assume that he is a special inspector who has come from Baghdad, and assume further that I am to be married to him directly."

I added, "And do not forget, of course, that you are not to mention any of this to anyone."

The warden, who had become confused, bowed and led the way.

"This is the ordinary prison. The dungeon is reserved for political adversaries and [death row] criminals."

We passed by a few soldiers and guards and reached a door that was kept closed with a large chain and padlock. The warden signaled one of the guards to open the door. The door opened onto a flight of stairs that led underground and into darkness. One of the guards gave the warden a torch, which lit our way down many steps. The air gradually turned fetid and dank.

We reached a crossroads at the bottom of the stairs. The sound of moans and prayers could be heard. I whispered to Qanwā, "What good criminals we have who spend all their time in prayer and communion with the Lord!"

She shrugged. Each of the passages led to a large catacomb that was like a cave that had been carved out of the earth. A well-like oculus opened above each catacomb, functioning as an air vent. The walls of each catacomb were ringed with large iron eyehooks through which a heavy chain was threaded. Smaller chains branched off this heavy chain, each of which attached to a separate prisoner, all of whom were shackled with handcuffs, leg irons, and a yoke around their necks. They could only move a few steps in any direction. They were hirsute, their long hair and long beards not having been trimmed for many months. Their clothing was sparse and in tatters. Whip marks could be seen on their bodies. The ground was wet, and its pungent stench stung the eyes and nostrils. There were various whips and clubs hanging on the walls.

"Please keep your distance from the prisoners."

I asked, "Are all of these wretched souls Shī'a?"

"At this time, yes. But sometimes, other criminals will be brought here prior to their execution."

There were over a hundred people locked up in these catacombs. All of them were gaunt and frail. Their cavernous eyes were sensitive to the light of the torch. I thought to myself, "If it is as Abū-Rājeh says, and the Shī'a have an Imam and leader [who is capable of helping them], why does he not save these poor souls from this torture and torment? The torment that these people are subjected to is much worse that what Ismael Harqalī suffered."

Among the prisoners, I spotted a youth whose facial hair was sparse. I felt so sorry for him that I completely forgot that he might be the person whom Rihanna had seen in her dream. With feigned surprise, I said, "Oh, you're Hamād!"

The young man whose torso was uncovered and whose ribs could be counted opened his eyes painfully in the light of the torch to look at me.

"Who are you?"

"You do not know me."

Qanwā whispered, "Who is he?"

"He is a hard-working and righteous young man. He and his father run a dye works."

The warden said, "That is correct. They are dyers. His father is here too."

"Safwān?"

"Yes, they are enemies of the Sultan and the Caliph. They have been imprisoned on the charge of conspiracy and sedition."

I said to Qanwā, "This cannot be true."

"How do you know?"

"I happen to know them. The truth is, I am obliged to Hamād. I almost drowned once when I was swimming in the Euphrates. If it hadn't been for him, I would have drowned. He and his father were there washing out skeins of yarn."

"Are you sure you are not mistaken?"

"Absolutely sure."

Qanwā turned to the warden and said, "This young man saved the inspector's life from certain death. Him and his father should be freed."

"Forgive me my lady, but such a thing cannot be done without the order of the Sultan or the Vizier."

"I understand. I shall talk to my father about it. Meanwhile, take them out of the dungeon and transfer them into the ordinary prison, until such a time that the order of their release reaches you."

"But this…"

"And I will of course let my father know of your excellent work and cooperation."

"I am grateful for your kindness, but if I may remind my lady that…"

"If you refuse to do this, it will end up costing you dearly!"

Frustrated, the warden said, "Your wishes shall be obeyed, my lady."

"Allow them to bathe and give them proper clothing to wear. Give them a good meal, and salves for the wounds left by their shackles."

She pointed at me.

"Not only is anyone who has saved this gentleman's life not our enemy, but they are to be considered as our friends."

Qanwā was saying these things while keeping a wary eye on a large rat that was walking along the thick chain that girded the room.

When we came out of the dungeon, I said, "You surprised me with your compassion. Thank you, Qanwā. You are most kind."

She was distracted.

"A strange feeling has come over me. When Hamād raised his head in the light of the torch and looked at me, it sent a shiver up my spine."

I was agitated. I too had seen Hamād's piercing eyes and sympathetic appearance. I was convinced that he was the one Rihanna had seen in her dream. Qanwā stared at me and said with humor, "Envy is a sign of admiration."

I had caused Hamād to be freed from that frightful dungeon. Maybe if I had not done so, he would have perished there and Rihanna would have forgotten about him in time. I shook my head and tried to reassure myself. I thought to myself, "What good would his death do? All that would mean is that Rihanna would marry Masrour."

Qanwā said mischievously, "Now that you envy Hamād, I will pay him a visit every day!"

Qanwā was right. I had no right to envy Hamād.

Chapter 17

I had never seen Abū-Rājeh as happy as he was that afternoon. He savored and delighted in my every word when I told him the story of my going down into the dungeon and seeing Safwān and Hamād. It was as if I was telling him some exciting adventure story. When I told him how Qanwā insisted that they at least be allowed to bathe, be given decent clothing, and be transferred to the ordinary section of the prison, he jumped up and gave me a big hug.

"You have done a great thing, Hāshem! Safwān's wife is going out of her mind with worry. She doesn't even know if they are still alive. I have to go and give them the good news and make them happy."

He stared at me.

"Think how happy they will become, and how much they will pray for you. We owe all of this to you. The most I had expected to come of this was for you to bring us some news of their state. But with Qanwā's help, you saved them from the catacombs of the dungeon. If only I could repay your kindness."

I wanted nothing more than to be able to muster up my courage, look him in his eyes, and say, "All I ask of you is for the hand of your daughter in marriage!" Abū-Rājeh was looking at me from close quarters, but he could not see the secret that tormented my soul. I thought to myself, "What use would that be? Even if he was to agree to this marriage, Rihanna would never consent to it. And even if she were to agree to it, what good would it be if she did not truly love me in her heart of hearts? What would our life be but a constant torment?"

Masrour was giving a large-boned man a massage on the opposite platform. It was evident that he was anxious to know what Abū-Rājeh and I were talking about. He had entered into a depression ever since Rihanna had rebuffed him. I got the feeling that he was more concerned about the loss of Rihanna's father's hammām than of Rihanna herself. The way he carried on with the customers when Abū-Rājeh was away, one would have thought he was the real owner of the place. On several occasions I had thought to tell these things to Abū-Rājeh, but I checked myself, thinking that perhaps I was mistaken. And Abū-Rājeh was very much against back-biting, and disapproved of vain talk.

"You and your grandfather are to be my guests on Friday, if you would be as kind as to accept my invitation."

It was the height of my aspirations to be able to enter Abū-Rājeh's home. It would perhaps give me the opportunity to see Rihanna again. I knew that there was a wall between Rihanna and I that seemed impossible to surmount, but for some reason that I did not understand, there was a bright ray of hope at the bottom of my heart. It was as if an angel kept telling me not to lose hope and to entrust my affairs to God, who was pure love. There were four days left till Friday. My heart told me that something good was in store. Although I was faced with a dark dead-end if one were to go by an every-day calculus, yet, I was elated at Abū-Rājeh's invitation.

"I accept your kind invitation with all my heart. Grandfather will be gladdened, as usual, to see you."

Moments later, Abū-Rājeh and I were on our way to Safwān's house. He was taking quick and long strides, and so I told him, "I will accompany you almost to Safwān's house. I have a question for which I would like to hear your answer."

"Ask away, and I will answer if I can. Forgive me for walking so fast. The quicker I put Safwān's family out of their worries, the better. But you have my ear."

"Why is it that your *Imām-e Zamān*, your leader and the Lord of your Age ﷻ, does not save the Shīʻa that are imprisoned in Marjān-e Saghīr's dungeon?"

It was as if he had his answer at the ready. He immediately said, "It is not in accordance with the divine will and plan for him to be directly involved in any and all human affairs. God's will is such that people should bring about changes in their own conditions themselves, and to strive for improving their own lots. For if it were anything other than this, everyone would just sit around doing nothing but waiting for the aid of His Eminence to reach them."

We were passing through the hustle and bustled of the bazaar. I was not paying attention to my surroundings, even though I was being bombarded with its colors and scents and the various characters that formed its rich sensorial texture; all my attention was rapt in Abū-Rājeh's words.

"This is not to say that he does not interfere whatsoever in our affairs. He has a mediating role, but one that is usually not felt, which is why the simile of a sun that is behind the clouds has been used to describe His Eminence. Sometimes we cannot see the sun, but its light and warmth nevertheless continue to sustain earthly life. And with respect to saving the lives of the Shīʻa who are stuck in Marjān-e Saghīr's dungeon, it could well be that the loving Imam is laying the groundwork for just such a thing this very moment. Can you be certain that His Eminence did not play a role in Safwān's and Hamād's rescue from the dungeon? I hold out hope that with his supplications to the Almighty, the prerequisites of the deliverance of the rest of the Shī'a from the dungeon will also come to pass.

We took a side alley out of the bazaar, leaving its hustle and bustle behind. I took pleasure in the tranquility of the empty streets and alleys we passed through. Abū-Rājeh had become short of breath and was panting, trying not to slow down. For my part, I continued my questioning.

"When His Eminence deems it appropriate to help someone such as Ismael Harqalī, and cures the abscess that he had on his thigh, it is only natural for one to expect him to also be concerned about the fate of the dozens of his devotees who are ensnared in that terrifying dungeon."

"There is no doubt that His Eminence is indeed concerned for the well-being of all of us, and that his prayers hold countless lethal dangers that would otherwise confront us at bay. If it weren't for his prayers and support, the Shī'a would have perished at the hands of Marjān-e Saghīr and his ilk. As I said, Ismael Harqalī was in a difficult bind. Sayyed Eben Tāwūs had taken him to the surgeons of Hilla and Baghdad, who had examined him and concluded that nothing could be done for him. At that point, Ismael realized that his cure was in God's hands alone, so rather than returning to Hilla, he went to [the pilgrimage city of] Sāmarrā and sought recourse in the intercession of the Lord of the Age ﷿ with such a correct spiritual understanding and sincerity of purpose that His Eminence rushed to his help with God's leave."

We passed a small procession of camels. Abū-Rājeh's panting constantly interrupted the flow of his sentences. He had a frail constitution.

"If you pay close attention, you will see that the matter of Ismael Harqalī's miraculous cure is not a strictly individual and private affair. A large number of people became followers of the Lord of the Age ﷻ after having witnessed that miracle, and it was a comfort and reassurance for the Shī'a to know that their Imam had not forgotten them. The enemies of the Shī'a reproach us, saying, 'If you do indeed have an Imam and leader who is alive, why is he not concerned about you, and why does he not help you?' Undeniable miracles such as Ismael Harqalī's miraculous cure is a definitive answer to their idle objections."

I took hold of Abū-Rājeh's arm, which made him stop.

"I must return to the palace if I am to keep my word. Qanwā has probably prepared the horses and is waiting for me. If I hadn't made her this promise, I would not have been able to enter the dungeon."

He kissed my forehead and said, "If you behave virtuously, God will be by your side. When I finish visiting Safwān's family, I will go to the mosque and pray for you. Today, you gladdened the heart of the Lord of the Age ﷻ. I hope that you too will attain to your purpose and become happy as a result of his prayers and ministration."

As I was making my way to the palace, I was so excited that it was as if I was walking on clouds. I wanted the days that placed a distance between me and my Friday appointment to pass by and to leave me alone with that appointed time.

Chapter 18

We had fish for lunch, exquisitely prepared by Omm-Hobāb. Omm-Hobāb's cooking did us proud before all of our guests. There were specially cured olives and mixed pickles, the latter of which was an Omm-Hobāb specialty. I didn't eat much food, which upset her.

"A cat eats more than that!"

Grandfather said, "If you are invited to a kingly feast in the palace, pray tell us so that we can join you!"

I took a sip of the grape and date nectar.

"I can't go horseback riding on a full stomach, now can I?"

"Oh, congratulations! No more theatrical performances? So the turn of horseback riding with the Sultan's daughter has arrived, has it? Well, well, well."

Omm-Hobāb said, "What's wrong with that? Qanwā wants to give her future husband a practical demonstration of what a skilled rider she is."

I had not yet mentioned Abū-Rājeh's invitation.

"Horseback riding with Qanwā is not what is important. What is important is that we have been invited to their house on Friday."

"The Sultan's giving a party?"

I shook my head.

"The Sultans soirées are a dime a dozen."

Omm-Hobāb said, "I have to find something appropriate to wear. But you didn't say who had invited us."

"Abū-Rājeh has invited us!"

Grandfather reclined back and breathed a deep sigh of relief.

"Oh, thank God! I was not at all inclined to go to a party at the palace, but what could be more pleasurable than going to Abū-Rājeh's house and spending time talking with him?"

Omm-Hobāb pouted and said, "Too bad I can't come. It's all this fellow's fault."

She was pointing at me. Grandfather said with suspicion, "It seems something has happened that I am not privy to."

"The day I was not feeling well and had stayed home, I sent poor Omm-Hobāb to Abū-Rājeh's house to bring me some news of Rihanna. Now if Rihanna and her mother see Omm-Hobāb in our company, they will realize that I had dispatched her over there. Then Abū-Rājeh will realize that I am fond of their daughter, and will regret ever having invited us to their home."

Omm-Hobāb said, "Well, there is a lot of time between now and Friday, and plenty of opportunity for some opportunity to arise. When one tosses an apple up in the air, it goes through a hundred twists and turns before it comes back down. We need to wait to see what fate has in store for us. Who knows, maybe it is God's will, and I am fated to come with you and to ask for Rihanna's hand in marriage for you from her father right there and then!!"

I told her, "I have never seen a woman as simple-minded as you, Omm-Hobāb! For the love of God, think a little before talking!"

Omm-Hobāb turned her back to me and sulked. Then she thought better of her silence and said, "Don't stand on ceremony; tell me how you *really* feel! Why don't you just come out and say I'm nuts?!"

I helped her clear the table spread to make it up to her, but it was to no avail. Before he headed to his room for his afternoon rest, Grandfather said, "During these last two weeks, I have asked God to guide Abū-Rājeh and his family to the Straight Path a hundred times a day. God knows how much I yearn for the day where we go to his house and there would no longer be any distance between us in terms of our creedal and sectarian beliefs. What a pity. These are nice aspirations that are unlikely to come to fruition."

Omm-Hobāb who was all ears said, "Why do you say that, Abū-Na'īm? This kind of thing is as nothing for God, if He were to will it. It's a piece of cake for Him."

I laughed and said, "What are you saying, Omm-Hobāb?? God doesn't eat cake, like us human beings!"

Grandfather laughed. Omm-Hobāb gave me a dirty look and headed for the kitchen. When she sulked, one had to move heaven and earth to get her to come out of her mood.

Chapter 19

I couldn't help but smile when I saw Qanwā. She had tucked her hair under a turban she had coiled around her head. Using all manner of tints of her own concoction, she had applied shades to her forehead and to either side of her nose that made her look tanned and more masculine. The effect was such that by looking at her, no one could guess that they were looking at a girl who had several servants at her beck and call.

"Hilāl! Well, hello! How are you? What news from Lady Qanwā?"

We exited from one of the palace's rear exists, mounted on two young and fast horses. When we had left the palace grounds, Qanwā said, "I went to see Hamād about an hour ago. They have transferred him and his father to the ordinary prison. And they allowed them to bath and gave them clean clothes, in accordance with my instructions. I was so pleased that I rewarded the warden with one of my rings!"

"I am curious to know why this made you so happy? And why did you say that you paid a visit to Hamād, as if he is important and his father is insignificant. Has something happened?"

She shrugged and spurred her horse forward.

"Hamād is a handsome young man. If you see him now, you wouldn't believe that he was the same dirty and raggedy person we saw yesterday; just as no one would believe that I am Qanwā."

"Did that please you?"

"I don't know why, but yes. When I saw him today, a special feeling came over me. Something I hadn't felt before."

"Did you get this feeling just today, or yesterday when we were in the dungeon?"

"Don't be mean-spirited! You want to get your own back with these probing questions for the games I played on you before, is that it?"

"If you have fallen in love with Hamād, my mind will rest at ease, somewhat. You'll leave me alone and go after him, and I'll be able to go and see to my work and my troubles. On the other hand, I'd feel sorry for you, because you'd be entering into the same dead-end that I am in, as it would be a forbidden love that could not be consummated. Your father would never consent to your marrying a Shī'a dyer who has been imprisoned on charges of conspiracy and sedition."

"It is a new experience for me, but I do know that love attacks without obtaining one's permission. Whatever it is, it is exciting. I feel good!"

We passed a few date plantations outside the palace grounds before reaching the Euphrates. We followed its shoreline and rode the horses to the bridge at a trot in order to warm them up. Crossing the bridge on horseback was a pleasurable experience. I was glad that no one was paying us any attention. We trotted the horses again for a distance on the other side of the bridge, then spurred the horses to a gallop when we reached an open and unobstructed area. Qanwā tried to overtake me, but I kept pace with her, shoulder to shoulder. When we reached a caravanserai outside of town, we stopped racing each other. Our horses had broken a sweat and were frothing at the mouth. The sun was sweltering. Qanwā asked, "When did you learn how to ride?"

The ride had invigorated me.

"When I was young, in the years when we used to go to my Grandfather's village during the summers."

"I was six when my father gave me a pony. He does not have any boys, as you know. I tried to fill that void in my father's life by learning the art of archery and horseback riding."

A caravan could be seen at a far distance on the edge of the Euphrates. It was not clear whether it was approaching or going away. A few farmers were working the fields. The sky reflected in the irrigation spurs the farmers had tapped off the river. The air was lighter out here, and it seemed that Qanwā liked to get as far away from the palace as possible, whereas I preferred for us to have returned to the city by dusk. We kept the horses at a trot to keep them from cooling down.

"Your father is a *nāsebī* and is an enemy of the Prophet's *Ahl al-Bayt* ﷺ and of their followers (*shī'a*), but you helped two Shī'a. Let us hope that he doesn't find out!"

"But my mother, on the other hand, is not only not a *nāsebī*, but in fact loves the Prophet's *Ahl al-Bayt* ﷺ."

"Hmm. How is it possible for such a husband and wife to live together?"

"It is not easy. My mother is against the persecution of the Shī'a, but usually has no choice but to remain quiet."

"Is the Vizier a *nāsebī* too?"

"I'm not sure. I don't think so."

"There is a good man by the name of Abū-Rājeh who has a beautiful hammām in the bazaar. He is Shī'a. I have never seen anyone who is as good and righteous a person as he is. A few days ago, I was in his hammām when the Vizier stopped by in order to get Abū-Rājeh's two beautiful swans, so that he could give them to your father as a gift."

"I hear they are beautiful birds. I wish I could see them!"

"The swans are in the pool that is located in the changing room. Abū-Rājeh and his customers are very fond of these two birds. Abū-Rājeh told the Vizier that he loves his swans, and that they bring him more customers and increase his income. The Vizier used some pretext and slapped Abū-Rājeh so hard across his face that the poor man fell to the floor and his nose started to bleed. The Vizier then threatened him and left. And he did all this even though Abū-Rājeh had not disrespected the Vizier, and had even consented to give the swans as a gift to your father."

Before spurring her horse into a gallop, Qanwā said, "The Vizier's religion is the worship of whatever advances his social status and station in life. He will do anything it takes to keep his position as the Vizier. He has forced his son Rashīd to think like him. The Vizier wants to betroth me to Rashīd in order to consolidate his relationship with my father, which is why he isn't happy to see me associate with a wealthy and handsome young man who goes by the name of Hāshem."

We slowed our pace as we approached the bridge. Qanwā said, "Now that I have made myself out to look like a boy, I'd like to go and take a look at Abū-Rājeh's swans."

She didn't give me the chance to try to change her mind. She struck the ribs of her horse with her legs and darted off like an arrow.

Fortunately, Abū-Rājeh was not at the hammām. Qanwā tossed a coin toward Masrour and said, "Go out and watch over the horses!"

Masrour nodded and left. There was no one in the changing room other than two old men. Qanwā sat at the edge of the pool and examined the swans carefully.

"These two birds are prettier than I had thought."

Qanwā's presence in the changing room was not a good thing. If Abū-Rājeh were to arrive, he would recognize her and would be upset with me for having brought her there.

"We should leave. We should not have come here in the first place."

Qanwā stood up and said, "You said that you wanted to see the dungeon, so I risked the ire of my father and took you to see it. And now I wanted to come here and see the swans, and you brought me here. It isn't worse than the dungeon here, is it?"

"I went horseback riding with you for that."

"Now you listen carefully. For saving Safwān and Hamād from the dungeon, I want these swans. I expect you to purchase them from Abū-Rājeh and bring them for me. I will pay whatever their price is."

"Don't forget that these swans are not for sale."

"Everything has a price. For instance: Abū-Rājeh would undoubtedly be happy to receive a hundred dinars to part with them."

I held the curtain at the end of the hallway up.

"I don't want Abū-Rājeh to see us here together. I'm going to go and pay a visit to my grandfather. If you want, you can stay here and talk to Abū-Rājeh when he gets here, even though I know that he will not part with his swans even for a small chest of gold and jewels."

I left the hammām. Masrour was busy grooming the horses. Qanwā joined us. Ignoring us, she mounted her horse and made it turn by tugging at its reins. Masrour stepped back in surprise. I gave the reins of the other horse to her and told

Masrour, "This fellow's name is Hilāl. He had come here at the behest of his master in order to exchange these two horses for the swans. But now that Abū-Rājeh is not here, he is returning emptyhanded."

Masrour said to Qanwā, "Abū-Rājeh didn't give his swans to the Vizier, so it's not likely that he will give them to *your* master."

Qanwā said, "Be quiet and do not speak until spoken to."

Turning to me, she said, "We will eventually get whatever it is that we want. It will not be long before you see these beautiful swans in the pool of my master that is made of carved jade."

She started to leave from the side of the hammām that was not crowded. I said, "We shall see."

Masrour and I watched as she and the two beautiful horses left. I said to Masrour, "Don't say anything about this to Abū-Rājeh. Let Hilāl speak to him himself."

"Are the swans that valuable?"

"For those who have so much money that they don't know what to do with it, yes, they are."

I was about to leave when Masrour grabbed my sleeve. When he saw me staring at him, he released it and, stammering, asked, "Wha- What's the deal with the party on Friday?"

"How did you find out about that?"

"I overheard something from Abū-Rājeh."

"Yes, you overheard something, but you overheard something wrong. Someone who stands and listens behind a wall can't understand everything he hears. If you have any questions about it, ask Abū-Rājeh."

"Abū-Rājeh keeps nothing back from me. Maybe you have proposed to Rihanna and maybe that's the reason for the party."

His simplemindedness made me laugh.

"You just said that Abū-Rājeh keeps nothing back from you. So then why do you say 'maybe'?"

I only wished that the party on Friday were for precisely that reason. I wanted to tell Masrour that I had not proposed to Rihanna and that the party had nothing to do with that, so that I would put the poor soul out of his misery, but I didn't. At the time, I had no idea what a calamity that short conversation of mine with Masrour would cause.

Chapter 20

anwā and Amīna were playing with two small monkeys. The monkeys were dressed in colorful silk clothing. The room had not changed; there was still no sign of working tools and instruments. It was now plain to see that I had not been invited to the palace to work on jewelry.

"Ladies! What is the program for today, then?"

Just as before, we passed a passageway that was half-lit, and just as before, the heavy door which was covered with metal strapping and large iron studs articulated on its heel, giving us access to the prison courtyard. This time, the courtyard was empty of people and devoid of the sounds of moaning. The warden led us to his room.

Moments later, Safwān and Hamād entered the room accompanied by a guard. Upon their entry, the warden stood up and said, "If you will permit me, I will give you some privacy," and then left, together with the guard.

Safwān was a broad-shouldered and handsome man. He drew me into his arms and thanked me. Hamād did the same, and like his father, gazed at me in curiosity. It was clear that they wanted to know who I was and why I had helped them. We sat on a wide bench in the back of the room. There was a bowl of fruit and dates next to us. Safwān sighed and said, "I am grateful to you for having saved us from the dungeon, but when I think of my friends who are still there, enduring those arduous conditions, I cannot be happy. If only we could at least feed them these fruits and dates."

Qanwā said in jest, "If you are so unhappy, we can return you back down there."

Hamād said, "I am willing to go back there in exchange for the freedom of an old man who is ill."

Hamād had a riveting and determined look on his face. The trace of handcuffs could be seen where they had pressed down on his wrists. Qanwā asked him, "Would you really do such a thing?"

"I am still able to tolerate the conditions of the dungeon, but that old man is no longer able to do so. God knows what I would give if only they would remove the irons shackles and yoke from his body, give him a bath and clean clothing, and allow him to return to his family."

Changing the subject, Safwān turned to me and Qanwā and said, "How can we repay your kindness?"

Addressing me, he continued, "Destiny shined on us when you came to the dungeon unexpectedly and recognized Hamād in the semi-darkness among all those people."

I said, "Rather than talking about these things, let Lady Qanwā recount yesterday's tale. It will be of interest to you, I'm sure."

Qanwā asked, "Which one, our horseback riding adventure or our going to Abū-Rājeh's hammām?"

Safwān and Hamād were taken aback at the mention of Abū-Rājeh's name.

"Tell them the story of our going to Abū-Rājeh's hammām."

I said to Safwān, "Abū-Rājeh is a trusted friend of mine. He is a good man. He has a hammām in the bazaar."

Safwān smiled and nodded. I had been able to convey to him that I had come to visit them at Abū-Rājeh's behest. He said, "I have heard of him. He is a man of good repute."

Hamād was intelligent enough to understand what was taking place between me and his father. He said, "I have heard he keeps two beautiful white birds in his hammām."

Qanwā said, "I had heard people talk of their beauty as well. Yesterday I was finally able to see them for myself."

Hamād asked in surprise, "You mean you went and saw them in the hammām?"

"Yes."

"But that's a men-only hammām!"

Happy in her being able to attract Hamād's attention, Qanwā told every detail of the story, elaborating and exaggerating for effect.

When we came out of the prison, Qanwā asked, "What do you think about Hamād?"

I replied, "His father is a righteous man, like Abū-Rājeh. Hamād is the son of this kind of a person."

"And providing that you are not jealous, of course, I can add that he is very handsome. There is a certain quality about his eyes that I love!"

We were passing through the lush verdure of the palace grounds. It occurred to me how happy Rihanna would be to hear of Safwān and Hamād's well-being, and of their deliverance from the dungeon. It pained me to think that Rihanna would be grateful to me for having saved Hamād. I thought it likely that she would thank me for this on Friday, and ask me to tell her how Hamād was doing. If I told her he was fine, she would think her dream was on the cusp of being realized. The question occurred to me as to whether it was fated that her dream would be realized and she would marry the husband of her dreams as a result of something that *I* had done. I reproached myself: "If you truly love Rihanna, her happiness ought to be more important to you than anything else. It is nothing but selfishness to want her to be happy only on the condition that she marries you. You must be content and accept her marrying Hamād if that is what will make her happy."

But this reproach was like a skin of water that is poured on a pyre the size of a mountain. This kind of justification and assuasive reasoning could not assuage and placate me. But I felt a modicum of tranquility in my heart when I recalled Abū-Rājeh's faith in God. I prayed to God, "Let all of my actions be only for the sake of seeking Your good pleasure. Thus, help me to be content with all that is pleasing to You."

Amīna waved at us from behind the railings of the second-floor balcony. She was holding the monkeys in her arms and waiting for our arrival. I wanted to take my leave, when Qanwā said, "The time has now come for me to tell you the truth."

I sat on the carpeted platform when we entered the room. I felt tired out.

"I hope that this is not another one of your theatrical plays. I am in no mood of such games, believe me!"

Qanwā sat down too and had Amīna sit next to her and held her hand.

"You are right. What you have seen over the last few days has been a show. As I said yesterday, the Vizier is driven by his ambition. He has tried to raise his son Rashīd to be like himself, and has succeeded, to some extent. Rashīd and Amīna love one another. Amīna is an orphan who grew up in the Vizier's household, where she served as a maidservant. Five years ago, I took a liking to Amīna and approached the Vizier, who agreed to allow her to become my lady-in-waiting. Rashīd did not agree with this decision, but his father convinced him that Amīna was beneath him, and that he should be thinking of marrying me instead. Rashīd's marriage to me would be completely to the Vizier's advantage. This bond would cement his position with my father, and Rashīd would become rich and powerful."

Qanwā gave Amīna a quick hug and continued, "Amīna is the one who told me all these things. So I decided to put the Vizier and his son in their place and spoof everyone concerned by putting on a big charade. I needed to pretend that I was in love with a handsome young man who was wealthy and whom I wanted to marry. And you happened to be the person I chose to play this role. You were both rich and handsome, and you came from a well-established family with a good reputation. I saw you when I had made myself out to be a gypsy and was telling fortunes in the bazaar. I followed you. You were going to your store. I then sent someone to gather information on you. When it was reported back to me that you were the grandson of Abū-Naʿīm the goldsmith, and that in addition to owning several jewelry stores and date plantations, your grandfather had recently entrusted a large consignment of goods to various caravans to be traded, your fate was sealed. I arranged for us to pay your store a visit. The rest of the story, you already know. I needed to have you come to the palace regularly, but at the same time it was imperative that you not be seen repairing or polishing jewelry or doing anything like that. It would not do for it to get out that you were coming to the palace on business."

I walked over to the window and looked at the view. Thinking about what I was doing made me laugh. Once upon a time, I dreamed of seeing the inside of the palace. And now that I was inside it, I stood by one of its windows looking at the view outside.

"You don't have to come here anymore. I will send someone to pay for the jewelry tomorrow."

I said, "It was a childish thing to do. If your father is determined to give you in marriage to the son of the Vizier, this kind of charade will not stop him from doing so."

Qanwā placed her chin on Amīna's shoulder and said nothing.

I said, "You have no choice in the matter! You are different from ordinary girls. Just look at where you are! Nothing matters here except power and the dominion of Baghdad. If your father does not serve its interests, he will be dismissed. Nor can he manage all of his affairs without the help of a wily Vizier. Tens of people have been buried alive in the catacombs of the dungeon to ensure that nothing threatens the political order. And with all this, you, the daughter of the Sultan, expect to be able to marry whomsoever you please?!"

"That's why I envy the ordinary people I see in the streets and in the bazaar for their simple and unadorned lives."

I looked at the pond in the middle of the palace grounds and the handful of people who were gathered around it. I was ill at ease with my own situation. Like Qanwā, I was worried about my future. I was not able to have a life together with my beloved. I wanted to leave the palace and take refuge in my work in Grandfather's workshop. It had not taken long for me to tire of being inside the palace walls. I disliked the indeterminacy that I was suspended in. The palace smacked of the greed for power and its sordid machinations. How could anyone continue to live out their life while being indifferent to the fact that dozens of innocent people were being tormented in a horrible dungeon and had no hope of surviving such a terrifying ordeal? I didn't know whether to feel sorrier for myself or for Qanwā. I felt bad for Amīna too, whose fate was also up in the air.

In the next moment my mouth was agape in surprise at what I saw by the pond. I saw Masrour running down the palace stairs towards the garden. He was leaving the palace grounds in a hurry. For the life of me, I couldn't think what business could possibly have brought him here.

Chapter 21

I turned to Qanwā and pleaded with anxiety, "Please help me! Masrour is leaving the palace grounds!"

"And who might Masrour be? What's going on?"

She came over to the window. I pointed to Masrour, who was now approaching the exit.

"Masrour is the person we saw in Abū-Rājeh's hammām yesterday, who you had tend to the horses. He is Abū-Rājeh's apprentice."

"So why are you so jumpy? What's the significance of his coming to the palace?"

"Send someone to bring him back. I must find out what business he had at the court. If Abū-Rājeh had sent him after me, someone would have called for me."

"He's probably here on some other business."

"I don't know why seeing him here has me concerned. He is not a trustworthy person, and he gets up to things that are suspect. I implore you to do something!"

Before Qanwā left the room with Amīna, she said, "Calm yourself! It is not necessary to send for him to come back. I'll just send someone to ask Sendi what his business was. We'll make inquiries with a couple of other guards as well."

"I am grateful to you both."

They left, but I was unable to remain put in the room. I walked back and forth in the hallway and by the balcony railings. Masrour's visiting the Sultan's court was a puzzle for which no solution came to my mind. Seeing an elephant in the palace grounds could not have surprised me as much. As far as Sendi was concerned, Masrour was no better than some vagrant, so why had he allowed him entry? Had Masrour come to pay the taxes for the hammām? No, Abū-Rājeh had already paid his taxes for the year. If Abū-Rājeh had some business with the Sultan's court, he would have told me. The thought then occurred to me that it was probably nothing important and would make Qanwā and Amīna give a good laugh at my expense.

Qanwā and Amīna returned. I was hoping that they would smile and make fun of me for having panicked for no reason, but they had somber looks on their faces. Qanwā said, "Sendi and the other guards say that Masrour had business with the Vizier. Masrour had said that there was an important piece of information that he needed to deliver to the Vizier."

Amīna said, "And he had succeeded in obtaining an audience with the Vizier."

I grew more concerned. I told Qanwā, "I was right to be concerned! What possible business could Masrour have with someone such as the Vizier? Please help me to get to the bottom of this. I have a bad feeling."

"We're not going to get very far with the Vizier; we have to go and talk to Rashīd."

Amīna said, "He is usually at his father's side and acts as his assistant."

We went down the stairs. After crossing the garden, we went toward a building that had rooms within rooms in which people were seated on small cushions working on clerical and official business. There was a small table with some ledgers in front of each of them. Two or three people were seated next to each official who was attending to their business.

We reached a large wooden door with ornate carvings and small inlaid stained glass. A sentry was standing guard in front of the door. Qanwā signaled us to stay behind and approached the sentry and said something to him. The sentry bowed and gently knocked on the door. A small window that was built into the door opened and a grouchy old man showed his pockmarked face. His frown was replaced with an obsequious smile when he saw Qanwā, and he nodded courteously several times. Qanwā exchanged a few sentences with him, after which the old man nodded and moved away from the window. Qanwā came back to us and said, "Let's go. We'll talk to Rashīd somewhere else."

We took the same path back to where we had come from. When we left the building, I saw several people who had been bound together with a chain. I asked Qanwā, "Who are these people, and what have they done to deserve to be humiliated in this way?"

"I don't know. Maybe they are a gang of bandits, or another group of Shī'a."

They didn't look like criminals. They had seated them in a tight bunch in a corner, and the guards were kicking them closer together and forcing them to get closer still with blows from the scabbards of their swords. There was an old man with a luminous face whose nose had been bloodied. He was whispering some prayers, but what was strange was that he stared at me and a smile came to his lips.

We stopped by the pond and water cascades. The sun was mercifully mild. Water cascaded from one pool into another, then another, in thin, transparent curtains. Some ducks and geese and pelicans were swimming in the largest pond, which was surrounded by dense bushes and shrubs in flower. Qanwā reached out to touch a pelican's pouch, but the pelican turned and drifted away in the water. Amīna chuckled gleefully. Her occasional glances at the entrance to the building we had just left indicated that she was expecting Rashīd's arrival at any moment. Eventually a tall and lean young man exited the building. Amīna whispered to me, "That's him."

Rashīd approached us. He resembled a better-looking version of his father. He gave a big smile to Amīna, which he tempered when he turned to me. He had probably guessed who I was. He offered his salaams to Qanwā and Amīna and asked them how they were doing. He then turned his attention to me. I gave him a salaam, to which he responded in kind. Qanwā told him, "This is Hāshem."

"Hāshem?"

He acted like he had not heard of me. Qanwā said, "You don't need to play coy. I know full well you know who he is and why he has been calling on me."

Rashīd calmly looked over to a few people who had just left the building, then looked longingly at Amīna, who was standing in the same general direction. For her part, Amīna tried to conceal her happiness and lowered her gaze.

"I have heard certain things, but I trust they are not true!"

"The truth is that I will never consent to marrying you. I will not allow your father to make of me a bridge by means of which you are to gain access to power and wealth. Everyone knows that you love Amīna, and that you have only agreed to marry me under the pressures that your father has exerted on you."

Qanwā placed her hand kindly under Amīna's chin and continued, "Are power and wealth so valuable that you would sacrifice someone you love and who loves you back for the sake of it?"

Rashīd sighed and said, "Someone who has become entangled in the swamp of the game of power and office will sacrifice even their spouse and children if they have to. Unfortunately, I cannot go against my father's will. If you refuse to marry me and marry Hāshem instead, for example, this problem will automatically be resolved, and my father will consent to my marrying Amīna."

Amīna looked at the two of them in hopeful expectation. Rashīd talked in such a way that it was as if he did not really believe what he was saying. I told him, "Qanwā and I are not to be married. Like you, my heart is set on someone else."

"Then why have you been coming to the palace to see Qanwā so much lately?"

"I am a jeweler. Qanwā has asked me to come to the palace in order to repair and clean the palace jewelry and precious ornaments. But what she was really doing was pretending that I was her suitor and that we were to be married."

"What would she do something like that for??"

"So that you and the Vizier would forget about trying to marry her. I prevailed upon her to talk to her father and to resolve this matter in a more fitting and rational manner."

Rashīd came closer to me and said, "My father wants me to be like him. He will stop at nothing to remain in the Sultan's good graces. And the chief magistrate will issue whatever ruling, edict, or *fatwa* (authoritative religio-legal opinion) it takes to maintain his position. A group of Shī'a were brought here about an hour ago. They are awaiting trial, but do not realize that they have already been found guilty before being tried and will be dispatched to the dungeon forthwith."

"The people who were chained together?"

"Yes."

"What have they done to deserve to be thrown in the dungeon?"

"They attended a meeting that was suspect. Someone has informed the court that they prayed for the downfall of the Sultan and the Vizier in that meeting, and that the old man, who is their sheikh, has told them that they are to pray to the Lord of their Age ﷺ [to intercede with God] to rid the Shī'a of the city of Hilla of the evil of them both! Father says that because there is no such thing as a 'Lord of the Age', what their old sheikh is referring to is their leader who is hiding out somewhere and who will rise up in rebellion against Marjān-e Saghīr with the help of the Shī'a of Hilla."

I was reminded of Abū-Rājeh's words. I said to Rashīd, "Unfortunately, your father has bargained his lot in the world that is to come for [the ephemeral pleasures of] this lower world and the tenuous [tenure of the] office of the Viziership. He stops short of nothing when it comes to crimes that are being committed against the Shī'a because he knows that Marjān-e Saghīr takes pleasure in tormenting and persecuting them."

"Yes, he has told me in the past that the Shī'a are the 'rungs of the ladder of our advancement', and that we tread on them and sacrifice them in order to increase our wealth and power."

"Strive to be different to your father."

Rashīd sat on the edge of the pond. He ran his hand through the water and said, "My father has a successful farm on the edge of town that he inherited from his father. Sometimes I feel like abandoning palace life, taking Amīna's hand, and going there and never coming back."

Amīna told me morosely, "It is a large and beautiful farm. That's where I was born."

Rashīd continued, "Before he became the Vizier, my father had such a dream too, but power and privilege are sweet. When one tastes it and becomes use to its taste, it is very difficult to let go."

I told him, "Living out one's life in a beautiful farm with a woman you love is a thousand times better than a position of privilege the price of whose maintenance is the sacrifice of one's felicity in the hereafter, and one's ultimate loss and humiliation."

Rashīd stood up. He squeezed my arm and said, "You are a man of noble character. It is strange for me to see you turning down marriage with Qanwā and the courtly life for Rihanna's sake."

We expressed surprised that he knew Rihanna's name.

"You are right to be surprised. Not only do I know who Rihanna is, but I also know who her father is."

This time Qanwā looked at me with surprise and said, "Oh, so Rihanna is Abū-Rājeh's daughter! I should have guessed. Now I know why anything to do with him is so important to you. So that is why Masrour's coming to the palace riled up your curiosity and concern."

Now it was Rashīd's turn to be taken aback.

"So you know about that too?"

I said, "Yes, we know about it, and we know that he spoke to the Vizier about an hour ago. That is why we wanted to see you."

Rashīd shook his head dolefully and said to me, "All I can say is that Abū-Rājeh and Rihanna and you are in grave danger. I wanted to say something before but didn't know how to broach the subject."

We were all shocked and I grew all hot inside. Qanwā asked, "What do you mean? What danger?"

Rashīd squeezed my arm again to bring me out of my shock and disbelief. After a few moments passed in silence, he said, "It's a long story. Masrour's grandfather is a *nāsebī*. His desire was for Masrour to gain possession of Abū-Rājeh's hammām after marrying Rihanna. Their plan was to have Abū-Rājeh thrown into the dungeon on some trumped-up charge and to take possession of all of his wealth and belongings. They were supposed to do all this without Rihanna finding out what they had done."

It was incredible. I asked, "Abū-Rājeh doesn't even know that Masrour's grandfather is a *nāsebī;* how do you know all this?"

"I talked to him in private for a few minutes. He is so dim-witted that he soon told me everything."

"I knew that he wanted to marry Rihanna for the sake of the hammām, but I didn't think him so base as to want to get rid of Abū-Rājeh in the bargain. Abū-Rājeh had been like a father to him! Pity all the kindness and help that Abū-Rājeh gave him and his grandfather."

"Masrour told my father that Abū-Rājeh had maligned the Companions of the Prophet ﷺ, and that he is the Sultan's and my father's sworn enemy. He also let them know that Rihanna is a well-read girl who agitates women against the political order in their home."

"May this treacherous liar be damned to Hell!"

"But as to what he said about you…"

"About me??"

"Indeed. He knew all about your comings and goings to the palace. He said that you come here to spy for Abū-Rājeh at his behest. My father put these words in his mouth, of course. He found out that you and Qanwā had two Shī'a transferred from the dungeon to the ordinary prison. When he said this to Masrour, Masrour claimed that Abū-Rājeh had asked you to do such a thing. In other words, that you tricked and used Qanwā to do this, so that Abū-Rājeh would give Rihanna's hand to you in marriage."

I said to Qanwā, "This is all nothing but a tissue of lies! What a despicable conspiracy! Abū-Rājeh doesn't even know that I love Rihanna. I have just told him that I have fallen in love with a Shī'a girl. And what he said is that I should forget all about such a marriage."

"But Masrour said you and your grandfather will be going to Abū-Rājeh's house on Friday to ask for Rihanna's hand in marriage."

"That's just another *lie!* The truth is that Abū-Rājeh had asked me to see if I could stop by the dungeon to obtain some news of Safwān and his son Hamād. No one knew whether or not they were even alive anymore or had passed away. And so that's what I did, and went there with Qanwā. I was deeply moved when I saw the way the prisoners were being treated and spoke highly of Safwān and his son, and Qanwā ordered them to be transferred to the ordinary section of the prison. When Abū-Rājeh heard of their being saved from the torments of the dungeon, he invited my grandfather and I to be their guests on Friday in appreciation of what had taken place. That's all."

Rashīd said, "There is no doubt in my mind that what you are saying is the truth. But something less than what you did is sufficient for someone to be accused of espionage and of abusing the trust of a member of the Sultan's family for someone else's benefit and for saving the Shī'a from the dungeon. Immediately upon leveling this charge, my father will claim that you intended to murder the Sultan when the opportunity arose. This is how he intends to eliminate you from the picture of Qanwā's marriage. And because he has it out for Abū-Rājeh, this plan of his will destroy him as well, and throw Rihanna and her mother in the dungeon in the process. And the Sultan will draw my father closer into his confidence and trust for having discovered this conspiracy and for saving his life, and will force Qanwā, the unwitting partner in crime, to marry me."

My legs no longer had the strength to hold me up. I collapsed onto the knee-wall that encircled the pond. The Vizier was a real satan.[20] By using Masrour as his cat's paw, he had arranged it so that everything would end up to his own advantage. I had no doubt that such an evil schemer ultimately had his eyes on the Sultan's position, and would eventually want to destroy him and ensconce himself in the Sultan's stead. Before leaving, Rashīd turned to me and said, "I advise you to leave town and go into hiding before your arrest warrant is issued."

I asked, "What has your father decided to do to Abū-Rājeh?"

He stepped back a couple of yards and said, "I am sorry, but he is done for! I am sure that the Sultan will have him executed, given the story that my father has concocted for him."

Rashīd left. The world had become occluded and murky before my eyes. Abū-Rājeh, Rihanna, Rihanna's mother, and I had become ensnared in a perfidious and terrifying conspiracy and were on the verge of destruction. I knew that if I were to die, Grandfather and Omm-Hobāb would also languish in the depth of their sorrow. All these crimes were supposed to take place so that Masrour and his grandfather could gain possession of the hammām which they so yearned, and so that the Vizier could get a step closer to his diabolical objectives.

Qanwā sat next to me and said, "I want to tell you something."

I looked at her. She had turned pale. She said, "I am not upset with you for talking me into taking you to the dungeon. I'm glad that you caused me to save them from there."

"What use is it, anyway? The Vizier will only send them back down there and treat them even more harshly than before."

I stood up and said, "We better go and tell Abū-Rājeh of the danger that he faces. If we have the chance, we all need to go into hiding together."

Qanwā said, "I'm still shocked at what I heard Rashīd say. I still can't believe that I have become embroiled in the coil of such a conspiracy. Would that I had never caused you to come to the palace. But know that whatever happens, I will protect you."

"Thank you, Qanwā. Even though, given the state we are in, you are in need of a powerful protector yourself."

Amīna's eyes were brimming with tears. It was difficult to tell what she was more upset about: about the possibility that Qanwā would be forced to marry Rashīd, or because of the snare that Qanwā and I had fallen into.

Nobody stopped me when I left the palace grounds. My arrest warrant had not been issued yet. Even though I was in danger myself, I wanted more than anything to save Abū-Rājeh's life.

Chapter 22

I took a shortcut through a small palm plantation to get to the hammām faster. I had no choice but to climb its walls, which soiled my clothes and left some scratches on my hands and forearms.

What I wanted to do when I entered the hammām was to grab Masrour by his shirt collar and force him to confess his perfidy before Abū-Rājeh's incredulous eyes. I was gnashing my teeth in fury as I ran toward Masrour. The least of his comeuppance was that he was going to be exposed for what he was, whereat he would be so ashamed as to wish the earth would open up its mouth and swallow him whole. It was not beyond the realm of possibility that Abū-Rājeh would be so angry at him as to lose control of himself and kick Masrour and beat him with his fists.

When I got to the hammām, I was stunned. The door was locked. A few customers were standing outside the door, waiting. I sounded the knocker. One of the customers said, "It's no use. No one answered, no matter how many times we knocked."

There was a store adjacent to the hammām that belonged to an old coal vendor. I asked him where Abū-Rājeh was. He slapped his sooty hands together and said, "I don't know what's going on. First Abū-Rājeh left with two other people. Then Masrour locked the front door and left to stop at Abū-Rājeh's house. The customers who were forced to leave the hammām were upset and were grumbling. Masrour told them not to worry, and that not only was he not going to charge them for this time, but that their next visit would be free too, and that he would serve them lime cordials and fruit bowls on the house. He then gave me a coin and told me to announce to anyone that came by that the hammām was closed for the day."

The old coal merchant joined the customers and had a brief word with them that sent them on their way. He then turned to me and said, "This is the third time I am sending the customers away. They ask me why the hammām is closed, but what can I say? Abū-Rājeh didn't tell me anything. And Masrour only said, 'The hammām is closed until tomorrow, or maybe until the day after tomorrow. Or maybe for a week'."

I could take a guess at the meaning of Masrour's mirth. What I couldn't figure out was why he wanted to stop by Abū-Rājeh's house. Anything was possible, except the possibility that he wanted to hide Abū-Rājeh somewhere safe.

I had no choice but to go to Abū-Rājeh's house to figure out what was going on. Had someone gotten word to him before me? That was doubtful.

I stopped by Grandfather's store on the way. I walked him back to the storage room in the back of the store and told him everything that had happened. He became so frightened that his pupils remained dilated. I had never seen him in such a state. He was flabbergasted. He said, "I think the two people who had accompanied Abū-Rājeh were law enforcement officers. Did you not pass them when you were making your way back from the palace?"

"No, I took a shortcut. If they've taken him there, I didn't see them do it."

He grabbed my arm and said, "Listen, Hāshem. You are in danger. You have to leave Hilla *right now!*"

I knew how difficult it was for him to utter these words. My absence would be hard on him. He closed the door to the storeroom, even though we were talking in low tones and it was doubtful that the customers could hear what we said. He was walking back and forth between the storage shelving and boxes and chests, staring at the floor anxiously. He had become deeply emersed in thought.

"I will bring all of my wealth to bear to make sure not the slightest harm comes to you. What good is any of this wealth without you? No one is to know where you are leaving for, do you understand? *No* one. You have to go somewhere where no one would guess you'd go to. Only I can know where you are going to and no one else. Is that clear?"

It was natural for Grandfather only to think of saving me. He was so concerned about my well-being that he could not think of the well-being of Abū-Rājeh and his family. Or maybe he had given it some thought and had concluded that there was nothing he or I could do for them. I understood where he was coming from, but I couldn't agree with him. He kept walking back and forth, looking down at the floor. It was as if his restless eyes were chasing an invisible mouse that kept changing direction rapidly. His reaction indicated to me that the situation was much more serious than I had thought. He suddenly stopped and looked at me with eyes that sparked in the semi-darkness like two large gemstones, and said, "I got it!"

He squeezed my biceps and sat on a chest in front of me. I was able to see that handsome and kindhearted man as he actually was for the first time. In that moment, it was as if I understood the meaning of the word 'grandfather' for the first time. There was an unbreakable bond between us, and we didn't have anyone else besides ourselves. I saw that he was willing and able to give his very life in order to protect me from harm. His eyes told me that he was only alive for my sake, and that I was to remain alive and live out my life for his sake and for the sake of my father. Given this feeling that had come over me, I could guess what he was going to say.

"Mother?"

He smiled and nodded his head.

"Bravo! You guessed right! You have to go to Kūfa and live with your mother for a while until the dust settles and the waters fall from the waterwheel."

"Why with her? I don't remember anything about her."

"I don't like you going to Kūfa and living with her for a while, but we have no other choice."

"What about her husband? He doesn't like me. Have you forgotten how he didn't allow me to live with my mother? We must also think of the possibility that he might get curious to know why I have come to stay with my mother after all these years. If he finds out what's going on, he'll give me up to the authorities. Or at least he will make life difficult for my mother, or milk you dry like a leech."

I was hoping I had convinced him, but he said, "I have already thought through all of these concerns, but you are unaware of what has happened!"

Given everything that I had heard from Rashīd, nothing could surprise me anymore. Nevertheless, I asked, "Has something happened to my mother?"

"Not to your mother, to her husband. Almost a month ago, a woman brought news of your mother's husband's death, leaving his family without a guardian. She said that they didn't have any income or savings and are in bad shape. I thought it was possible that your mother had sent that woman herself. She probably hoped that I would bring her and her children to Hilla and take care of them. But even if her own father was alive, he would not have done this. I gave some money to that woman to give to her, together with the message that because you have forgotten her, it would be better for her to remain in Kūfa. I didn't want to disturb our peace and tranquility, so I didn't tell you anything about it."

I had never forgiven my mother. How could she have abandoned me when I was only four years old and go her own way? All of my hopes were in her, yet she abandoned me and left. I don't know what calamities would have befallen me had it not been for Grandfather. He was not a wealthy man then. But he nevertheless accepted and took on the responsibility for my guardianship. A year later, Grandfather's uncle died and bequeathed all his wealth to Grandfather, who was his groom and right-hand man.

I said, "She knew that you are a rich man now, and was looking for a handout, which you gave her. In any event, her children are in better shape than I am. At least they have a mother to look out for them."

He wagged his finger severely.

"No, no. She is your mother, after all. Maybe it is fated that you go to Kūfa and spend some time with her. This would be in both your interests. You will be safe there, and furthermore, you will be able to bring some order to the lives of your mother and her children and look after them."

I conceded his point.

"Abū-Rājeh used to talk about my mother at times, and he would say that the fact that I did not go and visit her to see how she was doing meant that I was committing an injustice against her. Once I replied, 'If she had any feelings for me, she would have come to visit me just once over all these years that have passed.' But Abū-Rājeh said, 'Her husband is a rough and cold-hearted man, and does not allow her to come to visit you in Hilla from Kūfa.' But even if we suppose Abū-Rājeh to be right, why then has she not come to visit after the death of her husband?"

Grandfather stood up and signaled me to be quiet.

"Now is not the time to carry out this kind of conversation. The authorities could barge in at any minute and arrest you. I think it's possible that your mother might think that if she comes to visit now, we will think that she has only come to visit us after all these years because she needed money now."

I was determined to stay and help Abū-Rājeh in any way I could. I said, "In any event, I will never leave Hilla without Abū-Rājeh and his family."

He growled quietly, "Have you gone mad? Abū-Rājeh is not helpless and can take care of himself. It's even likely that he has already left town with his family. This could be the reason for the hammām's being closed."

"Who could have informed him so quickly that his life was in danger? Unless we assume that Masrour has."

"Masrour has his eye on the hammām. He will achieve his objective with this collusion. What's important for him is to separate Abū-Rājeh from his hammām. Masrour will reach his objective when Abū-Rājeh and his family become fugitives from this city. He might not be as base as to be indifferent to Abū-Rājeh being arrested and tortured and put to death, and for his family to be consigned to the dungeon."

I went over and opened the door of the storeroom.

"I will only leave this town on the condition that Abū-Rājeh's life and that of his family's are safe." If Abū-Rājeh is put to death, and his family is sent to the dungeon, how would I be able to forgive myself for only thinking of saving my own life in his time of trouble? No; if such a thing were to happen, my life would no longer have any meaning.

He reached his arms out towards me and pleaded, "Where do you want to go? What could you possibly do??"

I stood by the door and said, "I will go to Abū-Rājeh's house. If I am to go to Kūfa or some other town, I will go with them."

Grandfather realized that he could not stop me. He collapsed back on the chest and stared at me at the last moment. Neither of us knew whether or not we would see each other again.

Chapter 23

I kept praying to God that Abū-Rājeh and his family had not left town, for if they had, I would have to wander from town to town, and village to village, searching until I found them. Nor would it be at all certain that I *could* find them. How would I be able to find them if they had to live in such a furtive manner as to escape the clutches of the tenacious authorities? And this was not even taking into consideration the fact that looking for them would not be a rational endeavor as the authorities could use my inquiries and efforts and simply follow my lead to track them down.

I ran all the way through all of the back alleys, dozens of horrible and depressing thoughts streaming through my mind as I did so. If Abū-Rājeh and his family had been able to escape successfully, it was unlikely that I would ever be able to find them again. If they were arrested, Abū-Rājeh would be executed, and Rihanna and her mother would be thrown into the dungeon. How would Rihanna be able to tolerate that terrifying dungeon? I prayed to God that if Rihanna were to be imprisoned there, that I should also be imprisoned there with her. That way, I could see her occasionally and talk to her and share in her pain and suffering. This was much better than not ever being able to see her again, or than her marrying someone such as Masrour. I shivered at the thought that Masrour might ask the Vizier to make Rihanna marry him, although I knew that Rihanna was not one to give in to such a life of humiliation and abasement. She would never live with a traitor who had brought about the death of her father, but it was possible that she would never find out about Masrour's treachery. In such an event, Abū-Rājeh and I would be killed, and Rihanna and the hammām would fall into Masrour's lap. Nothing worse than this scenario was imaginable, although Qanwā knew about Masrour's treachery and would not stand idly by and say nothing.

Juxtaposed with all these painful and depressing thoughts, what gave me hope and lighted a corner of my mind like a lantern in the dark of night, was that I might succeed in seeing Rihanna. It was possible that she was still in their house. In that case, I could take them all to Kūfa with me. Or it was possible that Abū-Rājeh would take me along with his family to some other safe location. I liked to imagine that when we were escaping Hilla, we were being chased by the authorities. I would then take a stand above a precipice and would ask Abū-Rājeh and his family to flee while I distracted the posse. Then Abū-Rājeh and his family would take refuge in a safe haven that could be on top of a mountain, from where they could see how I neutralize several of the police officers with my bow and arrow. The officers would then gradually tighten the noose of their search party around me, forcing me to draw my sword in man-to-man combat, and to take several men on at the same time. It would not take long before the blows I had received from the swords of the officers finish me off. Then Abū-Rājeh would beat his fist on a boulder and say with deep regret, "It's just too bad we didn't recognize Hāshem for the hero he is. He was the best friend we ever had!" And Rihanna would weep next to her father and say, "He was selfless as a child too!"

Only God was capable of arranging a better and more beautiful and desirable death than this scenario for me. What possible scenario could be imagined that was better than this for someone who was being waylaid by death and who could not marry Rihanna?

I entered the street where Abū-Rājeh's house was located. My heart was beating so furiously that it was as if someone was beating a drum in my chest. I had accompanied Rihanna to their house a few times when we were kids. The door of the house was open, and someone was standing in the doorway with his back to me. The fact that there was still someone in the house sent a shiver of hope through my body. But my delight gave way to concern and then to anger just as quickly. The person in the doorway was none other than Masrour. I approached the door to the house and stood in the cover provided by the promontory of the entryway. Before anything else, I needed to find out what Masrour was doing there. He has taken a different route there, which is why I hadn't seen him. I heard Rihanna's mother's voice who was in tears, asking, "What will we do now??"

Masrour sighed and said, "You cannot stay here. They will be coming after you too."

"Where can we go?"

"I talked to someone before I came here. He is a friend. You have to hide in his house for a few days. Then I will take you out of town, all in good time. Trust me. Abū-Rājeh and you have been very kind to me. Now is the time for me to reciprocate your kindness."

Right then I heard Rihanna asking with a quiver in her voice, "But why did the officers arrest my father so unexpectedly? I can't figure that out, no matter how much I think about it."

Masrour let out another sigh and said, "You know that Hāshem has been visiting the palace lately, right? It's being said here and there that he is to marry Qanwā, the Sultan's daughter. I think he might have said something about your father to set the wheels of his arrest in motion."

Rihanna said with assurance, "Hāshem? You should never talk about him in such terms!"

Hearing these words of Rihanna's made me feel like I had grown wings and could fly. Masrour became flustered and said, "I heard that Hāshem, acting on Abū-Rājeh's suggestion, saved two of the Shī'a from the dungeon. Don't you think the Sultan's court found out about that? Maybe Qanwā said something to the Sultan or to the Vizier about it. Don't forget that the Vizier is still angry at your father because of what happened with the swans."

Rihanna and her mother said nothing. Masrour said in a sympathetic voice, "What I know is that two officers entered the hammām and arrested Abū-Rājeh on the charge of espionage and conspiracy to kill the Sultan. And it is possible that they might come here at any minute and arrest you as well. It's better that you get ready to leave instead of doing any more talking. I'll go and get to the bottom of this once I have taken you to a safe location. We have to leave this house immediately."

Rihanna's mother said, "We will not go to the house of someone we do not know. Let them come and arrest us as well."

Rihanna said, "You better go and find Hāshem and tell him about my father's arrest. He might be able to do something to save my father with Qanwā's help."

"Do you think that Hāshem would be willing to endanger his own life in such a dangerous situation?"

I could not take it any longer. I cast a quick glance to either side of me. There was no sign of any police officers. I came out from behind the cover of the entryway and pushed Masrour into the front yard of the house before he could see me and have time to react. Masrour let out a cry and fell onto the floor in the middle of a garden bed that contained rose bushes, some other plants, and a few palm saplings. He was frightened and turned and looked at me. I stepped into the front yard as he retreated on his hands and knees. I offered my salaams to Rihanna and her mother, who placed her hand on her heart and said, "Oh, is that you, Hāshem? You scared me."

Rihanna smiled and said, "Thank God you came!"

Her eyes filled with tears and she said through her tears, "They have arrested my father."

At that moment I was so excited at seeing Rihanna and her smile and her tears, and so affected by the danger that threatened us all, that I almost lost control of my tears. On the other hand, I was so enraged at Masrour that I wanted to suffocate him. I was beside myself. I was so excited and had become so faint at seeing Rihanna that I was only a small step away from fainting. I prayed to God to give me the strength to conceal my burning love for Rihanna. She had enough troubles of her own to deal with now. I didn't want to do anything that would reveal the secret of my love for her and to add to her troubles. I closed the door to the yard and went for Masrour, who crabbed his way back a few more feet. I landed a solid kick to his ribs and grabbed his hair and lifted him up. He held his hair with one hand and his ribs with the other and let out a cry.

Rihanna came closer to me and asked with a concerned look on her face, "What's going on here? Please let him go. If you have caused the arrest of my father for whatever reason, you shouldn't torment this poor fellow like this."

Looking into her eyes was too much for me. I said with a hurt frown on my face, "Do you believe that I am capable of doing such a thing?"

I forced Masrour to sit down on the edge of the patio.

"Ask Masrour how he came to know about Hamād and his father's release from the dungeon. You can be sure that Abū-Rājeh hasn't spoken a word about it to him."

Masrour didn't say a word. I grabbed him by the scruff of the neck and said through my clenched teeth, "Answer the question, you little snake in the grass!"

He stammered, "I overheard it when they were talking in the hammām."

You couldn't help but overhear, or were you spying? Now tell us what business you had that took you to the palace this morning?"

I could feel Masrour shaking in my hands.

"*I* had gone to the palace? For what reason? What business would I have at the Sultan's court?"

"This is the question *you* must answer! I saw you leaving the court from a second story window."

Masrour looked at Rihanna in fright and pleaded, "He is mistaken! He wants to place the blame of Abū-Rājeh's arrest on my shoulders!"

Rihanna stood up with her back to the door to the street and with incredulity in her voice said, "Answer the question, Masrour!"

Masrour made to stand up and said, "Was I wrong to have informed you of the arrest of your father? What would someone like me have to do with the Sultan's court? They wouldn't let me in to such a place."

I shoved him back down and said, "The Vizier's son Rashīd provided me with a full explanation of what someone like you would have to do with the Sultan's court!"

I then turned to Rihanna and her mother and said, "I have to go and get news of Abū-Rājeh, but before I do so, I need to reveal to you Masrour's intrigue and treachery."

I told Rihanna and her mother everything that had happened at the palace and everything that Qanwā and I had heard from Rashīd.

"Now my life is in danger. My grandfather wanted to ferret me away from Hilla and to send me to Kūfa, but I did not accept this. Why? Because what happens to Abū-Rājeh and to you is important to me."

Rihanna walked up to Masrour and said, "What a loathsome ingrate you turned out to be! The feral dogs of Hilla have more honor than you and your wayward grandfather. It was God's will that you come here on your own accord and fall into the well that you dug yourself."

Rihanna's mother cried through her tears, "Throw this traitor out of my house!"

Rihanna embraced her mother and said, "No, I will hold him prisoner in the cellar! If any harm comes to my father, I will kill him with my own hands."

Rihanna went to the door of the cellar which was under the patio. She unlocked its small door and opened it. I made Masrour get up and go to into the cellar, but not before I took the key to the hammām from his pocket. The cellar door opened up onto a flight of stairs that led down to a dark space. Masrour resisted our efforts to get him to go down the stairs and clung to the knee-wall of the water well in the yard. There was a pile of firewood in the corner of the yard, from which Rihanna picked out a piece of wood that was about the size of a club, and made to swing it at Masrour, who then ran half bent over to the cellar door and went down its stairs. I closed the cellar door behind him and closed the latch behind it, while Rihanna returned the piece of wood to the pile of firewood. Her eyes were filled with tears again.

"It was all Grandfather's fault. He made me do these things. Then the Vizier tricked me. Believe me, I love Abū-Rājeh. Take me to the palace and I will tell them the truth." This was Masrour's voice. I could see his face in the small window that was cut into the cellar door. Rihanna's mother asked me, "What are we supposed to do now?"

"You must go to a safe place. Too bad our house is not safe for you, otherwise I would have taken you there."

I remembered that they had seen Omm-Hobāb. If they were to go to our house, my secret would be out once they saw her there. Rihanna said in a voice that was lowered so that Masrour could not hear, "We'll go to Safwān's house for a few days."

It was as if someone was squeezing my heart. This proved to me that Rihanna thought about Hamād and preferred their house over ours. But then she immediately added, "Given that Safwān and his son are not there, we can be comfortable there."

I breathed a deep sigh of relief and reproached myself for jumping to conclusions. Rihanna's mother asked me, "What will you do? You are in danger too."

Rihanna said, again in a low tone of voice, "It would be good for you to go into hiding for a while too. If you do not have a place to go, Safwān's wife will set you up with a room somewhere in that same house."

The paths of our eyes crossed, and we looked into each other's eyes for a moment. Then Rihanna turned her gaze towards her mother.

"I am not one to abandon Abū-Rājeh in his moment of need and go into hiding. I will take you to Safwān's house, and when I no longer have to worry about you, I will go looking for him."

Rihanna said, "Then take good care of yourself."

I said, "With all of these diabolical plots afoot, I no longer expect to stay alive much longer and am not afraid of any eventuality."

Rihanna wiped her tears away and said, "I don't expect to hear this kind of talk from you. It would be best if we entrusted our affairs to God and are hopeful [of being recipients of His grace]."

Chapter 24

I delivered Rihanna and her mother to Safwān's house. I kept my distance from them on the way over there so that if I was confronted by any police officers, they would not be involved.

Safwān's wife was gladdened at seeing them. When Rihanna introduced me and she realized that I was the one who had saved her husband and son from the dungeon, she thanked me warmly. She was very saddened by hearing the news of Abū-Rājeh's arrest and of the danger that confronted us all. She was more than happy to give Rihanna and her mother the use of one of the two rooms of her small house. Parting company from Rihanna was difficult for me. I performed my noontide ritual devotions there, and told Rihanna before parting, "I will take the swans from the hammām and will go and see the Sultan. May God grant that I will be able to see him. I might be able to defuse the Vizier's intrigues with Qanwā's help."

Rihanna said, "I will pray for you and for my father. You were selfless in your childhood too."

Elated at Rihanna's words, I said, "Your happiness is important to me. I hope that Hamād and his father will be freed soon! Whatever happens, you and your mother should not leave the house."

"What will happen to Masrour?"

"Don't worry about him. That cellar has nothing on the dungeon. He wanted to take possession of the hammām as well as to marry you. I am glad that he no longer has any hope of marrying you. I told the story of his treachery to my grandfather. The whole of the bazaar will become aware of it by tomorrow morning. In any event, he will have no choice but to pack up and leave Hilla."

At the last minute I wanted to ask Rihanna whom she had seen in her dream. Before I could say anything, she said, "My father is gaunt and frail. He will surely die if they torture him."

Having heard these words and seeing tears well up in her eyes again, I thought better of posing my question to her, and I left the house after we said out farewells. Rihanna was standing in the doorway when she said, "May God grant that you and my father will return in an hour or two and may He put an end to all of our troubles."

I said, "I have a feeling that we will be saved with your prayers."

I was ambivalent about leaving. It was difficult to part company from her, especially as I didn't know if I would ever be able to see her again.

"It's possible that we will not be able to see each other again. I beg you to wipe away your tears. I don't want to remember you in tears like this."

It was as if what I said amused her. She smiled and even laughed a little and wiped her tears away. I went backwards for a few steps. The street was empty. Then I turned around and walked away with long brisk strides. At the end of the street, I turned around for a moment. Rihanna was still standing in the doorway. I let out a sigh and made my way to the next street.

I was perhaps going towards my death, but I was happy and light-headed. I had a turban with me, which I now placed on my head. I covered the bottom half of my face with one of its loose ends. I thanked God that I had been able to see and talk to Rihanna before Friday. The dangerous situation we were all in had given us the opportunity to see each other and talk to each other like we used to when we were kids. Our meeting was nothing out of the ordinary for Rihanna, but it has a special significance for me. I had placed my life in danger in order to save Abū-Rājeh's life. It was only natural that Rihanna should give me a smile and be grateful to me.

I passed the streets and alleys quickly. No one would believe how blithely and light-heartedly and nonchalantly I was heading to potentially lethal danger. I was heading to a place from which everyone fled. If the police officers arrested me, it was not possible for them to take me before the Sultan's court any sooner than when I wanted to get there myself.

I reached the hammām. I hurriedly unlocked the door and entered. There was an eerie feeling to the hammām because of its unusual silence. The swans were standing at the edge of the pool. The absence of Abū-Rājeh and the customers and the murmurs that could always be heard emanating from the baths was tangible. It was as if the swans were awaiting my arrival. When I sat next to them, they didn't move away. I gently held them in my arms and stood up.

I locked the door to the hammām with difficulty, and gave the key to the old coal vendor, telling him not to give the key to anyone other than Abū-Rājeh or one of the members of his immediate family.

He asked, "But what about Masrour?"

I said, "Never! He betrayed Abū-Rājeh to the authorities and caused his arrest."

"Why did he do such a thing?"

"So that he could take possession of the hammām."

The old man placed the key on a shelf under a package and said, "You can be sure that he won't see hide nor hair of it."

I nodded and took off, carrying a swan under each arm. Their beautiful heads and red beaks were right next to my head. They looked at the stores and the passersby with interest. It had been a while since they had been out of their home.

I was glad I hadn't asked Rihanna who it was that she had seen in her dream because if she had said it was Hamād, I would not have been able to go to the Sultan's court with such confidence. I was giddy and fervid with her love. I wished that she could see me from over the rooftops and the crowns of the palm trees, and how I was holding the swans under my arms and was heading into the belly of the beast, where my possible death awaited me.

I couldn't blame Masrour for seeking refuge in the cellar when she threatened to hit him with that wooden club! I too was taken aback by her fervent eyes. I had never seen her in such an agitated state when she was a child. While it is true that her beauty was mingled with a halo of faith and an exalted modesty of character, but at the same time her tenderness could turn into a harshness that was as abrasive as an emery board. I thanked God yet again for enabling me to see her and to tell her of Masrour's treachery, and for enabling us to bid each other farewell in a way that was warm and gratifying.

On the way to the Sultan's court, people kept asking me questions like, "What are these birds called? How much do you want for them? Where did you get them from?" And so on.

I could just make out the palace with my eyes when I was confronted with a terrible sight. Several police officers on horseback were dragging a convict behind them with a rope, while a few other officers were beating him from behind with whips and clubs. A large throng of people had gathered around the convict. They were less than a hundred yards from me. I felt sorry for the unfortunate convict. I asked someone who was coming towards me from that direction what was going on. He shook his head balefully and said, "It's Abū-Rājeh the hammām-keeper. He's been sentenced to death."

I felt like I was a tree that had just been struck by a powerful bolt of lightning. I was flabbergasted. For a few moments I was frozen solid and couldn't move. I was finally able to move my tongue and ask, "Abū-Rājeh? What are they going to do to him?"

"They're going to bandy him around town for a while, then take him to the main square and sever his head from his body."

It was incredible! He had been tried and sentence to death with such speed, and now his sentence was being executed without delay! It was obvious that he had been convicted prior to any trial. The whips and clubs kept moving up and back down his body. I asked, "What is his crime?"

He said, "They say he has spoken ill of and cursed the Companions of the Prophet ﷺ. They have also charged him with espionage and conspiracy to murder the Sultan."

I made my way towards the crowd with legs that were shaking and eyes that were wide open. One of the officers on horseback who was a loud-mouth moved ahead of the rest of them and, maneuvering his sword in the air, yelled, "This is the fate of infidels and hypocrites who are wolves in sheep's clothing. What you see before you is what happens to the enemies of Islam and of the government and of the Companions of the Prophet ﷺ. Let the blind-hearted, extremist *rawāfeḍ*[21] look and learn their lesson!

I stopped when I reached the periphery of the throng. The officers on horseback passed by me. One of them had a rope tied to the horn of his horse's saddle and was pulling on it. The other end of the rope was tied around Abū-Rājeh's thin hands. If that stranger had not told me it was Abū-Rājeh, I would not have been able to recognize him. There were lacerations on several parts of his head and face, which were covered with streaks of clotted blood. They had threaded a string through his nose, which was in turn tied to the rope. None of his teeth could be seen; they had all been broken by blows from a club. A long chain which had been attached to his tongue hung from his mouth, which was bleeding profusely and dripping down the chain. There were also chains that ran through his leg-irons to his hands, and to a neck yoke. The crowd was shocked at seeing the violent and merciless way he was being treated. I peeled back the end of the turban that was covering my face when Abū-Rājeh was passing me by. When his agonized and weary gaze fell upon me, he stood still for a moment. The brutal officers who were behind him landed several crushing blows of their whips and maces onto his back and shoulders. There was no more life left in Abū-Rājeh, who closed his eyes as he fell on his face to the ground. The back of his shirt was in tatters and congealed blood oozed from where the blows of the whip had pierced his skin. It took a while for the horse that his hands were tied to, to come to a stop, and until that happened, he was dragged on his face for a few yards. I gave the swans to someone and stood him up with the help of a couple of other people. His face was covered in blood and dirt. I used the opportunity and whispered in his ear, "Your wife and daughter are safe."

He opened his dust-covered eyes with difficulty and looked at me. A world of loving kindness could be seen emanating in waves from within them. There was no fear in his eyes. The horse moved forward and dragged Abū-Rājeh along with itself. The foot-soldiers separated me from Abū-Rājeh with a few casual blows of their whips. I covered my face again. I took the swans back and waited for the crowd to pass me by and continue their procession. One of them said, "The poor fellow is going to die before they get him to the square!"

Another one said, "Less work for the executioner."

My back and shoulders stung where they had been struck by the whip of the guard. I was astounded by the precariousness of life. On the morning of that same say, Abū-Rājeh was busy at work in his hammām, oblivious to the events that were fated to befall him. And now he was in this terrifying and pathetic condition, a stone's throw away from certain death.

I thought of his wife and his daughter who had sought refuge in a house on the outskirts of town, and who had no idea what had become of this poor innocent man. I could at least be thankful that they were not there to witness that terrifying scene.

I don't know what thoughts went through Abū-Rājeh's mind when he saw me with the swans. Had be become aware of Masrour's treachery while in the Sultan's court? Was he trying to tell me with his eyes that I should flee from there and get away from Hilla?

I could no longer feel the sense of determination and assuredness that I had. I had resolved to go to the Sultan in order to save Abū-Rājeh's life, but it was too late for that now. Even if Abū-Rājeh was not executed, he already had one foot in the grave. The best thing that I could do was to flee to Kūfa with Rihanna and her mother. At least we would be saved, and Grandfather would rest assured that I was no longer in danger. Seeing Abū-Rājeh in that pathetic condition had shaken me to my core. But a voice within me shouted out, "No! You can never abandon Abū-Rājeh in the condition that he is in, and to think of running away and saving your own skin!" Rihanna had said that it would be best for us to entrust our affairs to God and to have hope [of being recipients of His grace]. She had said that she would be praying for me. I needed to try my best, for her sake as well as for her father's. Nothing would come of returning to Rihanna under those circumstances other than grief and shame.

I don't know why I remembered "him" – the same person who cured Ismael Harqalī, and who was the beloved of Abū-Rājeh and the Shī'a. I addressed him in a prayer, saying, "If it is as the Shī'a believe, and you are alive and hear my voice, ask God to help me!"

The heat of determination and resolve began to boil up in me again. I cast a final glance toward the crowd that was receding from me in between the palm trees and headed for the Sultan's court.

Chapter 25

My arms were aching by the time I reached the palace. When Sendi saw me, he got up and knocked on the door three times, as usual, but was surprised to see the swans I was holding. Before the window opened, he yelled out, "Open the door, we have an important guest!"

The dry bolt squeaked as it was pulled back, and the heavy door rotated on its heel. Sendi gave me a smirk which made his fat cheeks close one of his eyes. He stood in front of me and blocked my way.

"What beautiful birds! Is their meat *halāl*[22]?"

He wanted to touch them, but I pulled back.

"You be the judge: would it not be a pity for the flesh of such beautiful creatures to go down the gullet of a person such as yourself?"

Sendi gaped his mouth as wide as possible and laughed like a madman.

"What is a pity is that you have come about an hour too late, for otherwise, we would have dispatched you with that old hammām-keeper! You are right, I am lame and fat and ugly, but you will soon die despite all your handsomeness, and I will still be alive."

"I have forgotten to give you a coin in these last few days. Is that what you're upset about?"

"I get my tribute from whoever comes and goes through this gate: a dinar here, a dirham there. And when I see someone who has been given the death penalty, I look at his face and ask myself, 'Sendi, this person is entering the world of eternality. Does he have anything that you would want?' Sometimes I choose their hair, and sometimes their eyes and brows, and at other times, their lips and teeth. I ask myself, 'Why shouldn't I be able to have the handsomeness of these people who are goners anyway, and substitute it with my ugliness?' I looked at that old hammām-keeper. He was a poor man. He had nothing to give me. Oh, but there was something special about his eyes. The whites of his eyes shone like pearls."

The whites of Sendi's eyes were more like a yellowish red. He was still standing in the middle of the doorway, blocking my way.

"But I look at you and see that you are among the world's wealthy people, which is why choosing something to take from you would be a difficult task. Everything of yours is beautiful and perfect. One can't say that your eyes, for example, are more beautiful than your teeth, or that your head is more valuable than your body. In a word, I want *all* of your being, even the way you talk and the look in your eyes. If only we could exchange our bodies now that you are knocking at death's door. No one would feel a smidgeon of sorrow if they were to see my head and body in the clutches of the executioner's hands. The Sultan's executioner is an extremely merciless fellow. I should make a note to remember to ask him tomorrow whether or not taking your soul was difficult for him. If he says no, believe me, I will never talk to him again! Hmm. Do you not want to turn around? I won't stop you."

I was spellbound by his words. I hadn't figured him as being someone with any compassion.

"No, that's alright."

"It's clear that you have come to try to save that old hammām-keeper's life. It's hard to believe that a handsome and wealthy young man such as yourself would want to risk his life for someone like him. In any case, your courage is laudable!"

"Thank you. Now kindly step aside and let me pass."

"If the Sultan had any taste, he would have a painter come and paint your picture on one of the walls of his inner chambers, and only *then* sentence you to death! It would be good for the painter to paint you just as you are standing now, with a swan under each of your arms. With the same contemptuous yet sweet and alluring smile. One must indeed praise Qanwā's taste! I didn't think a youth such as yourself could be found in Hilla. I feel sorry for her too, as she will not be able to save your neck even for one more day!"

When I made to pass him by, he interlocked his fingers together and said, "Tell me something that I can remember you by, then be on your way."

I said, "It's good that there's compassion in your soul, but it's a pity that you were not able to see the beauty that Abū-Rājeh's mind and soul are imbued with. I hope that I will be more beautiful than what you see before you at the moment I die and separate from this body of mine. This body will age and degenerate and turn to dust. Rather than spend a lifetime hoping for a beautiful surface appearance, it would be better for you to open the eye of your heart, if only once, and to take a look at your mind and soul. If your body is not subject to much change, you can instead purify and polish your mind and soul with the performance of worthy deeds and beautify them in that way. No one can blame you for not having your share of superficial beauty, as this is how you came into the world. But your inner beauty is subject to your own will, and you will be blameworthy if you do not give it any thought."

Sendi went over and sat on his stool and said, "These are heart-warming and heartening words. I have to think about them. I will not prevent you from passing if you want to go."

I entered the palace grounds. The heavy door closed behind me, and the deadbolt and latches creaked into place. I looked up at the window from which I had espied Masrour. It so happened that Qanwā was standing there. When I removed the end of my turban from my face, she waved her hand and disappeared from view.

I had reached the pond and water cascade unmolested by any guards, when suddenly the Vizier and his son Rashīd appeared before me. Upon seeing me, the Vizier chortled and said, "Ah, the Persian Prince! Have you come to save Abū-Rājeh, then?"

He had likened me to a Persian prince when he had come to Abū-Rājeh's hammām to get the swans. I said, "It was the swans that you wanted, so here they are. Take them and order Abū-Rājeh's release."

The Vizier signaled a guard to come forward, who duly obeyed with a bow.

"You brought the swans too late in the game. An hour earlier, I instructed the guards to return Safwān and his son to the dungeon. I doubt they'll survive in there. Now hand over the swans. I am surprised that you have come to rescue Abū-Rājeh rather than going into hiding. Someone needs to come to your rescue now, and bring something more than a couple of swans!"

Qanwā arrived, short of breath. She was wearing shoes made of a woven cotton fabric, which is why we didn't hear her approach. She said to the Vizier angrily, "The one who needs to come is me."

Qanwā took one of the swans from me and signaled the guard to maintain his distance. The guard remained, waiting for the Vizier's instructions. Qanwā said to the Vizier, "I see that Hāshem has come to the court himself and has no intention of fleeing. Tell the guard to go away; I don't want anyone to hear our conversation."

The Vizier gave a nod to the guard, who gave a bow and returned to his post.

"Give the swans to your father. Perhaps he will grant you clemency. But he is very upset with you!"

"Acrimony between a father and daughter is fleeting. I would be more concerned for yourself!"

"The Sultan is most pleased with me for having unearthed a dangerous conspiracy. Hāshem, Safwān, and his son had conspired to murder your father. The leader of the plot was Abū-Rājeh, who was tried and convicted to death before the Sultan about an hour ago, and will be executed in another hour or so in the square. By abusing your trust, Hāshem succeeded in infiltrating the government and implementing a part of Abū-Rājeh's evil intrigues. Therefore, Hāshem and anyone else who was involved in this conspiracy will be sentenced to death."

"Well, you have certainly spun an interesting story, I'll give you that much. The only problem with it is that it is nothing but a tissue of lies!"

I said to the Vizier, "Fear God, and keep His commandments! You know better than anyone else that we are innocent. Be sure that you will not attain to your objectives by shedding the blood of innocents!"

The Vizier sneered at Qanwā, "You see, this insolent upstart is as bold and impudent as Abū-Rājeh! He is his protégé. I should have guessed as much the first time I saw them together. This is unprecedented! For someone to look me in the eye and cast aspersions on my character within the palace walls! It is an outrage! He has been emboldened by your support. I fear your father will be even more cross with you."

Qanwā said, "Hāshem and I will go and speak with him."

The Vizier crossed his arms on his chest and said, "I cannot permit it. He intends to murder your father. Do you want him to succeed in his objective?"

"You cannot prevent us from seeing him. Stand aside or make an eternal enemy of me!"

"Do not do something that will force your father to hold you in a room for a time. A dark room crawling with rats."

"You know how determined I can be. Do not do something where you will have to get rid of me too or force me to cause a ruckus and shame you before the guards."

The Vizier raised his fists and brought them down on his thighs.

"Very well. Just remember, you asked for this yourself! Now that you insist, I will come with you."

The Vizier turned to his son and said, "You come along too. You can amuse yourself."

We made our way through the garden and patio and a flight of stairs and some passageways and the main hall and reached the Sultan's inner chamber. The Vizier had no idea that Rashīd had revealed all of the behind-the-scenes secrets of the intrigue to Qanwā and me. But this is why Rashīd was concerned and came along with reluctance. I whispered to him in a tone that made sure his father could not hear what I said, "The lives of several innocent people are at stake. If you remain quiet, Almighty God will never forgive you. Make your decision; you have a difficult trial ahead of you."

He whispered back, "Why did you come back here? You are truly a dolt!"

I said with a smile, "We will either all die, or we will all be saved. Sometimes, running away or staying silent is little removed from treachery and criminality."

Chapter 26

The Sultan's inner chambers was the most beautiful part of the palace. The Sultan was reclining against silk-covered cushions on a large carpeted wooden platform. He was not happy at his having to deal with us. There was a curtain hanging adjacent to the wooden platform, behind which could be seen the outline of the Sultan's wife. We were standing next to a beautiful pool that was made of carved jade. Beneath our feet there was the largest silk carpet that I had ever seen. It had a bright color, and gold and silver threads sparkled among its purple flowers.

Qanwā gently set the swan that she was holding free into the pool's water. She took the one that I was holding from me and went towards the Sultan. She sat on the corner of the platform and said, "Look at it, father! Isn't it the most precious and beautiful bird in the world?"

The Sultan's eyes sparkled in delight. But without betraying his elation, he said, "Release this one in the pool as well. We'll have plenty of opportunity to look at them later."

Qanwā smiled sweetly and signaled to me to take the swan and place it in the pool. I went forward. The Sultan pursed his lips and stared me down with a frightening look. I took the swan from Qanwā and released it in the water. The Sultan indicated to us with a movement of his hand that we should move away from the pool. We all moved away. The swans were happy to be back on water and floated around in gentle circles. The Sultan smiled and looked at his wife who was watching from behind the curtain. The walls and pillars and curtains and rugs and paintings and expensive armaments were all covered. There were multicolored tiles, intricate mirrored shapes, and beautiful ornamental plaster moldings in and around the ceiling, but the white swans added something truly special to the space. I had guessed right: seeing the swans in his jade pool had the effect of softening the Sultan's attitude somewhat. He dangled his feet from the platform and stood up.

"Too bad this beautiful pair of birds belong to Abū-Rājeh. He was my enemy and the enemy of the government. I spent a bitter hour dealing with him. What an impudent and insolent man he was! He made light of death itself! Would that I lived in a city in which there were no Shī'a, and would that intelligent and courageous people like Abū-Rājeh were not Shī'a!"

The Vizier said obsequiously, "We did not want to disturb, sire. But your daughter insisted that she had to have an audience with your eminence together with this wayward and perfidious youth. I objected that it was not wise to take such a dangerous creature to your presence, but she threatened to cause an embarrassing scene. I fear this treacherous spy might have evil intentions hidden under his pretext of surrendering himself together with bringing these two birds. One who has no hope of living is capable of doing anything. His crime and that of his accomplices is very clear. Permit me to entrust him to the guards."

The Sultan said, "And so it shall be. And all of you should leave too. Qanwā! I don't want to see you either. Away with you! What a sad day it is when my daughter has become an instrument in the hands of my enemies and is still fast asleep! I have thought of a punishment for you. A week spent in a dark room that is devoid of any furnishings whatsoever. After which you will marry Rashīd and will only be allowed to see me once a week for a period of two years."

The Sultan clapped his hands twice. Two burly guards entered immediately and bowed. Qanwā kneeled in front of her father and said, "Father! No outsider can claim that he is more loyal to you than me. Without you, I have no guardian and pillar of support, but there are people who would reach their objectives if you were no longer present. If I have indeed been the cause of your shame, I shall poison myself. And you know that no one would be able to prevent me from doing so. But now that I feel I am but a step away from death, I want you to listen to what I have to say for the last time."

"Save the playacting for when you have a large and appreciative audience!"

Qanwā stood up and said, "I do not regret that you will soon see that I was not putting on a show this time. What I regret is that you will soon wish that you had listened to what I had to say, so that you could see the nature of the real conspiracy that is hidden under the guise of a manufactured one."

"Get out of my sight!"

The Vizier said, "If it pleases you, sire, allow me to go and tend to my affairs."

The Sultan said, "You have wasted my time. All of you are dismissed!"

Qanwā's mother appeared from behind the curtain and said to the Sultan, "Whenever you see an outsider pretend to be more concerned for you than your own blood, skepticism is warranted. What possible harm can come of hearing your daughter out, that you have become so impatient with her?"

The Sultan sat on the edge of the platform and said to Qanwā, "That's what women do: undermine men's judgments. Say what you have to say, but be brief. I have no patience for long, drawn-out stories!"

Qanwā turned to the Vizier and said, "Abū-Rājeh has an apprentice by the name of Masrour. We saw him come to the court today. After asking around, we discovered that none other than the Vizier had given him an audience."

The Vizier went pale, but he held himself together and said, "Perfectly true! Masrour is the one who discovered Abū-Rājeh's plot, and I gave Abū-Rājeh's hammām to him in gratitude for this service."

The Sultan said to Qanwā, "Enough with your preambles! What is it you want to say, child?"

"We went to Rashīd and asked him what business a commoner such as Masrour had with His Highness the Vizier? Rashīd is a truthful young man. He has not yet become polluted with plots and intrigues like his father. Rashīd told us what had transpired between Masrour and his father. Hāshem, Amīna, and I are witness to what he said. The short version is that the Vizier used Masrour as his means to devise a conspiracy which involves sacrificing several innocent people's lives, by means of which he would draw several steps closer to fulfilling the wishes he entertains in his mind. It would be in your interest to instruct Rashīd to recount the story."

The Sultan yawned and said, "What is the significance of Rashīd's words?"

The Sultan's wife said, "You think you are a great statesman, and that your Vizier is so afraid of you that he doesn't dare to disobey you or to plot intrigues against you. It is hard for you to accept that your daughter might be right, and that she has discovered a conspiracy at the highest level that you are not aware of. Instruct the Vizier to wait outside so that Rashīd can speak in peace."

The Vizier gave Rashīd a portentous look and left after having been signaled to do so by the Sultan. The Sultan's wife signaled one of the guards to go and guard the Vizier. The Sultan gave his wife a disapproving frown and asked Rashīd to draw closer. Rashīd approached and bowed deeply.

"Be assured that you and your father have nothing to fear. Now tell me what you know without being afraid of any recrimination. Telling the truth is a cause of salvation, whereas telling lies, and especially to me, will be your perdition."

I thanked God that the truth was revealing itself. I was sure that at that moment, Rihanna was in the position of prostration in her supplications and was praying for the well-being of her father and me. My only concern was for Abū-Rājeh, whom I feared might already have expired.

Rashīd bowed again and said with a quiver in his voice, "I love Amīna. Hāshem loves Rihanna, who is Abū-Rājeh's daughter. My father wants me to marry Qanwā in order to cement his relationship with you. He was thus unhappy when he saw Hāshem visiting the palace over the last few days, with Qanwā paying him special attention. He felt that he would not reach his goal if Qanwā and Hāshem were to marry. That is why he was looking for an excuse to drive Hāshem away from the palace."

The Sultan let out a bitter chuckle.

"Who said these two are to be married?"

"My father thought you had agreed to this bond."

"All he had to do is ask me, and I would have disabused him of his error. Continue!"

"Masrour's coming to the palace gave my father the excuse he was looking for. Masrour's grandfather is a wicked old man. He had instructed Masrour to marry Rihanna, and to take possession of the hammām by getting rid of Abū-Rājeh. After being turned down by Rihanna and believing that Hāshem was about to propose to her, Masrour went to my father and gave false evidence that Abū-Rājeh had been slandering the Companions of the Prophet ﷺ, and that he had asked Hāshem to see if he could bring him news of his friend Safwān, who is imprisoned in the dungeon. My father had heard that Hāshem and Qanwā had gone to the dungeon, and that Safwān and his son had been transferred to the ordinary section of the prison at Qanwā's request. My father asked Masrour, 'Did Abū-Rājeh merely ask Hāshem to bring him news of Safwān, or did he instruct him to use Qanwā's influence to free Safwān and his son, so that when the opportunity presented itself, they could murder the Sultan?' Because Masrour realized that it was to his advantage to remove Hāshem who was an obstacle in his own path, he confirmed the words that my father had put in his mouth and said, 'It is exactly as you have described'."

The Sultan asked, "Why is it in Masrour's interest for Hāshem to be removed from his path?"

"Yesterday evening, Hāshem had told Masrour that he and his grandfather Abū-Na'īm were to be Abū-Rājeh's guests on Friday. Masrour thought that Abū-Na'īm was going to propose to Rihanna on Hāshem's behalf. Masrour was afraid that Abū-Rājeh would accept and marry his daughter to Hāshem. Masrour knew that Abū-Rājeh would not give the hand of his daughter in wedlock to a non-Shī'a suitor, but at the same time, he allowed for the possibility that he would do so in gratitude for Hāshem's having saved Safwān and his son from the dungeon. Masrour is fond of Rihanna and wants to possess her as well as the hammām, and because he saw Hāshem as being an obstacle to attaining one of these two objectives, he went along with my father's plot and testified that Hāshem was Abū-Rājeh's spy in the palace, and that he intends to murder the Sultan with the help of Safwān and his son Hamād."

The Sultan turned to me and said, "You are very quiet. Speak up!"

I said, "The truth is just as Rashīd has described it. He has given testimony against his own interests and against the interests of his father for the sake of the truth. People who are willing to do such things are worthy of our respect and praise. Masrour regrets having become a means to the Vizier's ends and is willing to confess and testify to that which Rashīd has stated. But Masrour's claim that Rihanna and her mother have talked against the Sultan and the government in their home is a lie. The Vizier has so much spite and rancor toward Abū-Rājeh that he will only be satisfied not just with his destruction, but the destruction of his whole family. Perhaps Masrour wants Abū-Rājeh's wife and daughter to be thrown into the dungeon so as to keep Rihanna at bay from her suitors, and then to be willing to marry him for having saved her and her mother from the dungeon. I suspect that Masrour and the Vizier have already agreed to such an arrangement."

Rashīd said, "That is indeed the case."

The Sultan asked me, "Why did you consent to come to the palace regularly?"

"I had no desire to do so, but my Grandfather said, "If you do not go to the palace, they might cause us trouble."

Qanwā said, "My mother is witness to the fact that we had asked Abū-Naʿīm to send Hāshem to the palace to repair and polish our jewelry."

"Tell the truth, child! Why did you do this?!

"I had heard that the Vizier wanted to ask for my hand in marriage for his son Rashīd. And I knew that Rashīd and Amīna loved each other. So I concluded that this was to be a marriage of convenience and that love played no role in it, and came up with a plan to bring Hāshem to the palace and pretend that he and I were to be married."

"You would have been better served to talk to me instead of carrying on with such antics!"

"Would talking to you have done any good?"

"Watch what you say, you impertinent child!"

"If talking with you is not useless, then order Abū-Rājeh who is innocent to be released. He is minutes away from his death."

"Your insolence is unacceptable! Nor have I reconsidered your punishment. What is the story behind your going to the dungeon with Hāshem?"

"It's true that because of his friendship with Safwān, Abū-Rājeh asked Hāshem to see if he could get some news of them back to him, as their family didn't even know if they were dead or alive. Hāshem asked me if we could take a look at the dungeon. I agreed, and we went down there together. Then when I saw Hamād, who is Safwān's son, I felt sorry for him and instructed the warden to transfer him and his father to the ordinary section of the prison. Hāshem had nothing to do with my decision to transfer them."

I said, "And of course the Vizier has ordered that they be moved back down into the dungeon for the crime of conspiring to assassinate Your Eminence. How someone who is in prison can have a role in such a conspiracy is beyond me!"

The Sultan frowned and said to me, "I will pardon you and Abū-Rājeh's wife and daughter for having brought me the swans."

"What possible meaning these pardons could have when we were all innocent I failed to understand." I said, "I beseech you to order Abū-Rājeh to be released immediately. If he hasn't bled to death yet, that is, as a result of the blows and lashings he has received."

The Sultan said with annoyance, "Do not overtax my patience! This I cannot accept. If I retract the sentence that I passed, my word would no longer be credited or relied upon as being authoritative."

The Sultan's wife said, "Abū-Rājeh is well-liked by the people. He is a pious man. Sooner or later, news will get out that he was innocent. Then it will become known that you have the blood of an innocent man on your hands, and this will alienate you from the people, who will curse and execrate you."

"Upon my word of honor with God, I will put every last one of them to the sword!"

"Listen, Marjān! Abū-Rājeh will die eventually anyway. Act wisely and do not allow your hands to be tainted by his blood. I cannot withstand all this iniquity and oppression any longer. Believe me, if you do not release him, I will not live with you anymore."

The Sultan hopped on the platform and said, "God save me from you women! I cannot be at peace in my own inner sanctum! Why should your daughter threaten to poison herself, or you threaten to leave me? I'll do it just so you'll leave me in peace. Very well, I hereby pardon that miserable and ugly man! Happy? I hope he has died already! Rashīd! You run along and announce the news of his pardon to the cadi and executioner. Now go away and leave me alone, all of you!"

We all quickly exited the Sultan's inner chambers, leaving the Sultan alone with his wife and swans. The Vizier was waiting at the railings of the belvedere that faced the palace grounds. Upon seeing us, he came towards us, wanting to talk to Rashīd, but Rashīd brushed passed him, saying, "There's no time to talk now."

All three of us passed the Vizier and left him alone in his bewildered state. When we reached the bottom of the stairs, Qanwā said, "Let's go on horseback. We'll get there faster that way."

I spontaneously fell into a position of prostration and thanked Almighty God. Rashīd took hold of my bicep and said, "Get up! We have to get to Abū-Rājeh as soon as possible. Let us pray that it is not too late!"

Chapter 27

We mounted three fast horses and left the palace grounds from its rear exit, which was close to the stables. We rode by a date-palm plantation and circled around to the front of the palace complex. On seeing us, Sendi got up from his stool and stood there frozen like a statue in disbelief. We were galloping so fast that anyone who didn't know what was happening would have thought we were in the middle of a race.

Rashīd who had fallen behind Qanwā and I yelled, "We have to get to the main square!" The shortest route there was through the bazaar, which is where they had marched Abū-Rājeh through in order to get him to the main square. I overtook Qanwā and yelled, "Follow me!"

Mercifully, the bazaar was uncrowded and most of the shops were closed. The people had abandoned their shopping needs and had joined the procession accompanying Abū-Rājeh to the public square. We passed by the hammām, as well as Grandfather's store, both of which were closed. The sound of the horses galloping hoofs reverberated under the squinched domes and oculi of the covered bazaar. The few people who were still in the bazaar struggled in alarm to get out of our way.

When we left the bazaar, we were flooded by the rays of the late afternoon sun. We rode through a couple of wider streets through the centers of which water flowed in shallow canals. Women and children and elderly men stood by the doors to their houses or in their second story windows and looked out onto the street and its surrounding environs. It was clear that the procession had only recently passed them by. When we finally reached the square, we came across a huge crowd.

The crowd filled the whole square. A deadly silence prevailed. I saw the cadi in the middle of the square standing on the sundial. He was busy counting out Abū-Rājeh's crimes and misdemeanors. The executioner stood next to him like a ghoul without horn or hoof. Two sentries were holding Abū-Rājeh up by his arms. His head was dangling forward. The rope and chains had been removed from his body. I thanked God yet again. I didn't know whether he was still alive. I was just glad that he had not yet been executed, and that there was still a chance that he was alive. I approached the silent crowd and yelled, "Make way! Clear the path!"

The crowd turned around alarmed, and when they saw us on the back of horses who were frothing at the mouth, they made way and cleared the path for our ingress. We headed towards the podium. The crowd had realized or suspected that we were Abū-Rājeh's emissaries of mercy and was cheering us on loudly. The cadi stopped speaking and the executioner shaded his eyes with his hand in order to see who was approaching.

When we reached the podium, the crowd went quiet again. Rashīd said to the cadi, "Stop what you are doing! His Eminence the Sultan has pardoned Abū-Rājeh. Release him!"

The cadi, who had a long beard and an amber-colored turban on his head, raised a hand and asked, "Do you have a written order from His Eminence that is sealed with his signet ring?"

Qanwā yelled, "Do you not recognize me or Rashīd? Are you calling us liars??"

The cadi opened his arms wide, as if he was playacting some role, and said, "The accused is ready for the execution of his sentence, and the executioner only follows my orders, and, alas, I can only release the accused if I am presented with a letter that has His Eminence the Sultan's seal. So do you, or do you *not*, have a letter that has His Eminence the Sultan's seal? Well, *do* you?"

At this point in our story, someone in the crowd threw a ripe mango at the cadi that hit him on the head and dislodged his turban. The crowd cheered and roared in laughter. Qanwā jumped off her horse onto the podium and forced him off it with a quick shove. Grandfather was in the audience and was smiling and cheering us on along with the rest of the crowd. Rashīd got up on the podium as well and signaled the executioner to sheath his frightful sword, which he did. I was very concerned for Abū-Rājeh. His dangling head had not moved at all. I directed my horse to the edge of the podium and asked the two sentries who were holding him up to bring him over to me. They brought him over and helped me seat him on my horse in front of my saddle. I held Abū-Rājeh in place with one hand, and held the reins of the horse with the other and started to move through the opening the crowd had made for us. I could feel Abū-Rājeh's heartbeat with my forearm. Grandfather made his way through the crowd toward me and grabbed hold of the horse's reins and walked us through the square. His face was wet with tears, and he looked at me with pride and joy. I told him, "I'll take Abū-Rājeh home while you see about finding the doctor."

Qanwā, who was following me, dismounted. She gave her horse to Grandfather and took the reins of my horse in her hands. Before we entered the street, she asked the guards to control the people who were following us. Rashīd and a few others helped the guards do crowd control so that we could get to the street. When we had put some distance between us and the noise of the crowd, I was able to hear the sound of Abū-Rājeh's breathing. He took deep, raspy breaths, like someone who was in a deep sleep.

Qanwā said, "It's been a very strange day. I hope that Abū-Rājeh will survive his ordeal after all of your efforts and your having risked your life to save his."

The passersby looked at us and Abū-Rājeh with surprise. They had no idea what had happened and couldn't surmise why Abū-Rājeh's head and face was covered in blood and dirt and wounded so badly, so I had no choice but to spread the cloth of my turban over his head and shoulders.

Qanwā said, "With the valiant sacrifice that you have made, Rihanna will forever be in your debt and will always be grateful to you."

I said, "Abū-Rājeh was and continues to be a good friend of Grandfather's and mine. I could not allow him to be executed given that he was innocent. Now I know that if Abū-Rājeh were to die, no one could fill the void that he would leave behind. He lit a fire in my heart with his words over the last few days. I hope that he does not leave me alone with the burning fire that he lit within me!"

"So it is not just Rihanna that has set your heart on fire; her father has done so too!"

I nodded and said, "Just so."

"I really want to meet Rihanna."

"You will be enchanted by her, and she will be enamored of you."

We were not far from our house when Qanwā said, "I am worried about Hamād and his father. We saved the poor souls from the dungeon, but they were thrown back in there before their eyes had had a chance to adjust to the light."

I gave expression to the feeling I had in my heart. "I get a feeling you have grown fond of Hamād."

"If that is true, then both of us are unfortunate people."

"How come?"

Qanwā said, "Isn't that obvious? You love a Shī'a girl and I have fallen in love with a Shī'a boy. We are rich and they are poor. But despite this, they are unaware of our love for them, and would not be willing to marry us even if they were."

"It didn't turn out badly for Rashīd and Amīna."

After a pause, I said, "I want to tell you something, but I'm afraid it'll upset you."

"Tell me, even if it upsets me."

"I'm almost sure Rihanna is fond of Hamād."

Qanwā turned and looked at me with chagrin. "What about Hamād?"

"I don't know."

"They're both Shī'a. They will marry and make each other happy."

"Rihanna's happiness is what is important to me."

"And Hamād's to me."

"Do you not envy Rihanna?"

"Do you not envy Hamād?"

"I don't know."

"I don't know either."

"We're in a pretty tough spot."

"God help us!"

Chapter 28

When Omm-Hobāb opened the door on us, she let out a shriek and staggered back. I entered the front yard just as I was, on horseback.

"What are you doing, Hāshem? Who is this man? Why is there blood all over his clothes?"

"Calm yourself. Its Abū-Rājeh."

"Abū-Rājeh?! Heavens above!"

Omm-Hobāb sat down on the wooden platform bed. She had placed her hand on her heart and was staring at Qanwā in shock.

"Who is this young lady?"

"My name is Qanwā"

"Welcome, child."

I turned to Omm-Hobāb and said, "Now is not the time for sitting around. Give me a hand so we can lay Abū-Rājeh down on the bed. Don't let his condition frighten you."

Qanwā, Omm-Hobāb and I placed Abū-Rājeh on the bed. When I removed the cloth of my turban from over his face, Omm-Hobāb let out another shriek and clawed at her cheeks with her hands.

"Lord have mercy! What happened to him? Did he fall down a well?"

Qanwā said, "Calm yourself. It's alright. He's been tortured. They were about to cut his head off in the public square when we arrived and brought him over here on horseback, that's all."

Omm-Hobāb was on the verge of fainting. I said to her, "While we are waiting for Grandfather and the doctor to get here, go and bring a pail of warm water and some clean cloth, and clean his wounds. Qanwā will help you."

When Omm-Hobāb left, Qanwā asked, "What are you going to do now?"

"I'm going to offer my evening devotions and then go and pay a visit to Rihanna and her mother. They are worried for Abū-Rājeh, and they still think that the police might arrive at any minute and arrest them. I have to go and put their mind at ease."

"Will you be bringing them here?"

"Unquestionably. It is best for them to be at Abū-Rājeh's side in these critical moments."

I looked at Abū-Rājeh. He was still unconscious and took in a deep breath once in a while. Qanwā shook her head in dismay and said, "You'd better hurry."

I got myself to Safwān's house quickly, dismounted, and knocked on the door. "Who is it?" Safwān's wife asked from behind the door.

"It's alright, it's me, Hāshem. Open the door."

Rihanna and her mother were pleased to see me. Rihanna asked, "Any news of my father?"

"He's at our house now. We are no longer in any danger. The Vizier's plot has been foiled."

Rihanna and her mother embraced each other in joy, but then Rihanna stared at me and asked, "How is my father doing? Why are you not happy?"

I tried to smile.

"I am. Can't you see I'm smiling? The danger has passed. Our innocence has been established. Your prayers were answered. Your father is fine too, it's just that he's a little…"

I couldn't finish the sentence. What else could I say? Rihanna's mother asked, "A little what?"

Rihanna's worried look was killing me.

"A little… he's been tormented a little."

Rihanna asked, "I don't understand. Do you mean to say that they have tortured my father?"

"Yes, unfortunately. They bound him and dragged him to the main square, where he was to be executed, and whipped him and beat him with their clubs on the way there. But we arrived in time and saved him."

Rihanna batted her eyes a few times, as if waking from a dream, and said in shock, "Execute? This fast??"

I told her what had happened. Outside Safwān's house, Rihanna's mother asked me to mount the horse and ride a little ahead of them, which I did. She and Rihanna and Safwān's wife followed me at a quick pace, and even broke into a jog in streets where there was no one to see them. The sun had set and it was getting dark.

I was surprised to see that a crowd had gathered in front of the house when we got there. There was a small stable in a corner of the front yard. I rode the horse over there and stabled it with the horse that Grandfather had brought over. A few people who were privy to what had taken place that day came over and embraced me and thanked me. Qanwā and Omm-Hobāb stepped out from one of the rooms that opened onto the front yard and came over towards me. I asked them, "Where have they taken Abū-Rājeh?"

Before Qanwā had a chance to say anything, Omm-Hobāb said, "Your grandfather came back with the doctor and a few of Abū-Rājeh's friends and they took him to one of the rooms upstairs. They say he has several broken ribs and a broken shoulder blade, a fractured skull, liver damage, and that he has sustained serious blows to his kidneys. He has also lost a lot of blood. I don't want to upset you, but there really isn't any hope."

She wiped away a tear with a corner of her head-covering. I said to Qanwā, "Abū-Rājeh's family and Hamād's mother will get here in a minute. It's a sad day for all of us. Look at this crowd; it looks like they're already in mourning. You'd best take the horses and return to the palace."

She whispered so that Omm-Hobāb would not hear, "I could have done that before you came back, but I stayed because I wanted to see Rihanna. And I'm glad I'll be seeing Hamād's mother as well!"

"It's a good idea, but it's not a good time to get to know them."

I was concerned about Rihanna and her mother seeing Omm-Hobāb. As fate would have it, they entered the yard that very moment. When Omm-Hobāb saw them, she shook her head despondently and went over and greeted them with an embrace. I was afraid she would embarrass me in front of them. Omm-Hobāb asked, "Do you remember me?"

Rihanna's mother who had become even more concerned when she saw the crowd of around a hundred people gathered in the front yard of the house, said, "Ah, so you made it over as well. How is my husband feeling? What are all these people doing here?"

"They have taken him upstairs. These people are friends of your husbands, and, like us, are worried about him."

"Rihanna said, "We know that my father has been severely beaten and is badly injured. We want to see him."

I didn't know whether their seeing Abū-Rājeh would be helpful. I needed to consult Grandfather in order to be able to make the right decision. I pointed to Qanwā and said, "Before anything else, allow me to introduce Qanwā to you. Without her unstinting help, Abū-Rājeh would not have been saved from being executed, and Safwān and Hamād would not have been freed from the dungeon."

Rihanna, her mother, and Hamād's mother embraced Qanwā warmly and thanked her profusely. Rihanna said, "I have very much looked forward to meeting you."

Qanwā said, "Me too. I stayed here until you arrived so that I could see you. Hāshem speaks very highly of you, and now I see that you are indeed deserving of all that praise. I'm sorry that my father, who had been taken in by the Vizier's intrigues, caused all this suffering, and that we had to meet under such distressing circumstances."

Rihanna's mother said, "For us, you and your honorable mother are much dearer to us than the Sultan and his Vizier. Know that we will never forget your kindness and the favor which you have done for us."

I was very pleased by the way in which they had hit it off. Qanwā said to Safwān's wife, "If only Hamād and his father were with us! A lady who has the good fortune of having such a husband and son is indeed blessed."

"Blessed is the lady who has raised a jewel such as yourself within in the midst of the intrigues of the Sultan's court!"

Omm-Hobāb said, "Why are you standing? Why don't we go and find a room to sit down in and get to know each other better? Hāshem will go and bring some news of Abū-Rājeh; the men have packed the upstairs quarters. Let us wait and see if they will make way so that you can go up and see Abū-Rājeh."

Qanwā, who wanted to return to the palace said, "Forgive me for having to leave you in these circumstances, but its late and I must get back home."

While Qanwā was saying her farewells, I walked the horses from the stable to outside the front yard. When Qanwā came out, I said, "Its dark. Do you want me to come with you?"

In response, she flashed a small and delicate dagger that she had on her.

"Don't worry about me. I'll come back in the morning. I feel that Rihanna and I can become good friends. I feel I have a duty to come and give her my condolences and try to console her. The sooner they see Abū-Rājeh, the better. The doctor didn't think he would make it through the night."

I waited until Qanwā and the horses turned the bend in the street, then went back in. The crowd was gradually thinning out. They were all leaving with the intention of coming back in the morning for the funeral. I didn't know how Rihanna would react when she saw how bad a state her father was in.

Chapter 29

Abū-Rājeh was lying down facing the direction of the Qibla.[23] His wife and Rihanna were sitting to either side of his bed, praying and shedding tears. It was now midnight and everyone had left other than Safwān's wife, the doctor, and a Shīʿa cleric. Rihanna's mother said to Omm-Hobāb, "You have been so kind and it is late. You should go home and rest."

Omm-Hobāb gave me a look and said, "How can I leave you under these circumstances?"

"There is no escaping fate. Whatever is meant to happen, will happen. We are happy to accept God's will."

"In any event, I will remain here with you tonight."

I took the doctor to a corner of the room and asked, "Do you think Abū-Rājeh can hear what we say, or is he completely unconscious?"

The doctor was about Grandfather's age and had hennaed his hair. He said, "He sometimes comes to, but then quickly slips back again. I think that when there is a frown on his face, he is conscious and can hear what is being said around him."

"He wife and daughter have been sitting next to him and weeping for several hours now. Have them leave for a while so that they can get a little rest at least."

The doctor went over to Rihanna and her mother and said, "It would be better if you went to the adjacent room and got some rest."

Rihanna's mother said, "Tonight is not a night where we will be able to get any rest. When I think of what they have done to my husband, and how they have whipped and beat him half to death, and the state that he is in now, it fills me with a powerful fire of fury!"

Rihanna looked at her father and said, "They hooked a chain through his tongue! They threaded a tether through his nose! And tied a rope around his neck and dragged him along with a horse. When I imagine this scene, I nearly go out of my mind and feel on the verge of feinting. I imagine myself in the place of Lady Zeinab, Ali b. Abī-Tāleb's daughter, whose front door was burned down [in an attempt to get her father to pledge allegiance to Abu Bakr immediately upon the Prophet's death]. And I see myself in the place of her mother Lady Fātema, the daughter of the Prophet ﷺ, who sustained injuries after being beaten with a whip, and slapped in the face [in that same assault on their home]. And I see myself in the place of Lady Zeinab's father, Ali ؑ, who had a noose tied around his neck and was dragged to the mosque. When we are certain that God witnesses everything and believe the Lord of the Age ﷺ shares our sorrow, it is a source of comfort for us."

It seemed as though Rihanna was saying these words in order to comfort her mother. The imām[24] who was busy praying in a corner of the room came over and, after saying his salaams, said, "Perhaps the doctor will want to examine Abū-Rājeh. It would be better for you to go to the other room for an hour or so. Don't forget that if Abū-Rājeh is not unconscious, he would be further pained by your bereavement and lamentations."

With the help of Safwān and Omm-Hobāb, Rihanna and her mother got up with reluctance and went to the next room, which was separated from Abū-Rājeh's room by a curtain.

The imam placed his prayer mat closer to Abū-Rājeh. The doctor sat on the other side of Abū-Rājeh in order to moisten his lips. A few minutes later, Grandfather entered the room with somnolent eyes. He asked me, "Anything new?"

"No," I said.

"Where are the ladies?"

"There're in the adjacent room here. They just went in there to get some rest."

Grandfather had gotten a couple of hours' sleep.

"You should go and get some rest too. We have a long, sad day ahead of us. May God grant his daughter and wife patience."

Before I left to go to my room, I went over to Abū-Rājeh. The doctor was at a distance and the imām was busy praying. Abū-Rājeh's lips and nose were still swollen. The area around both his eyes was dark with heavy bruising. I sat next to him. Now that his teeth had been broken, his face looked different and concave, and wasn't as elongated as it used to be. For me, Abū-Rājeh's being was a lantern that shone in the middle of a dark night. His face was so welcoming and luminous! Every time he saw me, he broke into such a wide smile, as if he was expecting me. I felt he liked me more than other people. I was so tired that I had no choice but to go to my room and get some rest. I was afraid that I would be woken up in the morning by Rihanna's and her mother's wailings and see that a sheet has been pulled over Abū-Rājeh's face. I regretted not having gone to the Sultan with Qanwā immediately upon seeing Masrour in the palace and hearing what Rashīd had to say, for if I had done that, Abū-Rājeh would not be in the state he was in now. It was hard to believe how fast he was tried and consigned to the executioner's blade. I didn't know what fate awaited Rihanna after the passing of her father.

Suddenly, Abū-Rājeh shivered all over, took in a deep breath, and let out a gentle sigh. The doctor was taking a nap and Grandfather was busy reading the Quran on the other side of the room. The imām was busy making supplications in the standing *qonūt* position and was oblivious to his surroundings. I had a feeling Abū-Rājeh was breathing his last breaths and that he was about to expire. He slowly opened his eyes, which were lifeless and bloodshot. His eyes were so lifeless that they were going through irregular repetitive movements. He opened his lips slightly. I dipped a clean ball of cotton in water and moistened his lips with it and dripped a few drops of water inside his mouth. I took his cold hand in my own. I moved my head close to his and whispered in his ear, "Abū-Rājeh, can you hear my voice?"

He squeezed my hand with the last ounce of his strength to indicate that he could hear me. It brought tears to my eyes. I said, "Do you remember how you told me the story of Ismael Harqalī? His condition was beyond the help of any doctor. You told me that the Lord of the Age ﷺ cured him in such a way that no sign remained of his abscess, and all of the doctors of Baghdad and Hilla affirmed that such a miracle could only be performed by prophets. Now your condition is worse than Ismael Harqalī's! No one can help you. Seeing as you have talk to me about the Lord of the Age ﷺ on so many different occasions, you should pray to him and ask him to save you from death."

A tear fell down from the corner of his eye onto his pillow. I was sure he had heard my words. Exhaustion overcame him and he closed his eyes like someone who has been drawn in by an undercurrent. He moved his head and let out a moan. I looked at him intently, trying to take in his pale and tormented face and entrust it to my memory. I kissed his shoulder with tears in my eyes and stood up. When I moved away from Abū-Rājeh and went toward Grandfather, Rihanna and her mother came back and sat next to Abū-Rājeh again. Rihanna told me in a low tone of voice so as not to waken the doctor, "I saw you from behind the curtain speaking with my father."

I nodded.

"Was he conscious?"

"I think so."

"What made you think he was conscious?"

"He moved. He sighed and let out a moan. I was holding his hand, and I felt him squeeze my hand, and when I talked to him, he shed a tear."

Rihanna and her mother looked at each other with hope. Her mother asked, "What did you say to him?"

Rihanna hastened to add, "If it is not private, of course."

I glanced at Grandfather, who had become curious also.

"I had gone to the hammām one day to see Abū-Rājeh, but he was not there. I went to the Station of the Lord of the Age ﷻ looking for him. I found him sitting by Ismael Harqalī's grave. He related the story of Ismael Harqalī being cured by the Lord of the Age ﷻ. Now that I thought he could hear me, I reminded him of that story and told him, "Now your condition is worse that Ismael Harqalī's and no doctor can help you anymore, so you should pray to him and ask him to save you from dying."

Rihanna wiped away a tear from her cheek and said, "My father loves the Lord of the Age ﷻ. What is the extent of your knowledge of and love for His Eminence?"

I was confused by Rihanna's question. I said, "But I am not Shī'a."

"But then if you do not believe in the Lord of the Age ﷻ, why did you ask him to make intercessory recourse with him?"

Rihanna was so intelligent that she had been able to entrap me with this clever question of hers. I replied sincerely, "I love Abū-Rājeh so much that I wanted him to be saved through whatever means that were possible."

The imām, who had just completed reciting another supplication, said, "There are so many reports about the Lord of the Age ﷻ helping his Shī'a[25] that it leaves no doubt for a rational person that His Eminence is alive and is acting as God's *hojja*[26] on Earth. The story of Ismael Harqalī is a drop in an ocean [of such evidence]. Happy the fate of Ismael Harqalī, whose eyes were brightened by the brilliant luminescence of the Lord of the Age ﷻ, who is extremely handsome and captivating. When someone asked Ali b. Abī-Tāleb ؏ to describe the Lord of the Age ﷻ, he said, 'He is the closest creature to God's Apostle ﷺ in terms of his character, handsomeness, and mode of conduct.' All of the perfections of character are gathered in his person."

The imām began to weep silently. After a few moments had passed, Grandfather said to me, "You had better go and get an hour's rest."

Leaving Abū-Rājeh and Rihanna under those circumstances was not easy for me, but I heeded Grandfather's counsel and went to my own room and laid down in my bed. A black cloud had obscured the moon. The wind rustled through the fronds of the palm trees. There was pandemonium in my heart. It again seemed that the ceiling of my room had come down and was putting pressure on me. I never thought I'd see Rihanna in our house at such close range, and under such gloomy and tearful conditions. I asked myself whether or not I would ever see Rihanna happy again. Would I be woken by cries of lament if I were to fall asleep? What would tomorrow bring? Would Abū-Rājeh be buried by this time tomorrow, and would he be spending his first night in his grave?

I tried to go to sleep. I had endured a difficult day, but despite all of its difficulties, I had also been able to see Rihanna and talk to her. There was no longer any doubt in my mind about the fact that I couldn't live without her. I had heard that Rihanna's mother's family lived in Basra. If Abū-Rājeh passed away, would his family sell the hammām and their house and move to Basra? Or perhaps Rihanna would marry Hamād or some other young man in Hilla, and her husband would take on the responsibility of running the hammām and their lives. In that case, I would have to leave Hilla. But wherever could I run to without her??

These thoughts were running through my mind when Grandfather entered the room holding an oil lamp.

Chapter 30

I sat up in my bed, and Grandfather came over and sat next to me. After he looked at me and around the room, he said, "I know you love Rihanna. She is a peerless young lady, but you have to accept that what you are feeling is a love that cannot be consummated and a love that will continue to torment you. We and the Shī'a of Hilla are brothers, but two brothers will also have their differences at times, and each lives in his own house. Your love of Rihanna should not incline you toward the Shī'a form of Islam. I am terrified by such a prospect! There are enough beautiful flowers in the garden of your own house for you not to want to possess a flower from your neighbor's garden. What's wrong with Qanwā, for example? She might not be as beautiful or as graceful as Rihanna, but she will certainly make a good wife for you."

He yawned and continued, "What you did today was extraordinary. I didn't think you had so much courage in you. If you had gone into hiding as I had advised, Abū-Rājeh would have been put to death already, and you and his family would still be wanted fugitives. Everyone congratulated me for having you as a grandson. And I congratulate you and thank God that the story ended well, and you no longer have to go to Kūfa and be far from me. I don't know; maybe it is the miracle of love that is at play."

I needed to spill my heart out to someone, so I was happy that Grandfather had come in and struck up a conversation. I said, "I too thank God that I have you. Sometimes I feel like talking to someone. At these times, my father and mother's absence weigh heavily on me. That's why I go over to see Abū-Rājeh. He is the person I would go to when I needed a shoulder to cry on. He was a good listener and I in turn would listen to what he had to say in response. He would talk to me and try to help me."

"The poor soul now needs help more than anyone else."

"No Grandfather! The one who is in worse shape is me! If Abū-Rājeh dies, he will be released from all of his woes and troubles. Rihanna will marry sooner or later and start her new life. And Abū-Rājeh's wife will start to smile again upon seeing her first grandchild. It is only me who has to somehow find a way to live with my torment. Nor is there anyone who can help me."

"Believe me when I tell you that I am willing to give up my very being in order to make you happy. I am willing to place Rihanna in the pan of a balance scale and fill the other pan with gold and gemstones, if doing such a thing would make it possible for her to become your wife. Alas, me and my wealth are powerless to do anything about this. What an ill-omened day it was, the day I asked you to come down from the workshop into the store. Would that Rihanna and her mother had never decided to purchase a pair of earrings from our store! If you hadn't laid eyes on her after all these years, it wouldn't have turned out like this."

The thought occurred to me that Rihanna was now sitting by her father's bed in our house wearing the earrings that I had made, and it occurred to me how close I was to her, but how far she was from me. She was as far away from me and as unobtainable as the moon.

"I feel helpless and humbled when I see I cannot save you from the torment you are suffering."

I rested my head on his shoulder.

"Don't worry, Grandfather. The best thing we can do is to entrust our affairs to God's good graces. Abū-Rājeh is dying in the other room, and his wife and daughter are obviously very troubled by this. It is not right for me to be so selfish."

He pressed my head to his chest with his arm and said, "You are right. I entrust you to God and pray to him to grant you happiness. I hope that I will see you happy before I die!"

I stared at him and said, "Please do not speak of your dying! I'm already losing Abū-Rājeh. I don't have anyone other than you beside him. You have to remain alive long enough to raise my children and to teach them the trade of goldsmithing."

Grandfather chuckled and said, "I would like nothing more, but we have to see what God wants."

"Last night, right here, I saw that you, Abū-Rājeh, Rihanna and her mother and I were sitting in a beautiful garden, talking about all sorts of things and laughing. When I woke up, I thought to myself how distant I am from that dream. Tonight, I feel more distant than ever from the possibility of the realization of that beautiful and splendid dream. I wish that I had never awakened from that dream! If sleep comes to me tonight, perhaps I will be able to chase that dream. Oh, how I dread waking up tomorrow! We have put a difficult day behind us; God only knows what awaits us tomorrow."

Grandfather stood up and said, "You passed a difficult day with distinction. Try to get some sleep. I hope that you will be able to pass tomorrow with distinction and pride as well. Life has taught me that patience and longanimity are the remedies of the bitter things in life, as that these are the cure for many afflictions and hardships. When your father died, I exercised patience and forbearance; you, too, must learn to do this, and it is something that I know you are well capable of."

"I cannot stay in this town and be witness to Rihanna's marriage. I want to go somewhere, where I will not even hear the name Hilla mentioned. Maybe in this way I might be able to stay alive and be patient and have forbearance."

He smiled bitterly and said, "We will leave together, and return to Hilla whenever you are ready."

I tried to sleep after Grandfather left. I was expecting Rihanna's and her mother's lamentations to break out at any moment. I hoped I'd get to sleep before anything happened. I didn't know how much longer Abū-Rājeh could resist. I longed for and rued the passing of the days when I would visit him and when we would talk about anything and everything. I never thought in those days that such a strange and bitter end awaited him.

I felt sorry for myself. Not only was Rihanna outside of my reach, but I was losing Abū-Rājeh as well. Until about ten days ago, I thought of myself as a successful young man with a bright future ahead of me. Now I felt that all of the sorrows of the world were heaped upon me like a mass of black clouds.

The moon and stars shone brightly in the midnight sky now that the clouds had cleared. There was a star close to the horizon that twinkled dimly, and I did not think of my future as even having a glimmer that could match the weak twinkle of that distant star. I saw myself as resembling someone on a safe harbor who had been placed on a small and precarious raft that was released onto a tumultuous sea without shore. I could see nothing but tall, dark waves. Was my raft about to fall apart under the pressure of the waves, with the remnants of its planks floating on the water and never reaching the shore, or was the good Lord going to save me from the abyss of this stormy sea?

I don't know when I fell asleep. When I slept, I also dreamed I was in a small boat on a stormy sea. The frightful waves positioned their shoulders under the boat like ominous giants who would then rise up as tall as a mountain. A bolt of lightning struck and a formidable wave demolished the boat. I clung on to a stray plank. After being thrown back and forth and being immersed by hundreds of waves for an hour, I saw an island in the distance. I was so tired out by the struggle with the waves that I was barely able to move my arms and legs. Somehow, after a gargantuan effort, I was able to inch my way to the Island's shore and drag my tattered body onto its sands. I was only able to thank God for having been saved before I passed out. Moments later, I heard a beautiful and alluring voice calling my name.

"Hāshem! ... Hāshem!"

It was Rihanna's voice. I opened my eyes with difficulty. It was light out. I saw myself on the shores of a beautiful and verdant island. Rihanna was sitting next to me with a beautiful smile on her face.

"Hāshem, wake up! You finally made it to the shore of your salvation!"

She was elated at my having been saved. Upon seeing her, I forgot all of my weariness and exhaustion, and stared at her captivating and luminous face.

Chapter 31

"**h**āshem! Hāshem!!"

I woke up. It was that same voice. Rihanna was sitting next to me. Grandfather was standing next to her, holding a lantern. For a moment, I wished I had not awakened. Had Abū-Rājeh passed from this world? But Grandfather was smiling.

"Wake up, my son!"

I rubbed my eyes. No; I was not mistaken. Grandfather had a big smile on his face. I looked at Rihanna. She too was smiling and shedding tears of joy! How beautiful her smile was! I wished that time would stand still so that she would continue to look at me with her hope-inspiring smile. Her eyes had a strange luminosity about them. It was as if her tears were intermingled with love and sweetness. I hadn't seen her this happy even in childhood. I couldn't peel my eyes away from her. I gradually sat upright and said jokingly, "How very interesting. I'm dreaming that I have woken up from my dream!"

Making no effort to conceal her loving smile, Rihanna said, "You really *have* woken up."

"But both of you are smiling and are happy. How can it be?"

"As you can see," she said, with an even bigger smile.

"How is your father feeling?"

Two tear drops could be seen falling from her cheeks onto her *chādor* in the light of the lantern.

"He's feeling completely better, just as I had seen it in my dream."

I lay back down and said, "Now I *know* I'm dreaming. I want this pleasant dream to last for at least a few more hours. I've been having nightmares for a long while now. Thank God I'm having a good dream, if only for once! I'm just afraid someone will come and wake me."

Grandfather took hold of my arm and pulled me up.

"Get up! You're so tired, you're delirious."

He made me sit up. Rihanna wiped a tear away with the back of her finger and said, "Get up so we can go and you can see it with your own eyes, even though it really is incredible!"

She stood up. The sounds of people sending *salawāt*[27] could be heard from the room Abū-Rājeh was in. Grandfather took me by my arm again and helped me stand up. I couldn't think straight. I kept shaking my head and raking my brain to figure out if I was awake or still dreaming.

"If I'm awake, did I hear correctly that you said your father was feeling completely better??"

Rihanna was so happy; she couldn't keep from smiling and shedding tears of joy. My greatest aspiration was to see her happy like this.

"Yes, my father has never felt so good in all his life!"

Grandfather said, "What Rihanna is saying is true. It's hard to believe, but true nevertheless."

"So, I am awake, and Abū-Rājeh is feeling fine, and that is why the two of you are so happy?"

Rihanna said, "Come and let us go so you can see for yourself."

I gradually changed from a state of astonishment and bewilderment to one of happiness and joy.

"But wait! How did this happen? He was at death's door, with all those broken bones and organ damage and bruising…"

Rihanna said, "You should know. After all, was it not you who told my father to ask the Lord of the Age ﷿ to help him get his health back?"

"The Lord of the Age ﷿?"

I felt the sting of tears welling up in my eyes. I asked in a voice that quivered with excitement and joy, "You mean His Eminence cured your father?"

She couldn't stop her tears. She hid her face behind her *chādor* and nodded her head. Grandfather said, "What has occurred is a miracle. It can only be the work of His Eminence, and no one else."

I gave out a hearty laugh.

"My God! What am I hearing? What are you saying, Grandfather? Was it not you who not an hour ago was counseling me not to…?"

He didn't let me finish.

"Forget what I said. What I say now is, may my life be sacrificed for his sake! Pity the whole life I wasted without having an understanding of that noble personage!"

Rihanna said, "Rather, praise God that you ultimately did come to know your Imam and master."

"You are absolutely right, my child. An hour ago, I pitied Abū-Rājeh for his dying in what I imagined to be his state of ignorance. Now I am regretting a whole lifetime that I spent in a wayward direction. But I am grateful to God for ultimately showing me the right path."

I stopped short of the room's door. I asked Rihanna, "You mean to say that there is no longer any sign of all those injuries and broken bones?"

Rihanna shook her head and said nothing. Grandfather nudged me forward.

"There are less than ten steps to that room. Let us proceed so that you can see the miracle for yourself."

We crossed the hallway and reached the room in which Abū-Rājeh had been bedridden. Grandfather raised the curtain and entered, followed by Rihanna and I. The imām and the doctor were busy offering their devotions. The third person who was in the position of prostration could not have been anyone other than Abū-Rājeh. The womenfolk who were seated in a corner stood up upon seeing me. Abū-Rājeh's wife was the happiest of them all. Two oil lanterns lit the room. Grandfather gave me the lantern he held in his hand so that I could see Abū-Rājeh in a better light. I offered my salaams to the imām and the doctor and sat next to Abū-Rājeh. He had a mantle over his shoulder and was wearing a turban on his head. I could not see his face. A few moments passed. I was trembling in excitement. Rihanna approached her father and gently said, "Father, Hāshem is sitting next to you."

Abū-Rājeh shifted and slowly raised his head from its position of prostration on the ground and turned toward me.

"Salaam, Hāshem!"

My mouth was agape in astonishment, and the lantern began to shake as I held it in my hand. Rihanna took the lantern from my hand and held it up to her father's face. Not only was there no sign of any injury on his face, but his usual gaunt and jaundiced look and sparse beard had also disappeared. His face had filled out and turned into a healthy rosy color, and his beard had become a full and thick beard. He smiled at me and said, "My dear friend! Will you not return my salaam?"

A beautiful and uniform row of teeth had taken the place of the overlong ones that had been broken. The light of youth and health shone brightly from his face. Seeing was believing and seeing Abū-Rājeh put me in a position of having to acknowledge and believe in the miracle that had taken place.

"Salaam to you too, Abū-Rājeh! May God's peace be unto you too."

When we embraced each other, I became aware that his body was no longer frail and gaunt. I kissed his face and said through tears of joy, "Abū-Rājeh! *You* tell me that I am not dreaming any of this!"

I ran my hands over his shoulders and torso.

"Are there no more signs of all those broken bones and bruising?"

He took a couple of steps back, thrust out his chest, and thumped his fists on his chest and belly and shoulders, and said with tears that were intermingled with laughter, "I feel that I have never felt as happy and healthy as I do now. I don't feel any pain or illness in myself, thanks to the *baraka* (or divine blessings) of my *mowlā* (master), Hojjat ibn al-Hasan."

The imām who was no longer himself said, "I envy you, Abū-Rājeh! May the sweetness of this honor and felicitous event be salubrious for you, for you appealed to and were graced with the divine bounty and blessings of the Lord of the Age عجّل الله تعالى فرجه الشريف."

The doctor said, "My worldview had been molded for a while under the influence of the medical books of the materialists. I no longer believed in His Eminence and didn't think of him or call upon him. I came here to cure you, or so I thought, in my ignorance, but I myself was cured, thanks to

His Eminence's grace. This sign is so clear and evident that it leaves no room for any doubt."

Rihanna held Abū-Rājeh's hands in her own and said, "Dear Father. Upon my word of honor with God, you now look exactly like you did when I saw you in my dream last year."

Abū-Rājeh stood up and said, "Indeed, the glad tidings of such a *kerāmat*[28] (or supernatural occurrence) was given to us a year ago, but we failed to take it seriously. Alas! If I were to spend the rest of my life in the position of a prostration of gratitude, I would not be able to repay an iota of this great blessing. How handsome and noble His Eminence was, and with what kindness and grace did he talk to me!"

I said, "Relate what happened so that I can know it too!"

He sat next to me and brought me close to him with his arm.

"In those moments that I had come back into consciousness, I heard your words. After that, my condition got even worse, such that I saw death with my own eyes. I could no longer move my tongue. I supplicated and petitioned my Cherisher and Sustainer (*rabb*), and asked my *mowlā*, the Lord of the Age ﷻ, for help, and asked him to intercede on my behalf with Almighty God. When I was a step away from death, when the mere act of breathing had become difficult for me, I had hope in none other than God. I suddenly felt His Eminence standing beside me. I opened my eyes and was elated to find that he was indeed present. That loving Imam caressed my body with his curative hands and said, 'Go out from your house and strive earnestly for the sake of your wife and daughter, for Almighty God has blessed you with good health.'[29] All of my pain and ailments were lifted with the motion of his hands, and I felt light-footed and healthy, just as I do now. When I arose in ecstatic delight from my bed, I no longer saw His Eminence. Everyone was asleep. I took the lantern and went halfway across the front yard so that maybe I would see my Imam one more time and embrace him, but I did not see him, no matter how much I searched for a trace of him. The bolt of the lock [of the door to the front yard] was secured. I returned disappointed and with tears in my eyes, and lay back down in my bed. I thought of various ways to wake you all without alarming you. I couldn't control my tears. First the good doctor woke up, followed by Abū-Naʿīm, both of whom then gently awoke the others."

Rihanna said, "I fell asleep in the position of prostration. Before I fell asleep, I was the saddest girl in the world, and now I feel I am the most fortunate and blessed person in the world. My mother shook me gently and said, 'Wake up! Your father is feeling better and is sitting up in his bed.' I rushed headlong and drew aside the curtain. My father gave me a beautiful smile that was bursting with health, and said, 'Get a hold of yourself. It is not so strange for our Master to pay a visit to one of his devotees and solve his problems'."

Rihanna turned to me and continued, "Like you, I had thought that I was dreaming these things."

We all laughed. Omm-Hobāb said, "I *still* think I'm dreaming!"

We all laughed again. I said to Grandfather, "I was the last one to be awakened. That was not very nice of you."

The sound of our laughter and hilarity reverberated throughout the room. If anyone heard us outside, they would think that we were wailing and lamenting Abū-Rājeh's passing. Grandfather said, "I wanted to awaken you just before dawn, but Abū-Rājeh said that I should rouse you earlier so that we could offer our night devotions communally."

Abū-Rājeh was wearing a fresh, clean set of clothes. It was clear that he had taken a bath before they had woken me.

I could smell the perfume of our house's soap when I embraced him. The imām said, "What an auspicious day we have ahead of us. With sunup, everyone will be coming to Abū-Rājeh's funeral, and will be shocked when they see him fully recovered and in even better health than he was before. The Shī'a will rejoice and our enemies will be shamed. Thank God for all of His blessings!"

He shed some tears and said, "Why did I have to be asleep when His Eminence graced us with his presence? I was deprived of being witness to his peerless magnificence!"

The doctor said to him, "We have to console ourselves with the knowledge that the Imam's kind gaze fell upon us as well when he was here."

The imām said, "Abū-Na'īm! You and your house are very dear to us! What honor and virtue could be higher than one's house being visited by the Lord of the Age ﷺ?"

Grandfather said, "I am indebted to my grandson Hāshem for this great honor."

Abū-Rājeh said to me, "I saw you holding the swans as you were heading to the palace. I knew why you were going there. I wanted to tell you to head back and to save yourself, but I didn't have the strength. Rihanna has filled me in with the rest of the story. I am just as happy for you and your grandfather accepting Shī'a Islam as I am for having gained my health back. I feel a sense of pride when I see that whatever I related to you about the Lord of the Age ﷺ and his miracles have been witnessed by you with your own eyes."

I could not get enough of seeing Abū-Rājeh's beautiful face. He stood up and was preparing to start his devotions. Grandfather and I sat next to the imām so he could teach us the necessary parts of the ordinances [having to do with the performance of the ritual devotions in so far as they differed to that which we were accustomed to from our previous rite].

Rihanna went to join Omm-Hobāb. I preferred to have Rihanna as my teacher. Now that I knew that hers was a true dream, I was extremely curious to know the identity of that fortunate young man who stood next to her father in her dream.

A few minutes later, we were all busy performing the night devotions communally. I had never prayed so earnestly in my whole life.

Chapter 32

The day was full of adventure. The sun had just risen when hundreds of people showed up for Abū-Rājeh's funeral, gathering in the front yard and spilling over into the street. Grandfather spoke to the crowd from behind the railing of the second-floor balcony, giving them the news of Abū-Rājeh's miraculous cure. The crowd roared in delight. Abū-Rājeh came to the balcony and told everyone present what had happened. The crowd shed tears of joy and celebrated.

People would come in groups to see Abū-Rājeh and hear the story of his being graced and cured by the Lord of the Age ﷺ, and this lasted until around noon. They would then take their leave and repeat the story of the incredible miracle to those who had not heard it.

I saw Masrour in the midst of one of these groups. I didn't know how he had gotten out from behind the door of the cellar. I let Abū-Rājeh know. He said, "I have forgiven him. Tell him to come back to work, and to honor his grandfather more than ever."

I approached him from behind and grabbed him by the arm. He became alarmed when he saw me. When I gave him Abū-Rājeh's message, he became wide-eyed. I was standing next to him when Abū-Rājeh came to the balcony and said a few words so that those present would be convinced of his being cured. When Masrour saw Abū-Rājeh in his new form, he fell on his knees and wept profusely, reproaching himself for his treachery. Before I left him, he said, "Tell Abū-Rājeh that I will serve him for the rest of his days for the clemency he has given me and for the magnanimity that he has shown me. He will not see me go astray after this."

It was around noon when a group of women from the Sultan's palace entered the front yard. The group included Qanwā and her mother and sisters. After seeing Abū-Rājeh and hearing the story of his miraculous cure, they joined Rihanna and her mother upstairs in order to congratulate them.

By the time the call to prayer was made at noon, there wasn't a soul who hadn't heard the story. There was news that hundreds of people had become Shī'a. Abū-Rājeh told me, "I pray to God to increase the blessings of this miracle!"

I said, "I don't know how Marjān-e Saghīr will be able to reconcile himself with the reality of this miracle. I would really have liked to have seen the look on his face when he heard the news. He's probably suffering from a paroxysm of bewilderment by now."

"May God grant that he leaves the Shī'a of this town alone from now on!"

I took in Abū-Rājeh's loving and luminous face.

"Happy your fate, Abū-Rājeh! You were able to capture the bird of your belief in and love for the Lord of the Age ﷿. You are the talk of the town of Hilla today. Your name will go down in history, like Ismael Harqalī's did. Anyone who hears about or reads your story will envy you and salute you."

"If Marjān-e Saghīr frees the Shī'a he has imprisoned, it will prove to you how sometimes our Master solves many of the problems facing the Shī'a through indirect means. If the Shī'a who are imprisoned are set free, the joy of the Shī'a community will be complete."

"You think that's possible?"

"Perhaps our Master's real intention in performing this miracle was the freeing of the Shī'a who are being held prisoner, and the conversion of large numbers of people to the Shī'a faith. I am nothing but a means; I should not take pride in myself. The person who is the beloved of everyone's heart and who is spoken of more than anything else is our Master, the Lord of the Age ﷻ."

As always, I took pleasure in the depth of Abū-Rājeh's faith, and in his nobility of character.

After we offered our noontide devotions and had lunch, it would have been a good time for us to get some rest, but just then, some men on horseback came from the Sultan's court and stood waiting in the street while their leader came in and told Abū-Rājeh that Marjān-e Saghīr requested the pleasure of his company.

Grandfather said, "Anyone who wants to see Abū-Rājeh can come here to see him, like everyone else."

But Abū-Rājeh got up and said, "I will go to see the Sultan."

"Perhaps the Sultan has some ill-intentioned scheme in mind."

"Don't be concerned. Marjān-e Saghīr is curious to see me in my new condition, that's all."

"Then we will come with you too."

"I'll just take Hāshem with me."

I was very happy that Abū-Rājeh had chosen me from among all his friends. I stood up and took my position next to him, beaming.

The riders, whose company included Rashīd, had brought a few extra horses along, two of which Abū-Rājeh and I mounted, heading toward the palace in front of the others. I introduced Rashīd to Abū-Rājeh, and explained the critical role he played in Abū-Rājeh's rescue. Abū-Rājeh thanked him warmly.

On our way there, anyone who knew or recognized Abū-Rājeh came to him and kissed his knee or rubbed their hand over his clothing. When an appropriate opportunity presented itself, I asked Abū-Rājeh, "Now that we know Rihanna's dream was an inspired and true dream, do you think you could ask her who the young man was who was standing next to you? As I understand it, he is to be Rihanna's future husband."

Abū-Rājeh nodded his head and said, "You are right. I will ask her as soon as I can. I am curious to know the identity of my future groom myself. He must obviously be a pious man and worthy of marriage to her, if he has been depicted by Heaven in Rihanna's dream."

"I suspect that the fortunate young man is Hamād."

"Possibly. He is certainly worthy; there can be no doubt of that."

We all dismounted at the palace door, and two of the riders took the horses to their stables. Sendi did his usual three knocks on the door upon seeing us. He then came over wide-eyed and, after inspecting Abū-Rājeh for a minute, kissed his hand and cheeks. The door opened and Abū-Rājeh and I entered the palace grounds ahead of the others. Sendi walked with me for a few steps and whispered in my ear, "Wow! What a transformation!! You were right when you said that we should pay attention to the inner aspects of ourselves as well as to our surface appearances. The Imam of the Shī'a transformed him into his beautiful inner self!"

Rashīd directed us to the reception hall. We passed through the crowd that had gathered there to see Abū-Rājeh. Everyone watched Abū-Rājeh in stunned silence, followed by quiet murmurings. There was a large door at the end of the hall. A sentry opened it and said to Abū-Rājeh, "His Eminence the Sultan is expecting you."

Chapter 33

The Sultan was sitting on his throne. The Vizier was standing beside him. Abū-Rājeh and I stood in front of them with a few feet between us and offered them our salaams. The Sultan stood up and looked at Abū-Rājeh in astonishment. The Vizier circled around Abū-Rājeh and examined him closely. They were both so shocked at what they saw that they forgot to return our salaams. The Sultan eventually said, "I wish I knew what kind of magic trick you have used!"

Abū-Rājeh said, "During the time of the Prophet ﷺ, there were people who said the same thing when they witnessed his miracles."

"If I had Moses' staff, I would throw it to the ground, so that it would turn into a serpent and swallow you whole, if any sort of magic is at play."

"I am Moses' staff myself: a clear and undeniable sign that swallows every false and corrupt thought."

The Sultan came closer and examined Abū-Rājeh's face and teeth, then returned to his seat and sat down. He was completely confused. Nor was the Vizier in much better shape. Abū-Rājeh said, "Stop your enmity with the Shī'a, and free them from your dungeons!" Believe that my Master exists and is alive and is the heir to the Prophet's knowledge and powers. Allow us to live with our brother Muslims in peace and security."

After a moment's silence, the Sultan turned to the Vizier and said, "Say something! Why are you just standing there silent like a dumb mute?!"

The Vizier said, "Your power, and the power of the Caliph himself, is as nothing compared with the power of the Imam of the Shī'a. Until today, I did not believe in his existence or in his rightfulness, and mistreated innocent Shī'a Muslims in order to curry your favor. I devised some intrigue in order to kill Abū-Rājeh and be rid of him. It is now time for me to repent, before I subject myself to the wrath and revenge of His Eminence the Mahdi ﷿. I have done things to make the people of this town hate me. My remaining in this position would be to your disadvantage. It would be best for you to release the Shī'a that are imprisoned, and to honor and respect their Imam."

Addressing the Sultan, Abū-Rājeh said, "There are a large number of Shī'a Muslims in this town. They are like the fingers of one hand with respect to their Muslim brethren. When you sow enmity and discord between us, your own position is weakened. Heed the counsel of your Vizier. I pray that Almighty God to forgive us our trespasses and to guide us all onto the right path!"

"I am glad that Hāshem stopped me from shedding your blood. Until today, my throne was positioned with its back to the Station of His Eminence the Mahdi ﷿, which was my way of debasing the Shī'a. But before you leave, I shall instruct my people to turn it so that it faces His Eminence's Station."

The Sultan said to the Vizier, "Go and free all of the Shī'a that are in the prison! Take them all to the bath and give them new clothes and give fifty dinars each to all who will accept it as a compensation."

I looked delightedly at Abū-Rājeh. The Sultan said to him, "The people of Hilla will now respect and pay heed to everything you say. Can I rest assured that you do not intend to overthrow me?"

Abū-Rājeh said, "I am but a hammām-keeper. I have no wish other than to see the Muslims having a good life and being able to live side by side as brothers in faith."

We were preparing to leave when the Sultan said to Abū-Rājeh, "How do we know that it was the Lord of the Age ﷽ who cured you? Maybe it was the work of the Prophet ﷺ."

Abū-Rājeh smiled and displayed his teeth, which shone like pearls, and said, "The name and patronymic (*konya*) of His Eminence is the same as the name and patronymic of the Prophet ﷺ. He is the closest person to the Apostle of God ﷺ in terms of his nature and the excellence and nobility of his character. For me – who is someone who was able to make pilgrimage to His Eminence the Lord of the Age ﷽ – it is as if I made pilgrimage to His Eminence the Prophet ﷺ. Do not forget that His Eminence is a progeny of the Prophet ﷺ, and it should come as no surprise that a son resembles his ancestor. Anyone who loves the Prophet ﷺ cannot help but love the Lord of the Age ﷽ also."

The Sultan and the Vizier accompanied us to outside the reception hall. When we were saying our farewells, the Sultan said to Abū-Rājeh, "How about you accepting my horse as a gift from me?"

Abū-Rājeh, who was now in the midst of a throng of people who looked at him in awe and touched his clothing with their hands [in an effort to receive some portion his *baraka*], said, "You are fond of your horse, and I do not have a place where I can keep it, nor am I capable of seeing to its needs. I accept your gift and present it back to you with my gratitude."

The Sultan said, "Do you want to take your swans back?"

"If I were to say no, I would be lying."

We all laughed and parted ways happily and in good cheer.

News reached us that evening of the prisoners' release and that they were on their way to see and thank Abū-Rājeh together with their families.

It was an impassioned meeting. Hamād and his father were among the freed prisoners. Abū-Rājeh wept tears of joy upon seeing them, and they thanked the Lord by falling into a position of prostration. No one could recall a day when the Shī'a of Hilla were as happy and hopeful as they were on that blessed day. From where I was standing, I saw Rihanna and Qanwā mingling among the womenfolk and looking in the direction where Hamād and his father were standing. The freed prisoners left after about an hour, leaving only Safwān and Hamād, who stayed behind. Safwān's wife, who had gone to her home in the morning, had come back and would give Hamād a hug and kiss him at every opportunity she got. Like the other women, she too shed tears of joy.

Omm-Hobāb gave me a bowl of fruit to take to the room where the men had gathered.

"My legs are killing me. After you have taken the fruit bowl, go in the kitchen and fetch a jug of water."

When I entered the kitchen, I was surprised to see Rihanna there, busy washing fruit. She was being assisted by an old woman who was arranging the fruit in different bowls. I returned without saying a word, then knocked on the door.

"God grant that you are not weary!"

Rihanna gathered her *chādor* about her. I picked up the jug and held it under the tap of the water urn. The old woman said, "Well done! Once you have taken the jug of water, come right back and take these fruit bowls, like the good lad you are. May God reward you!"

When I took the jug of water and the fruit bowls to the men's area, I waited for the mango nectar to be prepared. Rihanna was gathering grapes from the bottom of a tub full of water. I said to her, "There is so much work to be done here! Would you like me to ask Amīna or Qanwā to come and help out?"

The old woman, who was chewing on a coconut cud or some such thing, said, "Then what am I here, chopped liver? The aristocracy only know how to hand out orders and boss people around. They are no good when it comes to getting any work done. They sit on their high chairs giving orders, and we poor souls at the bottom have to follow their orders."

Rihanna said, "They came to help, but I asked them to see to the needs of the guests upstairs."

The old woman poured me a goblet of mango nectar and handed it over to me.

Rihanna said, "You have to forgive us. We stayed in the kitchen and the bother of serving the fruit fell on your shoulders. I told my father that we should go to our own house, but your grandfather wouldn't hear of it."

The old woman said to Rihanna, "Where could be better than here? There's no room in your house, girl."

I said, "What could be a greater honor than to be host to Abū-Rājeh?"

The old woman interrupted and said, "That's what I was afraid of: for someone to come and strike up a conversation with us."

Rihanna glared at the old woman's pale face and smiled in shame as she apologized for the old woman's awkward remark.

I said, "When I think about it, I see that it is a strange story. By allowing this miracle to occur, God enabled Abū-Rājeh to continue to cast his protective shade over us.[30] My grandfather and I, Qanwā and her mother, and hundreds of other souls were guided to the light of truth; and the Shī'a prisoners were all released. And I figure that Marjān-e Saghīr will treat the Shī'a with moderation from now on. Your father had already talked to me about Shī'a Islam and the Lord of the Age ﷿. His words had positioned me at a crossroads, or perhaps it would be better to describe it as a dead-end. Last night, Grandfather was counselling me against flirting with becoming a Shī'a Muslim. With this extraordinary occurrence, not only did I become certain that the Lord of the Age ﷿ is endowed with prophet-like [supernatural] powers and is the sole living *hojja* of God on Earth, but my grandfather became Shī'a too!"

Rihanna said, "There is a world of difference in my condition today, and that of my father and mother, and hundreds of other people, compared to what it was yesterday. The liberation of the prisoners made us incredibly happy! They had been reduced to nothing but skin and bones. It will take some time for them to recover. My father used to say repeatedly that even if we grant, for the sake of the argument, that Safwān committed some crime, that does not give them the right to imprison Hamād as well. Did you see his condition? He could barely walk."

I wanted to shift the direction of the conversation to where Rihanna would reveal the identity of the young man she saw in her dream. I said, "The dream you had was strange too. From what I understand from what your father told me, you had the dream about a year ago. Could you talk about your dream? Did you really see your father in his present condition in your dream?"

The old woman went over to check on a large pot whose contents were simmering on the stove. Rihanna went with her, placing a distance between us.

"Yes, I saw him in my dream just as he appears now."

"What did you think your dream meant at the time you dreamt it?"

"Sometimes I thought it didn't mean anything. I didn't think it was going to be so close to the events that are actually taking place."

She said to the old woman, "Here, let me help you."

"If you want to help, pour me a bowl of *dough*[31] from that waterskin over there."

I asked, "Did anything in particular cause you to have this dream?"

I could see that she felt ashamed. She turned her face away from me and said, "I can't say anything more about this to anyone."

Rihanna was busy opening the thong of the waterskin. What she said made me feel like the Heavens and the Earth itself had come crashing down on my head. I had no choice but to be content with God's will. How else could she say to me that I was not the young man in her dream, without coming right out and saying it? When I felt I was back in control of my voice again and that it would not quiver, I said, "Forgive me if I am too persistent. Perhaps I will be able to be of some help to you in this matter. Your father had told me some time back that a young man stood beside him in your dream, and that he had said to you in the dream that he will be your future husband."

The old woman drank up half of her goblet of *dough* as she was stirring the pot and nodded her head in appreciation. Rihanna said, "Now that half of my dream has come true, I have no doubt that the rest of it will also come to pass."

The old lady finished the rest of the *dough* and said, "Anyone who works in this bounteous kitchen will become nice and plump, like Omm-Hobāb."

I asked, "Now that we know it is a true dream, why do you not reveal the identity of the young man in the dream? Perhaps I can persuade him to…"

She interrupted me, interjecting, "Oh, that's all right. He will find his way to me himself. So I'm not worried."

"But how is he to know that you have seen him in your dream?"

"Well, *he* might not know, but God certainly does!"

I didn't know why I was so persistent in trying to identify who that young man was. Maybe I wanted to make sure it was Hamād. Hamād was more tolerable than some unknown person. Now that I had become a Shī'a, I was still far from being able to reach Rihanna. If she loved someone else, there was nothing that I could do.

"It was fated that your father was to be a breath away from death before being cured. But we did not sit idly by either. We had the honor of having a small role in actualizing the divine will. Were our efforts all for naught? Should we have done nothing? If that is not true and we were right to act, then it might also be the case that it is necessary for us to do something now [toward the realization of the rest of your dream]."

The old woman looked at me and smirked. It was clear that she was bored with our conversation.

Rihanna said, "You are right, but don't forget that it took a year for half of my dream to come true. How are we to know that it won't take another year for the other half to be realized? One mustn't pluck a fruit before it is ripe for the picking. It's possible that the young man will petition for my hand in matrimony with love and passion in due time. But what about now? If I tell him that I have had such a dream and am awaiting his proposal, he might say, 'Well, nice dream, but I have my heart set on someone else'."

Omm-Hobāb came in and said between breaths, "Where have you been, Hāshem? Your grandfather is looking for you."

Rihanna said to Omm-Hobāb, "Abū-Na'īm is truly precious! I have been fond of him ever since I was a small child."

When I left the kitchen, Omm-Hobāb told me quietly, "Did you cotton on to what Rihanna was hinting at?"

"What now? What did you 'cotton on' to that has apparently alluded my senses?"

"The fact that she said that Abū-Na'īm was 'truly precious' and how she has always liked him!"

I had no patience for her games.

"No."

"What she meant was that *you* are a precious young man that she has always liked!!"

I said, "Hush! She is waiting for Hamād to propose to her."

Omm-Hobāb was flabbergasted. She said, "*What*? Is that even *possible*?"

I climbed the stairs and waited for her to reach me, panting and moaning.

"Before you came, we were talking. If she liked me, she would have made some sort of indication, one way or another."

She stopped and turned around.

"Well, if you don't believe me, that's ok. I'll go and ask her directly so you'll know where you stand. Let's put an end to this once and for all. We can't go on like this forever!"

I passed her and blocked her from going down the stairs.

"What's the rush, all of a sudden?"

She moved me to the side so she could go down the stairs.

"*You* might not believe what I'm telling you, but that doesn't mean that *I* don't believe it! I'll ask her to give me one word: Do you or do you not want to marry that poor wretch, Hāshem! Yes or no? One word is all it will take to put an end to all of this! What's with all the dilly-dallying? What were you jabbering on about then, when you were talking for so long in there? You are like a bashful young girl, and Rihanna is like a chaste angel that is all modesty."

I grabbed her arm, forcing her to stop. I helped her up the stairs.

"Listen, Omm-Hobāb! Now is not the time for this kind of talk. One mustn't pluck a fruit before it is ripe for the picking. Especially in the company of that busy-body who is helping out in the kitchen."

"Well, if you ask me, there's no time like the present. When Abū-Rājeh and her daughter leave this house, it will be too late. Have you already forgotten how you sent me to their house just to get some news of her? Now, God, in His loving kindness, has brought them to our house. Can you believe it?"

I tried to give myself courage. I said, "I have to be content with whatever God wills. We have yet to thank Him for having guided us. Man is avaricious. I have to find a quiet corner and talk to the Lord of the Age ﷽. If it is fated that Rihanna will be made happy by marrying someone else, then I will probably be made happy by marrying someone else too. Do you accept this?"

Omm-Hobāb opened her eyes wide and said, "Certainly, I accept it. But I don't know whether *you* do."

She made her way to the room where the ladies were gathered without waiting for my answer.

Grandfather was seated next to Abū-Rājeh and Safwān and Hamād, carrying on a conversation with them. When he saw me, he frowned and said, "Come and see what Abū-Rājeh is saying!"

"What's going on?"

"He says he wants to go home. He thinks his being here is putting us out."

I became dejected. I could not stand them not being here in our house. I said, "If you go, this house will become dark and gloomy. As for me, I want you all to always be here, and for Grandfather and I to cater to your every need."

Grandfather backed me up, saying, "This house belongs to you now. This room will always have the fragrance of the Lord of the Age ﷿. You and your family have to stay here for at least a week. Hāshem is right: if you leave, this place will become dark and gloomy."

Abū-Rājeh said, "I will call on you much more frequently from now on. Today, you are dearer to me and to the people of Hilla, than at any other time. Safwān wants to go home, and we happen to take the same path home. So I will go and let you get some well-deserved rest."

Grandfather kept them for dinner by hook and by crook. An hour after dinner, Abū-Rājeh stood up and said, "It is time for us to take our leave, with your permission."

Everyone got up and after expressing their thanks and saying their farewells, left the room. The womenfolk came out of their room too. Qanwā and Rihanna were together again. I felt that Rihanna and Hamād cast their glances downward upon seeing each other. As we were going down the stairs, Hamād told me, "I have to talk to you as soon as possible."

I said, "I am at your service!"

He said shyly, "I love someone, and I want her to be my partner in our future life together."

It was as if he lit every inch of my body with a match. I asked, "What can I do to help?"

We entered the front yard. He said, "I want you to talk to her."

"Is she here?"

He nodded his head. I could feel the beads of sweat forming on my forehead.

"Why do you want *me* to talk to her?"

"She thinks highly of you. You can ask her what she thinks about me. In a way that she won't know that I have asked you to speak to her, of course."

I said, "You can be sure that she loves you too."

He said in surprise, "But you don't even know who she is!"

We exited the front yard along with the other guests. I said to Hamād, "I know who she is. The fact that you said she is here now confirmed it."

He embraced me with a big smile on his face and said, "You're right! We'll talk more about this as soon as we have the chance."

Abū-Rājeh and Safwān came over and embraced me and said their goodbyes warmly, but I was not listening to what they were saying. All I understood was that Abū-Rājeh was talking about the Friday get-together which we had talked about before. I stopped myself from looking at Rihanna. The street was lit by the light of the moon. We waited until everyone disappeared behind the bend in the street. Qanwā was the only one who was still with us. I no longer had any desire to go back in to the house. The only person who was happy was Omm-Hobāb. She yawned and then said, "I hadn't catered to so many people in my whole life! I have to rest for a good two or three days to recover from this!"

Qanwā said, "Rihanna invited me to come to their party on Friday."

I said, "I hope you all have a good time."

We went back into the front yard and sat down on a wooden bed. Omm-Hobāb gleefully closed the front door. A few minutes later, two litter bearers arrived bearing a palanquin that Amīna was in, and took Qanwā back to the palace. I remained sitting in the front yard, alone. I gazed at the moon. I was sorely heartbroken. If it were not so late, I would have set out to get some air to my brain and calm myself down. I suddenly thought of "him", which made me want to stay up and commiserate with my *mowlā* or Master.

Chapter 34

bū-Rājeh came to our store Thursday evening, all bright eyed and bushy tailed. We were happy to see him. He said, "A couple of the Sultan's men brought my swans back about an hour ago. What intelligent birds they are! They still recognized me, despite the change in my appearance. They immediately came up to me and took food from my hands."

I asked, "Has Masrour come back to the hammām?"

"Yes, though he feels sheepish."

He got up before long and said, "The hammām is very busy, and Masrour is on his own. I have to get back there. I just came over to remind you of our little get-together tomorrow. Come over after you have finished your morning devotions. My house is a small house of one who is not well to do, but we will have a good time, God willing, with your gracing it with your presence."

He said goodbye and left. I had decided not to go to the party. Seeing Hamād and Rihanna together would be a form of torture for me. I preferred not seeing her to seeing her with Hamād. Besides, Hamād wanted me to talk to Rihanna about him! How could I pave the way for their marriage with my own hands?

Before coming to the store, I had paid a visit to the Station of the Lord of the Age ﷿. My intention was to go back there Friday morning and recite the Nudba Du'ā[32] or Supplication. I had been fortunate in that neither Qanwā nor Omm-Hobāb had told Rihanna about my love for her, because it would only cause her distress if she wanted to marry someone else.

I had hoped that after being witness to such an amazing miracle, I would become indifferent as to whether I married Rihanna or some other girl, but alas, that was not the case. I could not get Rihanna out of my mind, even for a minute. It was as if the two of us had been made of the same clay. One of these days, Abū-Rājeh was bound to come up to me and say, "Whatever happened to that Shī'a girl you loved? Why don't you have me or your grandfather go and propose to her family on your behalf?" What would I be able to tell him? What would happen if I told him that I loved Rihanna? He could well share the information with Rihanna who, after recovering from her shock, would say that Hāshem is not the person she has seen in her dream.

Before leaving the house Friday morning, I told Omm-Hobāb, "You two should go along to Abū-Rājeh's house and not wait for me. I won't be coming."

She scowled and said, "Whyever not?"

"I need to try not to see Rihanna from now on. I am even thinking of going to Kūfa for a few years so that I can forget her.

"Now you want to go to *Kūfa*??"

"I'm not joking! I'm going to go to the Station of His Eminence the Mahdi ﷿, and then go and have a stroll along the bridge."

"What are you going to eat?"

"I'll come back home in the evening and find something to eat. Or maybe I'll grab a bite from a vendor at the bridge."

"Then I won't go to the party either. I'll stay and prepare a meal for you."

"If you don't go, I'll stay out until midnight."

"Have you told your grandfather?"

"You tell him."

"What are you going to say to Abū-Rājeh? This party will not be the same without you. The whole point was for it to be an appreciation of your efforts."

"If necessary, I'll tell Abū-Rājeh the truth."

The Station of His Eminence the Mahdi ﷻ was crowded. Many of the people whom I had seen in our house the day before were there. The murmurings of prayers and the sound of weeping and wailing in supplication could be heard everywhere. I found a corner to sit in and recited the Nudba Du'ā. It made me feel better, and made me weep. I said to the Lord of the Age ﷻ, "My dear Master: you were kind enough to save Abū-Rājeh, and as I expected, caused the prisoners to be liberated. You caused many souls, myself included, to be guided aright. Would that you had considered me to be worthy of being Rihanna's husband! Who could be a better and more worthy wife for me? Perhaps I am not worthy of her. If it is her destiny to live happily with Hamād, then make it so that I no longer love her, so that I am not tormented like this."

I stayed at the Station for a couple of hours or so, then I walked along the riverfront until I got to the bridge. The vast vistas there were uplifting and made me feel better. I leaned against the bridge's wooden railings and gazed into the clear water that coursed under my feet. There was a family riding in a boat having a good time. They made their way to the bridge and drifted under it. The thought occurred to me that life passes us by like the currents of a river and like the boats that float on it, relegating both the good times and the bad to the forgetfulness that comes with the passage and flux of time. But I didn't know how long it would take for me to be able to accept that Rihanna would be spending her whole life living with someone else.

In the distance, there was a man in a boat with a little boy and a little girl. Many years ago, Abū-Rājeh had taken Rihanna and me by the hand and taken us boat riding on this same river. Rihanna and I sat next to each other on the forward thwart of the boat. The up and down motion of the boat made us giggled so much that it eventually got Abū-Rājeh laughing with us.

The boat in the distance floated away from the shore and slowly made its way to the bridge. I heard the sound of the children's laughter and wished that time would go back and that those children were Rihanna and me. I was a fish out of water, yearning for the sea.

I saw the silhouette of a woman climbing the grade of the bridge. It sent a shiver up my spine. For a moment, I thought it was Rihanna. Then I laughed at my misplaced optimism: what would Rihanna be doing here? She was happily seeing to the needs of her guests now. She might not even have noticed my absence yet. It turned out to be a young woman who had purchased some *masqatī*[33] from a street vendor, and was returning happily to her husband who was waiting for her on the other side of the bridge. I envied them. My mind thumbed through the book of my childhood memories. One day, Rihanna had brought a few pieces of *qottāb*[34] for me, and told me that her mother had made them. I asked, "Have you had some yourself?"

"I don't want any. My mother will make some more."

The *qottāb* were in a small basket made of date fronds.

I had said, "If you don't have any, I won't have any either." So she accepted, and we sat down and ate the *qottāb* together. It was right at that moment that I realized how pleasurable it was for me to share a meal with Rihanna.

I began to grow weary after a while. Abū-Rājeh's house drew me to it like a magnet. I needed to occupy myself in order to liberate myself from the force of this magnetic attraction. I made my way down from the crown of the bridge and went to where street vendors and fishmongers and boat rentals and street magicians and snake charmers were to be found, to take my mind off things for a while. I entertained myself with these distractions for an hour, but I didn't want to go back home as being alone there was oppressive for me. I could pass the time better if my friends had been around. It had been a couple of days since I had paid them a visit.

I made my way back to the bridge. If Abū-Rājeh was looking for me, he could find me by the bridge. I asked myself, "What would you do if he came looking for you?" If I saw him before he saw me, I would hide myself. But if he saw me first, he would insist that I go back with him, and I would have no choice but to tell him the truth.

I hadn't had a proper breakfast and was feeling hungry. I gave a coin to a female street vendor, who proceeded to cut off a piece of *masqatī* with her knife, placed it on a fresh grape-vine leaf, and offered it to me. It had an alluring fragrance of saffron, cardamom and rosewater, and had been decorated with walnuts and hazelnuts. There were some carpet covered wooden platform beds for sitting on along the river on its opposite shore. I made my way towards them. When my friends and I came to the river, we would sometimes go there and have a fruit nectar or a *pālūdeh*[35] before going for a swim.

I didn't doubt that by now, Abū-Rājeh had asked my grandfather about my absence, and received the reply that I was not feeling well enough to come. His house was so full of people that no one would notice my absence.

I sat on our usual platform bed. I missed my friends. The old man who owned the kiosk there brought me over a bowl of cantaloupe *pālūdeh* on a plate. I placed the *masqatī* on the plate. The old man was deaf and mute. We signaled a greeting to each other. His familiar smile told me that he remembered me. He was the kind of person who became friendly quickly. I wished I could speak to him. But alas, that too was impossible. If I were to leave Hilla, I would miss this part of the river. There was an incredible view of the river and bridge from here.

In the evenings, when empty platform beds to sit on were hard to come by, a dark-skinned man who was the old man's partner would come and sing for the customers. People who knew how to judge voice quality said that his doleful voice was unrivaled. Too bad he wasn't here now so that I could give him a dirham to sing me my favorite poems.

The sky of my heart was overcast. I felt like crying. I had cried that morning, thinking of my kind and loving Master. I would have like to shed a few tears for Rihanna's sake too. I had found my Master, even though he was hidden from my sight; whereas I could see Rihanna, but it seemed that she was not destined to belong to me.

The *masqatī* and cantaloupe *pālūdeh* remained on the plate, untouched. A breeze rustled through the fronds of the date-palms, sending glimmering circles of sunlight over me and the stool in front of me. Then a shadow was cast over me and the *pālūdeh*. I thought it was the old man who had come over to ask me why I hadn't touched the *pālūdeh*. The shadow moved, and the person who was standing behind me moved over to my side. I wanted him to sit down so I could strike up a conversation with him, no matter who it was. I turned around a little and looked up. I wanted it to be Rihanna, but it was my grandfather.

Chapter 35

I stood up.

"Salaam!"

He looked at me with a look that was one of contentment or dismay and drew me into his arms.

"Salaam, my son! May God's peace be unto you, too." As we were embracing, his shoulders shook a couple of times. I didn't know if he was laughing or crying. When we separated, I saw that he was laughing.

"It seems that you've come here to sulk and are not on speaking terms with anyone, like a child. Come on, get up and let us get going."

I felt like I was still a child. I had a lump in my throat that wouldn't let up. Tears started to run down my cheeks.

I said, "Where do I have that I can go to?"

"To Abū-Rājeh's house, of course!"

"Is there some new development? If I wanted to come, I would have gone already."

"It is arranged that someone is going to ask for a girl's hand in marriage. And here you are, sitting here alone on your own."

"Propose to Rihanna? I know that already."

"Yes, I want to ask for her hand in marriage from Abū-Rājeh on your behalf."

I scoffed at my grandfather's naivete and sat back down on the bed.

"Don't bother. I'm not the one who she wants."

"Then who is that?"

"Its *Hamād.*"

"You are mistaken! That fortunate young man is *you!*"

Blood rushed to my heart and my temples. I stood up.

"*Me?* Are you sure you are not making a mistake??"

"Perfectly sure!" He said with a big grin.

"Who said this?"

He nodded and said, "Someone on whose word you can count on."

"Who?"

"Rihanna."

I could not believe it. I had talked to her myself.

"Emm… can you explain?"

He took me by the arm and said, "Not while you are standing here I can't. I have been looking for you for a long time. Omm-Hobāb said I might be able to find you around here. I am tired, and we have to get back."

I placed a coin next to the *pālūdeh* plate, and headed for the bridge with Grandfather. I couldn't wait to hear what more he had to say.

"What I am afraid of is that things are not going to be the way they have been reported to you when we get there."

"Why? Don't you have any confidence in what Omm-Hobāb says?"

I let out a groan of agony.

"*No*, Grandfather! I don't! If she has said something to you, you can't take her seriously!!"

He chuckled and said, "You have to be grateful to Omm-Hobāb! If it weren't for her talking with Rihanna today, you and I would not be walking toward Abū-Rājeh's house right now."

We walked away from the river shore toward a date plantation.

"Grandfather, why won't you tell me what happened in a few succinct sentences and put my mind at rest?"

"Oh! However will I be able to thank God? God only knows how worried I was for you. I couldn't think of any way in which there was any hope of an opening. Things had gotten to the point that we wanted to leave this town!"

We were close to Abū-Rājeh's house when Grandfather finally said, "About an hour ago, Omm-Hobāb took Rihanna to a corner and said to her, 'Is it not important to you that Hāshem has not come to your house?' Rihanna became flustered at hearing the question out of nowhere, and said, 'I heard them tell my mother that he was not well.' At this point, Omm-Hobāb placed her finger on Rihanna's heart and says, 'His ailment stems from *here!*' Rihanna said, 'I don't understand what you mean.' To which Omm-Hobāb replied, 'I think you understand perfectly well, young lady. He is in love with you, and because he thinks you love Hamād and that it is him that you have seen in your dream, he intends to leave Hilla. And if he leaves, Abū-Na'īm and I will leave with him, perhaps forever'."

Grandfather paused by a stone pillar in order to catch his breath.

"You were saying…!"

"Rihanna's face went pale. Omm-Hobāb told me that when she heard what Omm-Hobāb said, she almost fainted. She said in disbelief, 'But Hāshem is supposed to marry Qanwā! So how can he be in love with me and still want to marry Qanwā?!' Then Omm-Hobāb assured her that you loved her and no one else. Rihanna was elated and had become as red as a pomegranate flower. She admitted that she loves you too, and that you are the person whom she saw in her dream. Then Omm-Hobāb came and told me of her conversation with Rihanna with teary eyes."

Until I heard it from Rihanna's mouth, I couldn't believe Omm-Hobāb's words. When we entered Abū-Rājeh's front yard, Omm-Hobāb and Rihanna's mother were waiting for us there. Not bothering to beat around the bush, I whispered to Omm-Hobāb, "Are the things that I have heard from Grandfather true??"

Without saying a word, she pointed to Rihanna's mother so that she could answer my question. She gave me a big smile and said, "I talked to Rihanna. What Omm-Hobāb said is perfectly true."

I breathed a sigh of relief and thanked God. Omm-Hobāb whispered in my ear, "And don't you worry about Hamād, either. It's Qanwā that he loves, not Rihanna."

I felt like a heavy load had been lifted from my shoulders. Before I had a chance to pull myself together and enjoy the fact that fortune was smiling on me, Grandfather took my arm and took me to the room where the men were gathered. Abū-Rājeh sat me down next to him and said with good humor, "Wonders never cease! You don't seem to be feeling ill at all. In fact, you seem to be positively beaming! So what was all that your grandfather was saying then, hmm?"

I said, "I was not feeling well, but I am all better now, thanks to God's grace and loving kindness."

He was obviously up to speed with Omm-Hobāb's and Rihanna's conversation.

He said, "I thought that perhaps I had done something inadvertently to upset you."

I said with a smile, "Well, if the truth be told, I *am* a little upset with you!"

Everyone went quiet and looked at me with uninhibited curiosity. Abū-Rājeh squeezed my arm and said, "You know how much I like you. Tell me what it is that I did."

"After Almighty God saved you through the intermediacy of our Master, you became so preoccupied with seeing to the needs of your guests that you plumb forgot about me."

My grandfather interjected, "What are you saying, Hāshem? Abū-Rājeh came to our store yesterday and thanked the two of us."

I said, "The fact that Abū-Rājeh has forgotten about the big problem that I have is what distresses me."

Abū-Rājeh let out a hearty laugh and said, "Oh yes, I remember now, you are absolutely right. I should have done something in this regard. Forgive me. But it is not too late."

Grandfather said cunningly, "What's that all about? Tell it so I will know too."

Abū-Rājeh said, "Hāshem was in love with a Shī'a girl. He had talked to me on numerous occasions about this. I told him he should forget her, of course. One day, a girl and her mother came to your store to buy a pair of earrings, and Hāshem fell in love with the girl. And now that you and Hāshem rank among the best Shī'a of Hilla, it would be fitting for us to take steps to propose to that fortunate young lady on behalf of the most beloved young man in Hilla."

Hamād and his father and all the others were looking at me. Grandfather laughed and said to Abū-Rājeh, "May God grant you blessings and increase His favor towards you! Do you think the family of that young lady will approve of such a matrimonial bond?"

Abū-Rājeh raised his head and said, "It would be an honor for them, and they would fall down in prostration to their Lord in gratitude!"

Grandfather turned to me and said, "It would be well for you to introduce her to us now. I do believe that Abū-Rājeh and those present know her."

I took in a deep breath and said with a quiver in my voice, "Her name is Rihanna, the daughter of Abū-Rājeh."

Abū-Rājeh was stunned, and those present, who were certainly surprised, sent out a loud *salawāt*. After a few moments had passed, Abū-Rājeh said, "This is my ultimate wish, but my daughter saw a dream a year ago which, with my miraculous cure, we realized was a true dream. She had seen me as I am now in that dream. There was a young man standing next to me whom I described as her future husband, saying that he would be your husband within the year. So before anything else, it would be best if ..."

I said in an excited and still quivering voice, "I am the one she saw in her dream." Everyone again sent out *salawāt* and congratulations. Abū-Rājeh fell into a prostration of gratitude, after which he embraced me. Moments later, the sound of celebration could be heard from the women's quarters. It seems one of them was eavesdropping behind the door to our room, and had informed the others of the news.

Abū-Rājeh said, "I was always concerned for the future of my daughter, and always prayed that she would marry a worthy husband. And I love Hāshem so much that I wanted my groom to be someone like him. It was our destiny for me to attain to my dream after having undergone the ordeal that I went through."

Abū-Rājeh turned to me and Grandfather and continued, "In this way, our bond will become unbreakable."

I didn't know how I was to thank God for His blessings and loving kindness. After lunch, when I had a chance, I quietly asked Hamād, "You love Qanwā, am I right?"

He said, "My story is similar to yours. When I saw her, I fell in love with her. But because our rites and denominations were different, I reproached myself when I was in prison and then in the dungeon for falling for someone whose love could never be requited."

"But now, she and her mother have entered into the Shī'a rite."

"If only that was my only problem. How is Marjān-e Saghīr ever going to consent to giving away his daughter to a dyer? Besides, I don't even know whether Qanwā herself is amenable to such a marriage. She is accustomed to a life of luxury. How can I expect her to put all of that behind her for my sake?"

"I can give you the glad tidings that she loves you too."

Even though Hamād did not hold out much hope of sharing his life with Qanwā, he jumped up and asked elatedly, "Is that true?"

"You can be certain of it."

"Do you think she would be able to live with me?"

She has more than enough acumen to know whether or not she would be able to live with a dyer."

"It's doubtful that she would accept such a thing!"

"It is not something that anyone in her position could do, but she is certainly capable of it. What remains is her father's consent."

Hamād calmed down a bit and said, "He would never consent to such a marriage."

A few minutes later, I got word to Qanwā through Omm-Hobāb that Hamād loves her. When Omm-Hobāb came back, she said, "The poor child became so overjoyed that she threw herself in Rihanna's arms and started to weep."

Hamād said, "Maybe her tears were on account of the fact that she knows her father will never consent to our marrying."

Abū-Rājeh believed that one should not put off any good deed. And my Grandfather agreed with him. On the evening of the same day, Rihanna and I were married to each other in a simple ceremony. Later, when we were sitting next to each other holding each other's hands, I told her, "This morning I had lost all hope of living my life with you as my partner, but now you are my partner. I am afraid that all of this is nothing but a dream, and that I will wake up and see that I am lying down alone on one of the beds by the riverside."

Rihanna put her mouth to my ear and whispered so that no one else would be able to hear, "Do you remember when we were talking in your kitchen? Then, I thought that it might take a year for you to come and ask for my hand in marriage. But now I see that it is just as my father told me in my dream, and that you have become my husband within the year."

Omm-Hobāb said to us, "There's no hurry. From now on, you will have plenty of time to talk sweet nothings in each other's ears."

Then everyone laughed and the womenfolk sounded out in celebration.

Chapter 36

On the morning of the next day, Rihanna and I visited the Station of the Lord of the Age ﷻ and spent an hour there thanking the Lord and making pilgrimage to our Imam. After that, we went to the shore of the river and to the bridge, so that we could enjoy talking to each other while taking in the local scenery from the bridge.

The river was flowing calmly, and the city was brightly lit by a moderate sun. I said, "How I wished to be able to stand with you here and to look at the river and the houses and the palm plantations!"

Rihanna chuckled and said, "Ever since yesterday, it makes me laugh when I think that you sent Omm-Hobāb to our house on a spying mission!"

"She is an intelligent woman. She told me that you liked me, but I didn't believe her."

"Do you think that there is anyone happier and more fortunate than me in the whole of Hilla today?"

"Have no doubt about it."

"Who??"

"Me!"

We laughed at anything and everything at the slightest provocation. Rihanna's eyes and visage had a strange luminescence. Perhaps she saw a similar luminosity in my face, I don't know.

"Do you know what kind of fire you lit in my soul the day you came to the store with your mother? From that time on, I never had a moment's peace. Grandfather knows what you did to me. He said on numerous occasions, 'If only I hadn't made you come down the flight of stairs from the workshop to the store. If only Rihanna and her mother had not come into the store that morning. What an ill-omened day it was!' But now I say, what a blessed day it was! After you left, I went to see your father and told him that I had fallen in love with a girl who was Shī'a. He didn't know I was talking about his own daughter, of course. Your father told me that it would be best if I forgot about this girl. None of us had any idea what fate had in store for us."

"It is always best to entrust our affairs to God and to have hope [of being recipients of His grace]."

"What made you have that wonderous dream? It surprises me to see that you love me. Was it only because of the dream you saw that you became fond of me, and are now happy to have become my wife?"

Rihanna let out a sigh and said, "When I came to your store that day, it had already been a year that I had been stricken with your love."

It was difficult for me to believe what she was saying.

"How is such a thing even possible?"

"A year ago, me and my mother came to take a stroll by the river and to get some fresh air. I saw you sitting there on one of the platform beds with your friends. You were telling a story and making them laugh. It had been years since I had seen you. I was astonished by your handsomeness and poise and dignity. You had changed so much. What you saw in me that day in the store, I saw in you back then. When we returned home, I had become lovestruck and was bedridden for a week. I wept in my solitude."

"What are you saying, Rihanna?"

"It seemed to be a love that would not come to any satisfactory conclusion. I needed to liberate myself from it, for otherwise, death awaited me. One night, when I was feeling a little better, I wept profusely while offering my pre-dawn devotions, and asked God to free my heart of my love for you. After another hour or so passed in prayer and supplication, I fell asleep whilst in the position of [ritual] prostration, and that is when I had the dream. My father looked like he does now, and you were standing next to him. He pointed to you and said, 'Hāshem will be your partner in life. Entrust your affairs to God![36] What you see and what I have said will come to pass within a year.' When suitors came for me, I had no choice but to tell my mother about my dream, but I didn't reveal the identity of the young man who appeared beside my father in the dread, for two reasons."

"Firstly," I interjected, "because if you had said it was me, they would have told you not to give credence to your dream, because your marriage to someone who was not Shī'a was meaningless."

"Yes. And the second reason was that I was too embarrassed to give expression to the name of someone who was my husband-to-be."

"You suffered through this more than I did but were able to conceal your love for me. I take pride in having a partner who has such a high sense of modesty and nobility of character."

"Until my father was cured in such a miraculous way, I did not give my dream much credence. But when I woke up that fateful night and saw my father as he is now, I knew that it was a true dream, and that you were to be my life-partner. I had become so elated that when your grandfather went to your room to wake you up, I accompanied him."

After I related the dream I'd had that night to Rihanna, she continued, "After a year's anguish and torment, I saw you again last week in your store, and I knew then that my life would be meaningless without you. With my father's cure, I became more hopeful that my dream would be realized and that we would marry. But I had heard that you were going to marry Qanwā. I saw you with her constantly. The night we left your house, I was very despondent. I saw that Qanwā was at your side once again. I rued the time we spent talking to each other in the kitchen. In the dream, my father had told me that you would become my life-partner within a year. Recently, the thought occurred to me that a year has come and gone and still nothing has happened. Yesterday, I was curious to know why you hadn't come to the party. Whenever anyone knocked on the door, I would take a peek to see whether it was you. Omm-Hobāb had her eyes peeled. She came over and said, 'Are you expecting someone?' When I didn't answer, she said, 'If you are waiting for Hāshem, he won't be coming.' I was saddened. I asked, 'Why not?' That is when she told me everything. When I found out that you love me too, and why you hadn't come to our house, I was over the moon. This Omm-Hobāb of yours is such a lovely person. She is a sweet, unassuming person."

"When you come to our home, she will become your boon companion, I'm sure."

"And I will work in that large and beautiful kitchen with her every day and wait for you and Grandfather to come home from the bazaar."

"And we will have a lifetime to talk to each other like we are doing now."

At that moment, the pauper to whom I had given Rihanna's two gold coins passed us by. I called to him and gave him the coins that were in my pocket. He smiled and thanked me. I told Rihanna, "I had intended to keep your two dinars forever, but I gave them to our brother here. I asked him to pray to God to keep you for me."

Rihanna reached under her *chādor* and drew her earrings out from her ears and gave them to the indigent man.

"And I had made a *nadhr* or sacred vow before God, which I must now fulfill."

The pauper said, "With this capital, you will see me working at some trade from now on."

When the man left, I said to Rihanna, "Yesterday at the Station of the Lord of the Age ﷿, I asked our Imam, 'Seeing as you are so loving and kind, why don't you do something so that Rihanna becomes my wife?' And now I see that the tidings of this matrimonial bond had been given to you as far back as a year ago, and that I needed to witness this amazing course of events in order for me to be properly cultivated and guided aright. I felt that there was no solution to my problem, and I had lost all hope, when the doors opened before me, and I was allowed entry into a house in which you had resided from the start."

Rihanna said, "You deserve to be the recipient of this blessing. I will never forget your sacrificing your life in order to save my father's, and in order to do what you could to bring peace and tranquility back to me and my mother's life."

A boat was approaching from afar. We watched its approach in silence.

A week later, Rihanna and I were having breakfast with Grandfather and Omm-Hobāb on a platform bed in the front yard. Qanwā paid us a visit and brought news of Rashīd and Amīna's marriage, as well as news of the Vizier's resignation from his post. The Vizier and Rashīd planned to leave for the Vizier's father's estate in the country with their new bride in a few days. I told her, "All of us are going to go to Kūfa tomorrow."

"Are Abū-Rājeh and Rihanna's mother going with you too?"

I said, "You know that it wouldn't be the same for us without them."

She asked, "Why Kūfa?"

I said, "My mother and brothers and sisters are there. Rihanna insisted that we go and bring them to Hilla. She says that this house is large enough to enable them to live with us."

I told my mother's story to Qanwā. Rihanna said, "I won't rest until we bring them to Hilla with us. Hāshem's mother is my mother too."

Omm-Hobāb said, "We will be making pilgrimage to the shrine of the Imams as well. We will pray for you and Hamād."

Qanwā said, "I wish I could come with you!"

Grandfather said, "You and Hamād will be with us the next time we go there, if we place our trust in God."

Seeing my mother and brothers and sisters completed my happiness. When my mother saw me and her new bride, she fainted in our arms. She had become infirm and very weak. When she came to, I fell to her feet and wept so much, until she said that she has forgiven me for having forgotten her and for not having visited her over all these years. Rihanna was sitting beside me. She wept too. My mother embraced us and told me, "It is you who have to forgive me for being forced to abandon you. But now that I have found you again and have seen my beautiful and loving bride, I cannot bear to part with you again."

Rihanna and I promised my mother that we would be by her side forever. My mother introduced each of my brothers and sisters in turn, who were elated at having found a new brother. I told my mother, "Your days of anguish and hardship have come to an end. From now on, I will be your servant."

Grandfather said to my mother, "You are still my bride, and before I can teach the trade of goldsmithing to Hāshem and Rihanna's children, I must teach it to Hāshem's brothers. I am glad to see that our large and empty house will be made livelier by your presence."

"And I have to teach these beautiful girls cooking and sewing so that worthy suitors will call on them."

Our pilgrimage and tourism trip lasted two months. In this memorable trip, we made pilgrimage to the shrines of the Imams in Najaf, Karbalā, Sāmarrā, and Kādhemayn, under Abū-Rājeh's expert guidance. My mother's condition gradually improved, and she recovered her health and vitality. She was so taken by Rihanna and I, and with Grandfather, Omm-Hobāb, Abū-Rājeh and his wife, that when she saw the date plantations of Hilla, she said, "Before seeing you all, I had given up on life. But now, even the prophet Noah's years are not enough for me to spend living a life with you."

A gentle rain was coming down on Hilla when we entered its gate. The water of the Euphrates seemed clearer than before. The fronds of the date palms glistened in the rain. Even though it was raining, the sun still offered the city its light and warmth. It was as if all of the city streets had been washed down in anticipation of our arrival. Seeing Hilla reminded my mother of my father and brought tears to her eyes.

Before we did anything else, we made pilgrimage to the Station of the Lord of the Age ﷻ, where I thanked God for His loving kindness for giving me such a good and large family.

We had not yet left the grounds of the Station when we were informed that Marjān-e Saghīr had passed away. It had been forty days since he had passed. He had passed in a state where the miracle of Abū-Rājeh's cure had failed to open his eyes to the truth.

With the ascendancy of the new Sultan, Qanwā and her mother had left their quarters in the palace and were living in a large and beautiful house. The following day, Hamād told us that Qanwā's mother had purchased a house and caravanserai within the confines of the bazaar. Qanwā and Hamād were to be married soon, and Hamād was going to manage the caravanserai, which was located midway between Grandfather's store and Abū-Rājeh's hammām.

We all went to see Qanwā and offered her our condolences on the passing of her father. Rihanna asked her, "Is it difficult for you to be away from the life of the palace and all those servants and guards and power and wealth?"

Qanwā, who was gladdened by seeing our enlarged family, said with a reassuring smile, "Compared to what I have gained, all of that is as nothing. You will see I will change into a woman who Hamād and his family will like. Nor will there be any theatre or playacting involved."

The End

End Notes

1 The macron (ˉ) over the 'a' indicates that it is pronounced as a long 'a', as in Haashem (or 'halter').

2 Hilla, also spelled Hillah, is a city in central Iraq on the Hilla branch of the Euphrates River, 100 km south of Baghdad. It is the capital of Babylon Province and is located adjacent to the ancient city of Babylon, and close to the ancient cities of Borsippa and Kish.

3 These are the two great festivals that are celebrated by Muslims throughout the world each year.

4 A *chādor* is an outer garment or open cloak made of light cloth that is worn over the head and which comes all the way down to the ankles, which women wrap around their bodies to act as a full-body veil. It is considered the appropriate form of veiling by the clergy and practicing Muslims in Iran and Iraq.

5 The Abbasid dynasty ended with the conquest of Baghdad, their capital, at the hands of the Mongol hoard in the year 1258 of the Christian Era. The story can therefore be dated to the mid-Fourteenth century.

6 *Nāsebī*; plural, *nawāseb*: a term of disapprobation reserved for those takfiris among the Salafis and Wahhabis who try to pass themselves off as Muslims but harbor in their hearts hatred toward the Family of the Prophet ﷺ, and especially toward Imam Ali ؑ. As can be seen, this hatred has a long history.

7 The reference is to the Tigris and the Euphrates in Iraq.

8 The Mahdi ؑ is one of the titles the Shia give to their 12th Imam. Its literal meaning is, 'the guided one'. The coming of the Mahdi ؑ or universal savior has been foretold by the Prophet Mohammad ﷺ. The Shia believe that the Mahdi ؑ has already been born but is in a state of occultation (that he is alive but absent from the earthly

plane), whereas Sunnis, while believing in the coming of the Mahdi عليه السلام, do not believe he has been born yet.

⁹ This is the opening partition or "chapter" of the Quran. It is believed that its recitation has many spiritual rewards, and it is especially recited in cemeteries with the intention of sending the rewards of this meritorious act to loved ones who have passed into the next plane of existence, who might be in need of spiritual succor.

¹⁰ Another title of the Twelfth Imam عليه السلام of the Shia.

¹¹ The Occultation (*al-ghayba*) is the event whereat the Twelfth Imam عليه السلام disappeared from the physical plane (in the year 260 HQ/ 874 CE) at God's behest in order to protect him from being murdered by the Abbāsid authorities. The Shi'a believe that he will return to the physical plane at a time appointed by God to fill the earth with equity and justice, where it had hitherto been filled with iniquity and oppression. The Minor Occultation (*Ghaybat as-Sughrā*, 874–941) refers to the period when the Imam still maintained contact with his followers via deputies (*an-nuwwāb al-arba'a*). During this period, from 874-941, the deputies represented him and acted as agents between him and the faithful of the community. The Major Occultation denotes the second, longer portion of the Occultation, which continues to the present day, in which no specific deputy was designated by the Twelfth Imam to represent him, but in which the general class of persons, namely the magisters of theology and sacred jurisprudence (the *foqahā* or *olamā*) are named by him to act in a leadership capacity while the occultation lasts.

¹² *Tawassol* is a specific type of intercessory recourse in which someone resorts to or takes recourse in various instruments that have been made available to him by God (such as supplication to the spirit of a prophet or saint) as an intermediary means for obtaining help in his endeavors to recommend himself to the notice and favor or mercy of God. It is a practice that is rooted in the Quran and practiced by

Sunni and Shia alike. The great Sunni exegete of the Quran, Eben Kathīr, defines *tawassol* in his *at-Tafsīr* (1:532) as follows: "[*Tawassol* is when] man places an intermediary between himself and God in order that God fulfills that person's needs and desires on account of that intermediary."

[13] A form of ritual ablution of the entire body in accordance to directions provided by revealed scripture.

[14] *Tabarrok* is cognate with the word *baraka* and refers to the property of a relic or some mundane object which has been blessed (or charged in some other way) with sacral properties.

[15] Dinars are gold coins whereas dirhams are silver.

[16] *Jowhar* means ink in Arabic and Persian.

[17] The Purified and Immaculate (inerrant as well as sinless) Members of the House of the Prophet ﷺ, i.e. Lady Fātema ؑ, and the Twelve Imams ؑ.

[18] An authoritative report of a saying or deed of the Prophet ﷺ, and in Shi'a Islam, of one of the Fourteen Immaculates (the Prophet a, Lady Fātema, and the Twelve Imāms) ؑ.

[19] The Hadīth of Ghadīr Khomm refers to the appointment of Ali b. Abī-Tāleb ؑ by the Prophet Mohammad ﷺ as his heir and successor.

[20] Satan's minions are referred to as 'satans' (*shayātīn*) in the Islamic literary tradition.

[21] *Rāfeḍī* (plural, *rawāfeḍ*), literally means refuser or rejector. It is a derogatory term used by Sunni haters in order to demean and denigrate the Shī'a.

[22] Licit for consumption according to the sacred law of Islam.

[23] The direction of prayer, facing the Ka'ba in Mecca.

[24] When the word 'imām' is not capitalized, it has the generic meaning of leader and, more so, of a leader in religious matters. When it is capitalized, it refers to one of the Twelve Imams whom the Shī'a believe to be inerrant divine guides.

[25] Shia has the literal meaning of follower or partisan.

[26] *Hojjat* or *hojjatollāh*: The Proof [of God] [36:12] … *For of all things do We take account in a manifest Imām* (imām[in] mobīn) [who shall be called to testify and provide evidence on all matters on the Day of Judgment]. This is the meaning of the word *hojjatollāh* or God's proof for mankind, which is one of the names given to the Imāms by the Quran. The *hojjat* or *hojjatollāh* is the clear and perfect embodied evidence of, and unimpeachable authority for, all truth on Earth, and therefore the conclusive argument and evidentiary proof against all falsehood on the Plain of Assembly on Judgement Day.

[27] The invocation of blessings on the Prophet Mohammad a and on the purified and immaculate members of his Family. A highly recommended practice.

[28] *Kerāmāt*; singular, *kerāmat*: impossible wonders. God's munificence in His granting of supernatural knowledge or powers to those who have propinquity to Him other than prophets and Imams. These are so called in order to distinguish them from miracles which, strictly speaking, belong exclusively to prophets and to the Imams.

[29] Author note: This sentence is a word for word transcription of what His Eminence the Lord of the Age uttered to Abū-Rājeh, as it appears in the book *'Abqarī al-Hesān*.

[30] This is an expression used in hot climates where one needs to protect oneself from the harsh rays of the sun.

[31] *Dough* is a savory and slightly sour yogurt-based beverage of curdled milk and water that is seasoned with mint and salt and served cold. Because it contains live cultures of probiotic bacteria, it can become gaseous or fizzy with age.

[32] The Nudba Du'ā is a popular supplication whose main subject is seeking help from the Lord of the Age and bemoaning his absence from the earthly plane. This supplication was first related by Mohammad b. Ja'far al-Mashhadī in the book *al-mazār al-kabīr*.

Subsequently, Eben Tāwwūs attributed it to Imam Ja'far as-Sādeq in his *Eqbāl al- a'māl*. Its recitation on Fridays is a recommended (*mostahab*) act.

[33] *Masqatī* is a wheat-flour based sweet desert that is flavored with cardamom, saffron, and rose water. The saffron gives it a rich golden color, and it is usually cut into diamond shaped pieces and served topped with almond or pistachio slivers.

[34] *Qottāb* is a traditional almond or walnut-filled crescent-shaped confection that consists of pastry dough wrapped around a sugary cardamom and cinnamon filling.

[35] *Pālūdeh* is a traditional cold dessert similar to a sorbet. It consists of thin vermicelli-sized rice noodles that are zemi-frozen and topped with a sweet rose water syrup, and often served either with lime juice or with sour cherry juice.

[36] This is a rendition of a word that has appeared frequently in this book, which is *tawakkol*. Its literal meaning is allowing God to be the executor of one's affairs. In law, an executor is a person appointed by a testator to carry out the wishes expressed in his or her will, the testator being someone who is deceased. When one performs the act of *tawakkol*, one is similarly thought to be deceased in terms of one's own will, having self-surrendered it to that of God's. It is the very quintessence of the existential posture that is Islam, the literal meaning of which of course is the self-surrender of one's will to that of God's.